BLUE HILL

G. WAYNE MILLER

I looked seaward, at waves that had turned Blue Hill Bay angry. Further out, the unprotected ocean would be treacherous. On nights like this, my father always offered a prayer for mariners; when she was alive, Mom always joined in. Her grandfather, the guy who'd bought Blue Hill's blueberry fields from a Native American for a dollar, had been lost at sea on a night like this. His body had never been recovered, which meant no funeral or grave to ever visit.

"Can I ask you something?" Sally said.

"Anything you want."

"Why'd you call?"

I'd been expecting that question. I still didn't have the answer.

"I found the ring," I explained, "going through your letters."

I dug into my pocket and offered it to Sally, but she wouldn't take it.

Suddenly, the circumstances of our last encounter were with us—heavy and low, and nasty, like the clouds.

You stupid fuck, I thought. What possessed you to do that?

"I want you to have it," I said, struggling.

"Why?"

"Because it's yours."

"Was mine."

"Please?"

Sally took the ring, but she wouldn't wear it. Rather, she slipped it into her pocket.

"Things didn't turn out like we planned, did they?" I said, and that sentence sounds monumentally stupid now, but then— then, it seemed profound.

"They never do," Sally said. "The older you get, you learn that. And when you do, you reach a place of peace."

A place of peace.

How I envied her, this girl who'd become this woman.

First Edition

DEDICATION

To the frontline heroes of COVID-19: the childcare and health-care workers, grocers, food folks, drivers, therapists, clerks, first-responders, teachers, pharmacists, dads and moms, and so many other good-hearted people who practice courage and care when they are most needed.

And to the Sally Martins, Ruth Grays, Officer Bills and Rev. Grays of the real world.

A NOTE ABOUT THE PUBLISHER

Crossroad Press has published print, digital and audio editions of several of my books, and I remain grateful to publisher David Niall Wilson, who found faith in me years ago and has kept it. Folks, trust me: in the often cut-throat world of publishing, a true friend is priceless.

So, thanks again, David, to you and your team, with a special shoutout to David Dodd and editor Patricia Wilson.

INTRODUCTION

I began writing *Blue Hill* nearly a quarter of a century ago and I mostly completed the novel in 1997. I was juggling many other things at the time: fathering three children, working the day job as a *Providence Journal* staff writer, and penning horror and science-fiction short stories, many of them published and re-published by Crossroad Press. But by getting up *very* early, as I still do, I was able to indulge my passion for books.

I'd been lucky to have three published: the horror novel *Thunder Rise*, in 1989; and two non-fiction titles, *The Work of Human Hands*, in 1993; and *Coming of Age*, in 1995. Another non-fiction book, *Toy Wars*, was soon to be in print and many more would follow.

But fiction remained a passion, and so I wrote *Blue Hill*, originally titled *My Adult Life*.

My editor at the time, Jon Karp, then at Random House, liked it—but he wanted only more non-fiction, having published *The Work of Human Hands* and *Coming of Age* and having bought *Toy Wars*, which was destined to be a critically acclaimed best-seller. Also, I had begun work on *King of Hearts*, my last book with Jon until *Top Brain, Bottom Brain*, which he brought out years later as publisher of Simon & Schuster.

So *Blue Hill* went into the proverbial writer's trunk, to be resurrected when it was time.

The time is now. The themes explored herein—among them, family, faith, memory, celebrity and truth—remain as relevant now as then. You might argue even more so, with dangerous clowns masquerading as leaders.

You will also find in *Blue Hill* a fictional chronicle of an epochal real time that many of us remember: the dawning of the mainstream Internet Age, when the culture churned and the world (a part of it, anyway) was entering a virtual other-existence. Chat rooms. AOL. Dial-up. Five-and-a-quarter-inch floppy discs. Files measured in kilobytes. Modems that connected to land-line phones. The dot-com boom. Play Station. Nintendo. Super Mario 64.

Here we are today, the fruits of our labor realized, so to speak, with Facebook, Twitter, Instagram, disinformation, viral conspiracy theories, deep-fake videos, etcetera.

A new world has arrived, and the real-life artifacts in this novel are its roots.

On the literary level, I hope the farcical elements of *Blue Hill* elicit a laugh (a cringe will also do). I hope you will acknowledge truths you find. Some may be your own.

Mostly, I hope in this time of pandemic, you will find *Blue Hill* a good read—something to pass the time as we move toward yet another new world, as yet undefined.

G. Wayne Miller

G. Wayne Miller
June 21, 2020
Providence, Rhode Island

CHAPTER ONE

B efore the madness, I honestly believed I had things together. I did not drink to excess or even smoke weed anymore. I did not have a prescription to Prozac. God knows I'd never been wanted by the police and I certainly had no desire to become a caricature of myself, or anyone else for that matter.

I did not consider myself superficial, far from it. I was crazy for my kid and I loved my wife. Like anyone, we'd had our difficulties, but we'd worked through them on the conviction that parental responsibilities, shared ownership of property, and periodic lust were sufficient reasons to stay together in the late Nineties. Somewhere during our marriage, which was in its sixteenth year, it had become difficult to remember ever being with anyone else.

Was that good?

I thought so, at the time.

I enjoyed my job, no mean feat these days, when capitalism is bent on eating its own. So many drag themselves off to work day after day, year after year—and for what? To keep fat cats in Mercedes, mostly. I was fortunate: I not only liked what I did, I made money. Not untold millions, but partner Phil Grace and I owned our own company, CreativeWare, and word that we'd soon make an initial public offering of our stock had sent excitement through the software industry. CreativeWare's most profitable line remained our flight simulator games, but you didn't need great genius to see that 64-bit technology was going the way of the floppy disk. Our latest venture was in virtual reality, which was on the eve of going big.

I had few passions in my life at that point, and VR was one of them.

On September 25th, 1997, a woman from New York became another.

Her name was Allison O. Manchester, and she was funny and smart and a terrific flirt, and I knew before long I'd go to great lengths to spend an evening with her. I knew, even though I'd never seen her in person, only been tempted by her electronic image and her words—which, I fully understood, could have been outrageous lies.

We met on the Internet, and before you label me a hopeless loser, understand I was not one of the millions who'd gone digital only after America Online had mailed me one of their stupid disks. I did not get my rocks off on kinky-sex newsgroups, nor was I enthralled by Nicholas Negroponte, a drone for the ages. I thought Bill Gates was the essence of a nerd, albeit a very rich one whose MS DOS had revolutionized life and helped enable my good fortune.

Phil and I saw business opportunities in online, and when VR was finally fully deliverable by fiber-optic cable or some other means, we intended to become friends with those millions. We could already claim acquaintance with some 300,000 of them—subscribers to CreativeWare's gaming service, CreativeLine, which in its first year had outperformed all expectations, as my old bean counter partner liked to put it.

Allison's e-mail started like the hundred or so others I received after the *Wired* piece appeared—with congratulations and shameless praise, the sort of happy horseshit that inevitably precedes requests for bling and free beta software.

Then I reached her last three paragraphs. My heart raced as I read and re-read them—how else to describe it, except in teenage terms?

She wrote:

Well Star, I'm not into flying (that kind, anyway), but with all the pseudo-crappo-stuff out there I would definitely buy VR that worked. I'd even model for your program! Are you hiring? Not to brag or anything (OK, I'll brag) but my friends tell me I look like Julianne Moore. (You know who she is, right?) The only difference, I'd say, is I have a better body. You can check that out yourself real soon, once I get my homepage up and running. But hey—what makes me think a big software Star like you gives a shit about that?

Anyway, it must be great making money and having fun, all at the same time. That's how I try to live. It could even be my motto: Money and Fun. By the way, you are a very good-looking guy. (Except for the glasses. Tortoise shells aren't a happening thing.) You're also very funny. Comparing microchips to potato chips—it was one of those lines that shouldn't make you laugh but did!

I know you're probably getting tons of mail since the article, but if you respond to only one person, I hope it's me. I promise you won't be wasting your time.

Fondly,

Allison Manchester

Charlie Goldman, the guy who'd done the piece for *Wired*, was a groveling little nebbish who wanted to work for a firm like mine, not write about it.

I had no intention of hiring him but after one conversation I figured he'd write a positive piece, and he did. He even got most of his facts straight—the most glaring error, which I did not intend to correct, was that CreativeWare had marketed the first home flight simulator. In truth, we were third or fourth or tenth, with a game called *Attack Ship*, which we'd followed with *F-16*, *Tomcat*, *Carrier Deck*, *Stealth Striker*, and our latest, *Shuttle Saga*, a title that pissed Sega of America Inc. off royally, particularly when their lawyers concluded they had no grounds for a suit.

You may have read Goldman's profile—once the madness generated all those headlines you surely remember, it became the *Wired* website's most requested story ever, an accomplishment I understandably do not mention with great pride. The piece traced the history of our firm: how a young video-game nut, me, had met a slightly older venture capitalist, Phil, at an opportune moment. It outlined our strategy in plunging into VR but gave no details of what we were developing, only vague speculation about space travel.

What we really were working on were VR versions of board games that would connect players anywhere in the world. Our first title, under development with the good folks at Hasbro, was *Virtual Clue*.

CreativeWare had a PR agency, and over the years they'd gotten us into *The Wall Street Journal*, our hometown *Boston Globe*, all the gaming zines, *PC World*, and a bunch of other geeky publications like that—but never any place as hip as *Wired*. My nebbish friend's story, a 5,000-word opus entitled "CREATIVEWARE'S CREATIVE STAR," was hugely flattering—my mom, may she rest in peace, would have been proud.

"Star!" Phil kept saying.

"Get real," I kept replying, but I didn't actively discourage the description, nor could I stop sneaking onto *Wired*'s homepage, where downloadable audio and video clips of me were available. While the unfolding of my life had always seemed serendipitous to me, Goldman had connected the chapters in a way that suggested a fine logic leading to just such modern-day celebrity had been at work. He was helped, I should add, by a harmless white lie or two I couldn't resist telling, and figured he wouldn't catch, which he didn't.

It was all there: my childhood love of baseball, followed by my astronaut phase, which in high school was replaced by the conviction that someday I'd direct Jack Nicholson in a big-budget Hollywood movie. Goldman wrote about New York University, where I took first place in the student film festival for *Eating People*, a comedy about bad table manners and cannibalism. That's right, I had found a way to connect those two dots.

Goldman had talked to my dad, who mercifully revealed nothing of our troubled relationship. He'd tracked down an old girlfriend, Sally Martin, who was surprisingly complimentary in light of our final farewell, six hours after she'd had an abortion.

But Goldman's crowning achievement, in my humble opinion, was how he'd captured the critical turning point: the summer of 1979, when, living on Venice Beach, I hung with a crowd that was heavy into roller skates, movies, booze, weed, coke, hallucinogens and screwing. Here again, Goldman was on my side. His re-creation of that period was painstakingly detailed—the name of the bar where I played my first video game, the capacity of the microchip that powered my first computer, stuff like that—but only a hint of all the drugs and sex, presented in the noble context of "artistic blossoming," to use his phrase. Hey, I didn't say the guy was Updike.

"Today, as president and director of R&D," Goldman wrote, "Gray brings these diverse interests together in products that excite the consumer while enhancing the bottom line. The power of his imagination is not something competitors can afford to take lightly."

The power of his imagination—I liked that.

Goldman had hung out with us at corporate headquarters for most of a week, and we'd put on a great show: shooting each other with Nerf guns, throwing Gak around, staging Super-Soaker fights in the cafeteria—our "Nickelodeon behavior," in Charlie's apt words. I even pulled one of my infamous practical jokes: Supergluing old Charlie's tape recorder to my desk when he'd gone to take a leak. Charlie included that in his piece—he found it a regular hoot—but not a mention of the shitty reviews *Shuttle Saga* was getting in the game zines.

I mean, the guy was pushing the ass-kissing envelope. Even the art was a big smooch on the derriere. Goldman's photographer had studied with Annie Liebowitz and her photos—of me with joystick, me at keyboard, me with my arm around CEO Phil—were visual dynamite. The killer was the cover: a formal portrait of me in chinos, penny loafers, and signature Spiderman tie. Heck, that was me, the way I saw me, before the madness, anyway.

By the end of the piece, I almost felt a moral obligation to offer Goldman a job.

So, there with a hundred or so others was this communication from Allison O. Manchester. Allison could have been a corporate spy or some loser living in a trailer for all I knew, but wasn't I in the business of risks? Wasn't risk what life was all about? Besides, I had nothing against losers living in trailers—their kids bought my games, same as anyone.

I responded immediately.

Dear Allison,

You're right: the article has flooded me with e-mail. Of all the letters, though, yours is the only one that really caught my eye. Thanks for the compliments, but what about you? You said nothing about yourself except you're into money and fun (who isn't?) and that you look like Julianne Moore. Do I know who she is??!!! Would you believe she is my absolute favorite actress?

She wasn't. I'd only seen one of her films, Robert Altman's *Short Cuts,* and been singularly unimpressed with her abilities. But her looks—now that was a different story.

I continued:

Do we hire models for our games? As a matter of fact, yes. Let's meet online to discuss it further! We could also discuss 'software types' like me and which details about the opposite sex they might or might not appreciate. You'd be surprised!

Best,

Mark Gray

P.S. I'm with you on the glasses—it's definitely time for a change. The tie's pretty cool though, don't you think? See ya!

In the interest of full disclosure, I should note another e-mail that I received after *Wired,* one that, at the time, left me more excited. It was from Jack Nicholson—the real Jack Nicholson, as my secretary confirmed with a call to his agent. Jack wrote to tell me how much he enjoyed the article, how delightful it was to learn, as he put it, "the story behind the man behind the games" he'd played for so long.

I was deeply flattered, even if it was evident he had not the faintest memory of us meeting, many years ago.

CHAPTER TWO

I lived with my wife and son in a custom colonial on two acres in Marblehead, a seaside suburb of Boston. Our property bordered the ocean, a dead-end street, and the fourteenth hole of the Atlantic Country Club. We had an in-ground pool, underground sprinklers, a three-bay garage, a baseball diamond with backstop and stands, and a 25-foot sailboat. To my certain knowledge, there was no technology that captured or played image or sound that we didn't own. We had a wine cellar and our towels were monogrammed. I had over a thousand cassettes in my movie collection and almost as many video game titles, for every conceivable platform dating back to the original Atari. I mention all this not to boast, which would be pathetic, but only to illustrate the magnitude of the changes since Venice Beach.

My wife, Ruth, was a more telling illustration, and as I pulled into our driveway one evening two weeks after Allison came into my life, it was not the ambulance that I focused on for one micro-moment, but my wife. She'd been leaving for her daily run when Timmy, our son, had his attack, and there she was in her Reeboks and J. Crew jogging outfit, her hair—that magnificent auburn hair—down to her shoulders.

It's funny, what the mind can do.

As Timmy was being carried out of the house on a stretcher, Ruth at his side, I didn't see the woman who'd quietly added calcium to her diet and successfully campaigned for president of PTA. I didn't see the face across the breakfast table for sixteen years or the body beside me every night. For one fleeting moment, I saw the college girl who'd taken me by the hand into a Cape Cod dune one long-ago July afternoon and made love to me with such power and urgency that, had I closed my eyes, I would have been there again: feeling her skin, smelling her Coppertone, letting her pull me under to drown in a sea of lust.

I know: I'm dangerously close to sounding like Rod McKuen. But I don't believe you get more than half a dozen moments like that in your life, and that was one of them for me. If there was a sadness (and there was, though I did not recognize it then), it was realizing how long ago that day had been.

"How is he?" I asked.

"Okay—now," Ruth said.

"Did they intubate him?"

"No."

"Thank God."

This was the eighth time an ambulance had come since Timmy was born. I'd lost count of the times his asthma had sent us to the pediatrician.

"What triggered it?" I said.

"Three guesses."

"Pierpont."

Pierpont, a golden retriever, lived next door with Bob and Sue Morgan, two of the most sickening yuppies you'd ever want to meet—they'd made their millions in frozen yogurt and now spent it on Range Rovers and Sherpa-guided treks through Nepal. Definitely not our kind of people. Pierpont was electrically fenced, but of course that didn't stop Timmy, whose only pets were tropical fish, from getting to him.

"Sue called. By the time I got there, he was in shock."

I climbed into the ambulance.

"Hey, Scooter," I said, smoothing my son's brow.

His eyes brightened and he managed a smile. He was always so good about this.

"Everything's going to be all right now," I said.

Timmy lifted his oxygen mask and whispered: "I'm sorry, Daddy."

"For what?"

"Playing with Pierpont."

"Don't be silly."

"I promise I won't do it again."

"I know you won't."

Timmy took a breath—that terrible, wet breath we knew all too well.

"Daddy?"

"Scooter?"

"Will I always be sick?"

"Of course not."

"So, I'll be able to have a dog?"

"Of course," I said.

"And play Little League?"

"A hundred bucks say you will."

In truth, the doctors didn't know when, if ever, Timmy could play, or tolerate fur, or so much as climb a flight of stairs without struggling for air.

"Now no more talk," I said. "We've got to get you better."

An EMT beckoned: It was time to go. It was Ruth's turn to ride with Timmy. I would follow in my car.

It was an unusually warm night in early October. I had the window down and I heard crickets, and the last of the cicadas, and car radios tuned to rock 'n' roll.

And it was spooky, how much it was like the night Timmy was born. This was the same route we'd taken, to the same hospital where we were headed now, at almost the same hour and day of the month—Timmy's sixth birthday was in a week. Spooky, not only because the memory was so clear, but because it followed so closely my Cape Cod flashback. A shrink would've found something, I bet, exploring the link between the two.

Let me skip over the early stages of Ruth's labor and get right to when the baby began to crown—how, seeing white gloves streaked with crimson, I had one of my absurdist software thoughts: *Wouldn't this make one hell of a game, especially if you pushed it toward dark sci-fi, calling it* Alien Creation, *say.*

From absurdity, my thoughts shifted to the philosophical, a place they did not regularly visit. I was reminded of how profoundly our lives would change; of the awesome responsibility of having a child; of how our yard was big enough for a regulation-sized ballfield; of what kind of player our kid, girl or boy, would be—I was not sexist, you see. I thought of the extraordinary journey a human travels from single cell to infant—a being with the potential to fly F-16s or drive baseballs out of 75,000-seat stadiums. I thought of the innocence of babes and how they should not be punished for the sins of their parents. I was damn near metaphysical when, with one final humongous push, Timothy M. Gray came bawling into the world.

"Congratulations on a baby boy," the doctor said.

"He's beautiful!" Ruth said.

"He looks just like you, Dad," the doctor said.

I didn't respond to that.

Ruth didn't, either.

"Do you have a name?" the doctor said.

"Timothy," I said.

"Here," the doctor said, handing me a scissors. "Cut Timothy's cord."

"Isn't that what you get paid the big bucks for?" I said.

Pathetically enough, I had actually rehearsed this line, convinced it would make for a great comic moment.

It did not.

I cut the cord, and the doctor handed me my son. I whispered into his ear and kissed his nose and I did not notice that his skin was blue, his breathing labored, as if life already was a struggle.

"We have to take the baby now to clean him off," the obstetrician said. She wrapped Timmy in a blanket and took him out of the room.

"Come here," Ruth said. She took my hand and squeezed it with what little strength she had left. "Isn't he wonderful?" she said.

"He's the greatest."

"Do you love him?"

"More than anything."

"Honest?"

"I swear to God."

"I'm sorry for everything," Ruth said.

"That's behind us now," I said. "Let's never talk about it again, okay?"

"Okay."

I don't how much time had elapsed when a man in a lab coat entered the room.

"I'm Dr. Lindquist," he said. "I'm the neonatologist on duty tonight."

Neonatologist? I didn't like that.

"Is everything okay?" I asked.

"We're not sure," the doctor said.

"Oh my God," Ruth said.

"Your son has been transferred to intensive care," Lindquist said.

"What's wrong?" I asked.

Ruth was starting to cry. I wasn't too steady myself.

"We're concerned about him getting enough oxygen," Lindquist said.

"His lungs?"

"We're not sure of anything at this point," Lindquist said, "only that your son is in good hands."

Timmy had open-heart surgery on the second morning of his life and spent the next month at Massachusetts General Hospital. After so many return visits, they considered us family, which is why we were greeted by first name tonight.

"Back so soon?" the head nurse said as Timmy was settled into a bed with an oxygen tent. "You must've missed us."

Timmy smiled.

"Dr. Davis is on his way," the nurse said. "As a matter of fact, here is now."

We made small talk as our pediatrician adjusted Timmy's oxygen, started another IV, and ordered a portable chest X-ray.

"You're lucky," Davis said. "I wouldn't be surprised if he went home tomorrow."

Half an hour later, Timmy was sleeping comfortably. It was almost eleven, when I had a very important appointment.

"Go home," I said to Ruth.

"But it's my turn this time," she said.

"But what about your presentation tomorrow?"

"I'm ready," Ruth said. She was vice president of development at Harvard College. They were in the middle of another of their capital campaigns.

"And you expect to be clear-headed after a night here?"

"I'll manage."

"No," I said, "I'll manage. All you've talked about for two weeks is this presentation. Go home."

"If I didn't know better," Ruth said, "I'd think you were trying to get rid of me."

I was suddenly panicked. Did I sound overly solicitous? Flat-out devious? Despite how the media would soon be portraying me, I was not well-practiced in deceit.

"No," I said, recovering nicely, "I only want you to give the presentation of your life."

"Well, it is a big one," she conceded. "You sure you don't mind?"

"Not even a little. I brought my laptop."

"You're such a snore," Ruth said, with a laugh. "Always working."

"The shit never ends."

"I think it's almost time for Vermont," Ruth said.

"I'm sold," I said.

"Columbus Day weekend?"

"You've got a deal. Now go home."

We kissed, lightly, and she was gone.

It was ten past eleven. I knew Ruth would not call until morning.

I pulled the bedside phone from its jack and plugged in my modem.

CHAPTER THREE

"I'm sorry I'm late," I typed into my laptop.

"I was beginning to think you were standing me up!" Allison responded.

"Like that's possible. Timmy had another asthma attack. He's in the hospital. I'm here with him now."

"Are you alone?"

"Except for the nurse. She comes and goes."

"I have something for you," Allison typed.

I knew what it was: her picture. For two weeks, she'd promised it. Two weeks and—nothing. She was such a tease.

"Not your GIF," I typed.

"That and more."

"A video clip?"

"After a fashion. It's not up to your exacting standards."

"I think you already know you exceed my standards!" I typed.

"So, you want it?"

"Is the pope a Catholic?"

It was amazing, how inane I could sound with Allison. Ruth would never have believed it. Allison maintained it was part of my charm.

"You're the very first one to get this," Allison typed. She gave me the address of her new homepage, which had become operational only this afternoon.

"I'm honored."

"I'll meet you back here in five minutes. Hope you like me."

"You could have two heads and I'd like you!" I typed.

"Silly. See ya in five."

I'll spare you the details of how what began with e-mail had become, in only two weeks, a relationship, if that was the word (it wasn't), I could barely go an hour without rumination. You might conclude that the true underlying pull was sexual, and I would be hard-pressed to refute that in light of what was to come. But until tonight, there had been nothing overt. Only innuendo, sprinkled into small talk and digitally rendered.

This is what Allison had revealed about herself: She was twenty-seven, single, and unattached. She lived on the Upper East Side with her father, a senior vice president at World Bank. Her friends included poets, filmmakers, musicians and artists. She loved the Yankees and was into movies big-time. She was a skilled video gamer and she repeated, every conversation we had, her desire to model for CreativeWare's VR. I admit that laid out like this, Allison sounds like some stereotypical Gen X character—Zelda Fitzgerald for the '90s, if you will. At the very least, Uma Thurman in *Pulp Fiction*. Of course, that was the point. Allison was somewhere I wanted to go, and whether it really existed was increasingly irrelevant.

So those were the bullets on the bio card; beyond them was shadow.

Allison never offered to explain, and I never asked, why she had no boyfriend. She told great tales of a summer she'd spent on Venice Beach, but drew a blank when I mentioned the Santa Monica Pier. Twice, she signed off abruptly when someone was at the door. And despite our growing electronic intimacy, there seemed dead space where I expected dazzling emotion—I couldn't see what was in her heart, if you want to get country-and-western about it. Naturally, I'd had one of my absurdist software thoughts: that some particularly clever hacker had created a robot woman, and unleashed her on the net. I bet a guy like Gates would get his jollies that way.

Except Allison was flesh-and-blood.

I knew, because I'd found an "A. Manchester" in the Manhattan phone book and when I'd called, claiming, in an amateurishly disguised voice, to be a telemarketer, a woman identifying herself as Allison answered.

Only two weeks into it, and the madness already had a firm hold.

Truth was, I'd become a puppy at her feet. I couldn't open up enough to Allison, couldn't tell enough stories and infantile jokes, couldn't have asked for a better audience. And you'd think she and Charlie Goldman were in league, the way she poured it on.

Allison thought it was ultimate cool that I owned a 1967 Corvette Sting Ray and had built my own Field of Dreams, as she called it, in my backyard. She said I would have made an awesome film director—still could, if I wanted to. How did she put it? "Channel your creative genius in more cinematic directions," I believe it was. "The power of your imagination could take you anywhere."

The power of your imagination. I like the phrase now more than ever.

I was blindly rushing into things, of course, and now that I've had opportunity to examine why, what I keep coming back to is something simple, and sobering, and ultimately pathetic and sad: In all the years I'd been faithful to Ruth, no one had ever come on to me like this stranger who bore an uncanny resemblance to a certain Hollywood movie star.

Temptation, a taste of fruit in the Garden of Eden.

"What do you think?" Allison typed when we were connected again.

"You're even more beautiful than I imagined."

"Thank you."

"You belong in Hollywood."

"Silly."

"I mean it. You could be Julianne Moore's twin."

"You know where I really belong—in virtual reality."

"I'm working on it," I said, and I was. Just this week, I'd given one of my engineers a special assignment.

I wasn't exaggerating about Allison's resemblance to Julianne Moore. This was Weirdsville, folks. I mean, in the similarity department, certain people remind you of someone else, some are worth a double-take, and then you've got your clones. Allison was a clone. I could speak with absolute certainty because I'd bought all of Julianne Moore's videos and watched them, several more than once, after Ruth was asleep, in the privacy of my study.

And I must tell you, the more I saw of the actor, the more I was taken. Even the titles of her films seemed rich with meaning: *Roommates*; Steven Spielberg's *The Lost World: Jurassic Park*, blockbuster of the year; *Boogie Nights*, in which she played porn actress Amber Waves. There was a thin line between my fascination and the insanity that drives a stalker.

Like Moore, Allison had long red hair that fell to her shoulders in waves, and her skin was fair and completely without blemish. Her eyes were a cat-like green, her lips soft and full and almost—almost—pouting. And you would have lingered on that face if your eye hadn't been drawn to her neck and her white dress, cut low. She was wearing a pearl necklace and I wondered if she removed it before making love...and somehow knew she didn't.

That was the still, the GIF, I found on the opening pane of her homepage. From the purely technical point of view, her video clip was less stunning, but what it lacked in digital sophistication it more than made up for in its power of suggestion. Fifteen seconds long, it showed Allison, in a diaphanous gown (could it have been anything else?), moving in seductive slow motion through a rooftop garden, the twinkling lights of Manhattan visible beyond.

And I was wondering which character in *Virtual Clue* best suited such an ethereal but oddly stereotyped presence when I was reminded of a strange thought I'd had watching Julianne Moore kissing Hugh Grant in *Nine Months*:

Those incredible lips...they're Sally Martin's lips.

Sally was the first girl I ever kissed—a sweet, plain-looking, unassuming soul who had genuine goodness in her heart. Sally had been on my mind a lot lately, since sending me an invitation to our twenty-fifth high school reunion, which she was organizing. I hadn't seen Sally in over twenty years.

"Ran into your dad," her letter said, "and he tells me you're doing real good. I'm not into computers or anything, but it sounds like you're the Star of Our Class. That's what I told the magazine guy anyway, I forget his name. I know September is late for a reunion, but it took a while to get my act together. Like that would surprise you! Anyway, hope you can come. You know, for old times' sake and all that. There's lots to talk about. I work as a CNA at the Blue Hill Rest Home and I'm divorced now (married a cop, you wouldn't believe what a jerk he was) but considering everything, I've got nothing to kick about. Let me know.

"Love, Sally.

"P.S. Remember the night we spent on Blue Hill? Will you ever forget the sunrise the next morning?"

I didn't go to the reunion. I didn't even write to decline the invitation, which was awfully shitty of me, no way around it, but what would I have said—water seeks its own level? I wasn't being insensitive. I just wasn't up for it, not then.

You should know that at the time of Sally's letter, I wasn't big on the hidden meanings of dreams.

A horse was a horse, not a symbol; the dead didn't speak; past lives didn't surface. That was touchy-feely New Age stuff, and if you could make a buck or two off it, I had no problem. But that parting line about Blue Hill—why did Sally put *that* in there? It stuck in my skull like some Top Ten song and incorporated itself into a dream.

In it, Sally and I were sitting atop Blue Hill, the highest point in our hometown, which is halfway up the coast of Maine. Nothing happened—that's what was so spooky. We didn't make love as the sun came up, as we had in real life so many summers ago. There wasn't any cool dream metamorphosis—her turning into a bird and flying off over the ocean, say, a scene that, for all my cynicism, might have symbolized something. We were just together, Sally and me. She was talking, but I couldn't hear what she was saying. Then she was gone and I was at Massachusetts General Hospital, holding my son and marveling at how tiny he was, and how sick.

When I awoke, I had two thoughts, neither of which I could dislodge from my brain. The first was: Can old lovers still carry a flame after two decades?

And the other was: When Sally had made love to her ex-husband, had she ever, even once, thought of me?

"Do you like the dress?" Allison typed.

"I love it."

"And the necklace?"

"Exquisite."

"They're real pearls. You wouldn't want to know what they cost."

"Five grand?"

"You must be kidding."

"Ten?"

"Try twenty."

"That's a lot for a necklace."

"But worth it, don't you think?"

"Absolutely."

"Have you ever bought Ruth jewelry like that?"

I had, on our tenth wedding anniversary.

"Never," I said. "But it's something I'd buy you."

"You're so sweet! Here we've only known each other two weeks and you're already offering to buy me pearls!"

"That's pretty presumptuous of me, isn't it?"

"Yes...and I love it. To hell with the feminists—I still believe women can accept gifts from men."

"Not only can, but should."

"I like your style."

"And I like yours."

"Excuse me one second," Allison typed.

I used the break to check on Timmy. He'd gone to sleep in his Red Sox cap.

"Here I am," Allison typed.

"Welcome back."

"Did you notice anything else in my video?"

"Only how much you really do look like Julianne Moore."

"You didn't notice I wasn't wearing a bra?"

Now this was something we hadn't gotten into before.

"If you look carefully, you can tell," Allison went on.

"You're right," I said.

"I need to ask you a question," Allison said. "It's something I've wanted to ask for a while."

"Shoot."

"It's a very personal question."

"I promise a very personal answer."

"Have you ever had a fantasy about me?"

Jesus. Her sentence hung there on the screen.

"Did I offend you?" Allison typed.

"No," I answered. "It's just not your run-of-the-mill question."

"Who ever said I was run of the mill?"

"Good point."

"Maybe I'm smitten. It's not something you can control, you know. Or maybe I'm high. Cocaine loosens inhibitions."

"Believe me, I know."

"Of course—Venice Beach. We've talked about that! Well? You haven't answered my question."

"I'm thinking."

"Don't. Let it come from your soul."

"You want me to be honest?"

"Brutally."

"Yes, I've fantasized about you."

"Tell me about it."

"Boy!"

"I've opened up to you," Allison said. "Now it's your turn. Fair's fair."

"We were at your place…." I began.

"And?"

"I kissed you."

"Was it good?"

"Better than good. You have the most amazing lips."

"Thank you. Was there anything else?"

"Well…."

"Go on."

"I touched your breasts."

I felt like I was 15, writing that sentence. I felt naughty and embarrassed and like a total low-life creep…and deeply aroused.

"Which turned me on," Allison wrote. "But you didn't stop there. You couldn't stop there."

"No."

"Did you have a whip?"

Excuse me?

"Or chains? Don't answer," Allison wrote. "I don't want to hear any more yet."

"Okay."

"But keep the fantasy in your head. Is it there?"

"Yes."

"Imagine I was there…but not there."

"I don't understand," I said.

"And you're supposed to be the Software Star! Imagine you were in Boston and I was in New York but we were having sex together."

"Through VR."

"Exactly. If we wanted to, someone else could join us. Maybe someone from your past. Maybe Julianne Moore!"

"It would be awesome."

"Wouldn't it? Forget Clue, Mark. Clue's for kids."

I held my breath and typed: "Would you model for a game like that?"

"In a New York Minute."

I couldn't believe the shift we'd taken in the last five minutes. What did it matter if Allison were horny or high or only cunningly opportunistic in some freaked-out MTV kind of way? I was thinking about watching her undress in our digital actor motion capture room and I was getting *wiggly,* a word she'd soon be introducing me to. I was one hurting pup.

And I was about to type some unbelievably lame line— "Shouldn't we rehearse in real life first?" I believe it was—when an alarm started ringing.

Timmy, was my initial reaction, but it wasn't Timmy; it was the boy in the room across the hall.

"Just my luck," I typed. "There's a code or something. I better go."

"Talk tomorrow?" Allison replied. "By phone?"

"You mean it?"

We'd never actually spoken before.

"I do."

"I'll be at the office at nine."

"I can't wait!"

"Me too."

"Toodles, Mark!"

"Sweet dreams, Allison."

A nurse was wheeling a machine with paddles down the hall. It was not the end to the evening I would have written. It made me think of my childhood hero, for reasons I didn't want to explore—but did, nonetheless, as I tried to sleep.

CHAPTER FOUR

A week later, the Red Sox were in the playoffs.

I won't get sidetracked here on an examination of the Red Sox soul—to the fan, I need say nothing, and for the rest of you, nothing I could say would make sense. Suffice it to say that Red Sox seasons begin with extraordinary hope and end in extraordinary despair, so that on those rare occasions when they make the playoffs, the faithful will do anything to get to Fenway. In my case, it was no problem. CreativeWare had season tickets.

I brought Timmy. He'd been returned to health, such as it was for him, and for an extra-special treat we took my Corvette. We parked in an attended lot and walked to Fenway through a whirl of vendors. Timmy held my hand and every few feet, there was a tug.

"Can I have peanuts, Daddy?"

"Not unless you say the magic word," I said—as if I'd ever refused.

"Please?"

I bought the peanuts.

"Can I have a Coke—please?"

I bought a Coke.

"Can I have a pretzel—pretty please?"

I bought a pretzel.

Was that good parenting—a chronic inability to say no? I didn't give care what Doctor Laura would say. The way I figured it, asthma had tipped the cosmic scales against Timmy and it was up to Ruth and me to restore balance. Toys, video games, computers, McDonald's, Fenway, the circus, Disneyland every

February, Six Flags every July—maybe after piling all that on Timmy's side, the needle might budge, however slightly, in his favor. I honestly believed this attitude was the cornerstone of being a family man.

We had four box seats: first-base side, two rows from the field, yet more proof that CreativeWare was doing just fine. Phil was already there, with his new girlfriend.

"Hey, Scooter!" he said when he saw us.

"Hi, Uncle Phil."

Timmy showed off his glove. It was a carefully oiled Wilson—finest glove there is.

"You're going to catch one tonight!" Phil announced.

"You always say that," Timmy said.

"But tonight, I feel it—I swear I do. Don't you feel it, Markie-boy?"

"I feel something," I said.

"I look at Mo Vaughn warming up," Phil went on, "and I know it'll be one of his."

"Do you think he'll autograph it for me?" Timmy said.

"Without a doubt."

"Aren't you forgetting something?" I said to Phil.

"What?"

"Your friend."

"I'm Lisa," the woman with him said softly.

"Oh, right," Phil said. "Lisa Tessier, I'd like you to meet Mark Gray and his son, Timmy. Mark, Timmy—Lisa."

"Hi," Timmy said. "You can call me Scooter."

"Okay, Scooter."

"Pleased to meet you, Lisa," I said.

"Same here," she said. "Phil's told me so much about you."

And Phil so much about you, I could have replied, *including the fact that you give great head, the scum.*

No question, Lisa was hot—leggy and blonde, like Alicia Silverstone in Batman and Robin. She was wearing a white T-shirt and denim cut-offs, and she'd done her hair in a ponytail that dangled out the back of a Red Sox cap. She was fast approaching thirty, but her posture, smile and makeup all shouted high school cheerleader—not that I was opposed in principle to the look, mind you. She was the quintessential Phil babe, all right: divorced, childless, a paralegal. He'd gone out with so many women like her that you had to wonder if someone were bioengineering them for him.

"This is my first Red Sox game," Lisa said.

"No kidding," I said.

"It's my sixth game this year," Timmy said, "but Daddy never took me at night before."

"Why not?"

"'Cause of this."

Timmy showed Lisa his inhaler.

"I have asthma."

"I had it too when I was his age," Phil said. "I keep telling him he'll outgrow it."

"You poor thing," Lisa said, and gave her boyfriend a kiss.

I looked at Phil tonight and thought, hardly for the first time: *Thank you, Jesus, I am not like him.*

Phil was short, fat and bald—not the sort of guy who should have fancied gold chains and Rolex watches, but he did. I mean, he was an aesthetic nightmare. If he had any saving grace, it was that he didn't wear a toupee. So, what did the Lisas of the world see in him? The flippant answer is money, but that was only part of it. Like Lyle Lovett, Phil had made ugliness an asset: He projected sensitivity and need. It was all practiced art—I'd seen him part venture capital from Wall Street investors often enough to know he didn't have a vulnerable cell in his body— but women like Lisa instinctively wanted to mother him. It seemed a perversity of nature.

Timmy tugged on my hand. "Dad," he said, "if I don't catch a ball will you buy me one?"

"Of course," I said.

"With Mo Vaughn's autograph?"

"Aren't you forgetting something?"

"Please?"

"We'll see."

"Pretty please?"

"All right," I said.

"You're the best dad in the whole wide world!"

"Softie," Phil said.

"I think he's cute," Lisa said, and I knew what was going through her mind: that someday, sooner rather than later, she wanted a kid like him.

I never could visit Fenway without thinking of my father.

I would never have admitted it to him, of course, because it would have plunged us into issues I never intended to revisit, but it was true. Just seeing the Citgo sign in Kenmore Square set me off.

Dad was an Episcopal priest until his retirement a few years back, and my guess is when he gets to the pearly gates, Saint Peter will wave him straight through.

And not only for the collar he'd worn.

Dad believed in social justice, believed that principle mattered more than ascending the Episcopal hierarchy, even though principle had cost him a bishopric. He believed life was about more than desiring things, and my mother, who'd been raised in a house without plumbing, agreed. Dad went stratospheric over war. He'd been a conscientious objector during the Second World War, not exactly the launchpad for a Great American Hero, and his sermons on Veterans Day and Memorial Day were thundering tirades against the military-industrial complex. It was scary, watching the guy who read me Thornton Burgess starting before I could walk transformed into Cotton Mather of the nuclear age. And when I was too old to be scared, I was pissed.

Lest you imagine him as all fire and ice, it must be noted that Dad had two—exactly two—earthly indulgences.

One was Sunday dinner, which he always cooked to give Mom a day off.

The other was the Boston Red Sox.

Dad had played ball as a kid, well enough to be invited to tryouts the year he graduated from high school. He idolized Foxx and Williams, and he was at Fenway with my grandfather the day in 1946 that the Sox clinched their first pennant in three decades. Once a year, in August, we drove down to Dorchester, where my mother's brother lived in a triple-decker. It was our vacation, all we ever took—me and Dad at Fenway while Mom bought school clothes at Filene's Basement, where goods after three weeks were automatically marked down 75 percent.

If I had one certainty in my young life, it was that I was going to play for the Sox when I grew up. I was going to have my face on Wheaties boxes and drive a red Corvette with a 427 V-8 and when I pulled into Fenway, I was going to be mobbed by fans seeking autographs. In other words, I was going to be just like Tony Conigliaro, youngest player in history to hit 100 home runs.

I still had my Little League scrapbook and sometimes, for no reason at all, I flipped through it. "Gray Hits Third Grand Slam of Season," is one of the headlines from the Bangor Daily News. "Gray Leads Blue Hill to Maine Title," is another, from the June 21, 1967, edition. I was ten that year. Ten! No other starter was so young. We went to Hartford for the regionals, and it was there that I faced the best fastball pitcher in all of New England.

I remember watching him warming up and thinking with a fear worse than going to the dentist: *The ball's a blur! I'll never be able to hit it!*

His first pitch to me was a ball, his second a strike. I didn't see his third until it was too late to duck: It hit me in the left temple and I fell, unconscious.

When I came to, I was in an emergency room, an ice pack on my head.

"You were very lucky, son," the doctor said. "I've seen kids in comas from less."

And I can still see it—the knowing nod he and my father exchanged.

Mom got sick right after that.

"I don't feel myself, is all," she started to say, and pretty soon, she was spending most of every day on the couch.

That part of that summer is a blur—no matter how I've tried to bring it into focus, all I come up with is Mom under an Afghan and the TV on without the sound. She didn't make the trip with us to Boston that summer, but she insisted Dad and I did. We stayed with Uncle Bob, and on August 18, the day everything changed, we were at Fenway Park.

Let me wax mildly philosophic for a moment, even if it's alien territory for me until now, when I am making amends, as you shall see.

You get to be forty-some years of age and you've lived something on the order of sixteen thousand days, roughly half the allotment to the average guy, and the great percentage are blanks in the memory file. Of the remainder, most are fuzzy. What's left are those rare days when your angle of vision shifts, if only by a degree, leaving you forever with a different view of your world—days when things happen that you don't anticipate, can't control, and will never forget.

A July afternoon on a Cape Cod dune is one of those days for me.

Christmas and Valentine's Day the year before Timmy was born are two more.

Friday, August 18, 1967, is still another.

I close my eyes and I can see the sun setting over Fenway, can feel my hand inside my glove, a Wilson that Mom gave me for my ninth birthday. I hear Dad, happy for the first time since Mom took sick, explaining with uncharacteristic enthusiasm why the bleachers are the statistically proven best place to catch a Tony C. home run because of how he pulls the ball—nothing, of course, about how the bleachers are all we can afford. I didn't come to that realization until much later.

"Today's the day, Mark," he said, "I feel it."

I said: "Does He feel it, too?"

And Dad saying impishly: "Who—the Big Guy?"

This was Dad at his wickedest—you knew he'd be good for an extra Coke, a day like this.

"Yeah, the Big Guy," I said.

"Oh, yes, He feels it, too," Dad said. "I can tell, because we've been doing a lot of talking lately."

Talk was what Dad called prayer, when explaining it to little kids.

Even if you're only marginally into baseball, you know where this one goes.

Jack Hamilton was pitching for the California Angels when Tony C. came to bat. I had Dad's binoculars and I followed

Conigliaro as he left the warmup circle. The first ball was a strike. Conigliaro fouled the second off behind first base. The next pitch, a fast ball, caught Conigliaro in the left cheekbone. I heard it—I swear I did, three hundred and seventy-nine feet away—a sound like a hammer on wood.

Tony C. fell.

The crowd went silent, and Fenway Park suddenly seemed frighteningly huge, and then the woman next to me began to cry.

She was a woman like Lisa: pretty, ponytailed, dressed in cut-offs and a tee shirt with Tony C.'s number. I remember having stared at her breasts when she wasn't looking—how I saw Dad sneaking a look, too. I remember her telling me how she went every weekend to the club where Tony C. hung out. I remember the smell of the baby oil she rubbed onto her arms and legs, tanned to bronze, like Bridget Bardot, whose picture I'd secretly cut from a Look magazine from the library. I was a boy, discovering, awkwardly like all of us, sexuality.

I remembered all that and could not but wonder, sitting there at Fenway now with my own son more than thirty years later, where she was now and did she still feel good enough about herself to tan or did she heed the emerging warnings about skin cancer, and was she a grandmother—and did she have even the faintest memory of the boy sitting next to her that day.

I didn't cry, at first.

I knew that any second, Tony C. would get up, brush himself off and take first base, and the next time he faced Hamilton, he would send his darn beanball all the way to Kenmore Square. Yaz would knock one out, too, and maybe George Scott also for good measure, and that would teach the Angels a thing or two about messing with the man.

But Tony C. didn't get up.

He lay in the dirt, motionless, as men in white rushed out with a stretcher.

I started to cry then. Dad talked soothingly and held my hand, and when I didn't stop, he led me out to Landsdowne Street. I didn't know, of course, that he'd already decided I would never play baseball again, or that the tumor inside Mom would kill her before New Year's Day.

Tonight featured Wakefield against Martinez, the Indians' ace. Naturally, the Sox would go on to blow it, but the game started as a classic pitchers' duel and by third inning, Timmy was itchy.

"*You* were the one who pestered me to come," I said, "on a school night, no less."

"But I'm bored," Timmy said. "Nobody's hitting anything. I'm never going to catch a ball."

"If you'd like," Lisa said to me, "I could take him for a walk."

"Can we look for my ball?" Timmy asked.

"Of course—and get a hot dog, too," Lisa said.

"Please, Daddy?"

"Are you sure it won't be an imposition?" I said.

"I'm sure," Lisa said. "Can I get you anything?"

"No, thanks."

"Phil, honey?"

"A beer. And make it a Budweiser—not Bud light. I hate that shit you drink."

"I know," she said, kissing him again on his gerbilly cheek.

I could prattle on about how Lisa didn't exactly have the best taste in men, but the truth was I was starting to like her. She wanted to please and be pleased, sincerely wanted to be happy, and when I looked at her, I saw what I'd seen in Sally Martin before our relationship took its final plunge: reality about to dash hope. I watched Lisa being so solicitous of Phil and I wondered what he'd told her—whether about his two failed marriages, or the daughter in Texas he saw once a year, or the multitude of women like her that he'd fucked, only to dump when he wanted fresh meat, as he sometimes disgustingly called it. I wondered, and realized it probably wouldn't change a thing for her. Hope can be a blinding agent, until it's not.

"So, what do you think of her?" he asked when she and Timmy had gone off.

"She's very nice," I said.

"She gives great head."

"I believe you've already noted that."

"I keep telling you: You ought to find yourself a girl like her," Phil said. "Before you're too old to get it up."

I hadn't come to Fenway planning to mention Allison to Phil. I hadn't intended to swap war stories or solicit his advice, although he could have taught a doctoral course on adultery. I was...is *adolescent* the right word? I believe it is. You listen all those years to a guy who measures success with a penis and it has to affect you, subconsciously if nowhere else. And the truth was Phil had continued living a life I'd once led, too.

"You're the last person I should show this to," I said, handing Allison's photo to Phil. I'd had one of our engineers punch it up some. It was almost gallery quality now.

"Good-looking chick," Phil said.

"Remind you of anyone?" I said.

Phil gave the photo another look. "No," he said.

"Not someone in the movies?"

"Here we go again. You and your goddamn movies."

"Not like, say, Julianne Moore? The actress in Nine Months?"

"Maybe there's a vague resemblance."

"Vague? They could be twins, for Christ's sake. Look at those lips."

"It's not where my attention was focused," Phil said. "Who is she?"

"Her name is Allison Manchester. She's from New York."

"How'd you find her?"

"I didn't," I said. "She found me."

I filled Phil in, ending with yesterday, when I'd blown off a quarterly financial meeting to talk two hours on the phone with Allison.

"You little devil—you're in love!"

"I didn't say that."

"Then you're in lust. It's okay, Markie-boy."

I hated it when he called me that.

"So long as she's not a spy," he said.

"She's no spy," I said. "She wants to model for Clue."

"As who—Miss Scarlet?" Phil roared. "I thought you were an R&D guy, not a comedian."

"I'm still working on the details," I said.

"To hell with details—get a hotel room. This one's a slam dunk."

"No," I said, "this one's a friend."

Phil put his arm around me. I hated that worse than when he called me Markie-boy. It reminded me of one of the sleazeballs in *Good Fellas*.

"Listen to your Uncle Phil," he said. "How old are you—forty-two, right? And I'm forty-three. A guy our age has no business turning down a girl like that. Who knows when opportunity will knock again? Go for it."

"There's nothing to go for."

Phil reflected a moment.

"I get it," he finally said. "You're afraid of being caught."

"No."

In truth, I hadn't gotten that far in my thinking.

"Please don't give me some shit about a moral crisis," Phil said. "This isn't about morality. This is about pussy."

"You're a fucking pig," I said, and I meant it.

"No, I'm a fucking realist. How often have I told you—it's nature. You can no more change that than stop taking shits."

He'd given me this crap before: How every life form, from amoeba to man, is driven on the most primal level to procreate—how, given the realities of sperm, males are predestined to ceaseless conquest. Sociobiology provided Phil an excuse for his affairs and even a rationale for his exclusive pursuit of younger women: fresh eggs. It was as elaborate, and disgusting, a justification for zipper trouble as there could be.

"You remember the *Time* magazine piece?" Phil said.

I did. *Time* a couple of years back had done a cover story on infidelity, packaged under an even hipper name than sociobiology: *evolutionary psychology*, I believe it was.

"Remember what it said about guys who have been monogamous too long?" Phil said.

"No."

But I did. I'd read that section carefully.

"Something to the effect that their mental health is at stake," Phil said. "I say go for it, big guy."

We left it there—Lisa was back with Timmy. He bounded

into my lap while Lisa handed Phil his beer.

"Did you get the ball?" I said.

"Nope," Timmy said, "but I got a hot dog and a Coke."

"I hope you don't mind," Lisa said.

"Certainly not. As long as he said thank you."

"Thank you, Lisa."

"You're welcome, Scooter."

And I thought not how she was in bed but: *What a good mother and wife she'd make.*

I saw her hand in Phil's and while I've never been called a softie, it saddened me.

CHAPTER FIVE

November 29, the day I finally met Allison, began like any other in the Gray household.

The coffee machine started. The automatic thermostat brought the temperature up. Ruth woke Timmy. I turned on CNN and checked for overnight e-mail and faxes. Timmy fed his tropical fish. Ruth fixed Timmy's Cheerios…and on and on and on, the humdrum but reassuring mechanics of everyday existence.

I'd never really dissected the routines of my adult life so carefully before, and now that I had, the results were chilling. Ruth, not Charlie Goldman, was right: Spiderman tie and all, I was the total snore. Except for baseball, I basically worked, played an occasional game of tennis, and watched old movies, alone, on a VCR. When had the pattern been set? Was there a single day that marked the transition? If I'd been able to identify it, would anything have changed? Or was this the best I, or anyone for that matter, had the right to hope for?

"Early start today?" Ruth said as I reached for my keys. She was still in her bathrobe.

"And I'm going to be late tonight," I said.

"You're always late," Timmy said.

"Not always," I said, "just recently. It's this darn VR."

"You promised I could play it," Timmy said.

"But Timmy, you know it's only a prototype."

"Yeah, but you still promised I could play it."

"How about this weekend?"

"Scout's honor?"

"Scout's honor."

"Awesome!"

I closed my briefcase and gave Timmy a kiss.

"Aren't you forgetting something?" Ruth said.

She put her arms around me.

"When did you get *those?*" she said.

Oh, fuck, I thought. As careful as I'd been planning tonight, I'd forgotten to mention my new glasses.

"A couple of days ago," I said. "I got new sunglasses, too," I hastened to add. "John Lennon style."

"I love them," Ruth said. "Horn rims were no longer you."

Exactly Allison's point, I thought. But it was spooky, hearing it from Ruth. I didn't know whether to be flattered or alarmed. She'd never had an opinion on my choice of eyeglasses.

"Must be a mid-life crisis," I said, forcing a laugh.

"Thank God you're not like *that!*" Ruth said.

"Thank God. I'll call you."

"Please do," Ruth said. "I love you."

"I love you, too."

Ruth kissed me—light and polite—but kept her arms around me.

"There's something I want to say," she said.

"What?"

"Sometimes I take you for granted."

Jesus, I thought. *Who wrote this script? And is it a dark comedy, tragedy or farce?*

"Sometimes I take you for granted, too," I said.

"I mean it," she continued. "I joke about you being such a snore, but all your hard work—I want you to know it's appreciated."

"Thanks. I appreciate everything you do, too."

"This is not a test," Ruth said, smiling. "You are not required to return my every compliment."

"That's a relief!"

We laughed, and as Ruth let me go, she said: "That's it. Today's Hallmark moment is officially concluded. Call if you're going to be later than—?"

"Midnight."

"Boy, you *are* into this VR."

"Hey, it pays the rent."
"Have a good one."
"You too."
"Bye Daddy!"
"Bye, Scooter."
I kissed Timmy again and went out the door.

An e-mail from Allison awaited me at work:

Dearest Mark,
I'll be enroute by the time you get this, but I had to tell you how wiggly I am thinking about tonight! Has the Corvette got plenty of gas? Who knows, maybe we'll decide to drive to Venice Beach! Or maybe we'll tour CreativeWare, like you promised.
Dinner will be fantastic, see you at 8!
Affectionately yours,
Allie ;)

The day flew by—I'd deliberately loaded up the schedule to eliminate dead spots in which I'd have too much time to think. I brainstormed with our PR guy, who was helping plan our appearance at the Video Gamers of America conference in New York next month, a regular dog-and-pony show featuring me as keynote speaker. I met with our V.P. of sales to ponder the disappointing results of *Shuttle Saga* in our Midwest test market. My spirits were restored talking to my market research chief, who'd gotten an excellent response from a *Virtual Clue* focus group. Phil took me through third-quarter results, and, as usual, I was dozing once he got into the detailed accounting. I met with my blue-sky folks to discuss an interactive magazine we would soon offer CreativeLine subscribers. I flipped through my Little League scrapbook, wondering, for about the millionth time, if Tony Conigliaro even knew who the Red Sox were during the last eight years of his life, when he was essentially brain-dead and incapable of lifting a spoon.

And I called Ruth when I knew she'd be at lunch and left a message on her machine confirming how late I'd be.

"Love you," I said.

I'd rehearsed those two words, and still I sounded like someone else, someone I didn't want to be.

After telling my secretary I was in desperate need of some of the "Imagination Time" Charlie Goldman had gone on at such length about, I left early—to visit the dry cleaner and the carwash. I swam my usual half mile at the health club, showered, then parked myself at the sink.

You'd think I'd never seen a mirror before the way I examined myself. You'd think I'd never shaved, or brushed my teeth, or combed my hair. I was like a teenage girl, preening for the prom.

Don't misunderstand—ordinarily, I'm no more vain than the next guy. I do not whiten my teeth, use cologne, frequent a hair stylist (a barber does just fine, thank you), or even shave every day. My first wrinkles did not send me running to a plastic surgeon, and I did not go into deep denial when my ophthalmologist said I'd need bifocals soon.

Not that I was Forrest Gump, happily oblivious to the passage of time.

My first gray—I'd watched it spread and figured there'd come a time I'd be tempted to have my barber quietly erase it. I'd cut my fat intake and stepped up the fresh fruits and vegetables. I drank red wine, not white—the miraculous protection of resveratrol, you know—and took a baby aspirin a day. Enteric coated, no less.

But what really counted, I believed, was not cholesterol or subcutaneous tissue.

It was attitude.

Here I was, officially middle age, and I was still on the cutting edge of the digital revolution, supposedly a young man's game—one of its gurus, in fact, a bonafide star, as Goldman had said, someone who in his own way was as vital as Steve Jobs.

I may have had a newfound appreciation for mega doses of Vitamin C, the Linus Pauling cure-all, but I hadn't gotten into line dancing or poetry slams or considered moving to Montana. I didn't hang wind chimes and crystals around the house to satisfy Feng Shui, nor had I embarked on some quest to find my Inner Child or returned to the Episcopalianism of my youth. I could read the sports pages without a twinge of depression, even though I was well aware that not a single professional athlete contained therein was older than me. NASCAR drivers don't count. *Look at Jack Nicholson, I sometimes thought, with a sense of reassurance. Sixty-one and still the toast of Hollywood.*

A hand brushed my shoulder. It was goddamn Phil.

He was naked and sweaty—not a pretty picture. He must've popped into the sauna while I was doing my laps. That's all Phil ever did at the club: park his porkish self in the sauna and read *Vanity Fair* and *Fortune* magazines. I wondered why he bothered coming.

He put his arm around me.

"Tonight's the big night," he said. "Not chickening out, are we? Remember: young snatch—nothing like it in the whole wide world."

"You're a pig, Phil."

"Like where am I supposed to believe this dinner of yours is headed—the opera?"

"I wasn't aware dinner had to lead anywhere."

"Relax," Phil said. "An affair should be fun."

"This is not an affair."

"Whatever. Just remember to have some for me."

"I ought to punch you."

"No," he said, "you ought to thank me for being your friend. Without my support, you'd be going home to the same old leftovers."

"You've crossed a line," I said, and I honestly did consider punching him. If my job hadn't been at stake, I would have.

"Sensitive, are we?"

Well, yes. *All your hard work,* I could hear Ruth saying. *I want you to know it's appreciated.*

Talk about fucked-up—until this morning, I believed I'd reached accommodation with that.

Have I left the impression I went blithely toward Allison?

I didn't.

Believe me: I may have taken leave of my senses, but even in the depths of the madness, I was no moral cretin. That's what I told myself, anyway.

I'd wrestled with Allison in ways Phil could never have imagined, and where I'd netted out was here: what Ruth didn't know wouldn't hurt her. Not the most sophisticated ethical argument, I'll grant you, but it worked, especially since I wasn't looking for anything beyond dinner—I just wanted to be in the same non-digital space with Allison, if only for an hour or two. I swear that was the limit of my desire, as disingenuous as it sounds now.

So why was I replaying this morning, an hour from dinner with Allison?

Because of who my wife was.

Ruth was a wonderful mother—I mean, it wasn't lip service with her, God knows Timmy had been a true test of that. She had a marvelous sense of humor, and not because she still laughed at my sophomoric practical jokes. She'd succeeded where many fail: developing into a whole person despite a pathologically deficient parent. She was pretty, which shouldn't have counted more than if she weren't, but it did. Ruth was forty, and I suppose I could have been hung up about that, since Americans are mostly blind to beauty in women that age and older, but God's truth, I didn't care that she had wrinkles and pregnancy had left varicose veins. I looked at our wedding album and I could honestly say I liked how she looked better than the day we were married, a decade and a half before. I could look into the future, and see better ahead.

No, it had to be something other than the mild effect of oxidants on Ruth that had brought me this far with Allison. It had to do with familiarity, though I would have been loath to admit that to Phil. It had to do with loss. I'd looked for that Cape Cod girl a lot since Allison's first e-mail and realized how rarely she was around anymore.

Maybe this was just aging, the circle of life.

Or maybe it was something else. Something requiring crucifixion in order to achieve redemption, is how my father would later put it.

We stood silently, a ludicrous-looking duo: me Q-tipping my ears, Phil arranging the hair over his bald spot.

Friend.

It had a troubling ring coming from Phil.

I'd had friends once, lots of them.

Bud Robbins, college roommate and best buddy from eighth grade, had been a friend. Doris Wong and many of our NYU classmates had been friends, or so I'd thought. Chris McCauley and the Venice Beach crowd. But they'd faded away, every one of them, until all that remained was Christmas cards and an occasional birth or wedding announcement, the latter more likely than not following finalization of a divorce. Paper communication with me was ironic, considering we lived in the communications age and I, CreativeWare's Creative Star, had been proclaimed one of its visionaries. And to think this was one of the simple issues.

What about the bigger ones?

Did all guys turn out like me—lone wolves who left the pack to run on their own?

Or was I an exception—an incomplete man who had room only for a family, a job, and a womanizing partner who was brilliant with money, which benefitted my bottom line.

Except for the philosophers and theologians, whose job it is to go that deep, did we all move more or less blindly through our adult lives?

Was I therefore an imposter—a guru whose intellectualism was as shallow as binary code?

A star that glittered on the outside but was a black hole within?

A man who couldn't even decide if pondering any of this was worth the time?

These were very basic questions and you would have thought I'd have answered them by now, but I hadn't; until this autumn, I hadn't even raised them in a serious fashion. Maybe I *was* like Forrest Gump, after all. Or maybe I was something less. Maybe I had the depth of one of the characters in my games. No deeper than the surface of a screen.

Phil broke the silence.

"Look at you," he said.

"What?"

"You're getting a double chin. I've never noticed it before."

"You're crazy."

"Turn that way."

Phil moved my jaw. I should have punched him.

"See?" he said. "A double chin."

"It's the light," I said.

"The hell it is! Take it from one who's onto chin number three—that's a double. And your Adam's Apple is gone. Subsumed by the spoils of success. Consider it a badge of honor."

Like I needed this shit right now.

"Fuck off, Phil," I said, heading to my locker.

"Just remember what I said about you-know-what," he called after me. "Nothing like it in the whole wide world."

Allison was late and as I waited, I tried to recall my last date—not that this was officially a date, mind you. Except for Ruth, it must have been a woman from Venice Beach whose name I couldn't remember, only the appeal of her body as she lay, legs spread, on a waterbed in a candlelit room that reeked of incense and weed.

Despite her homepage, I still had this nagging fear Allison would prove a fraud. Loser in trailer would introduce herself in that sultry voice, and I'd be out of there.

But Allison did not disappoint. The moment she appeared, I knew it was her.

"Mark?"

"Allison."

We shook hands and I planted a stupid sisterly kiss on her cheek and then, like some fumbling Jim Carrey. And I held her chair.

I have only a vague recollection of what we said those first few minutes—probably chit-chat about the restaurant, which was one of Boston's finest: the four-star Maison Robert. I was focusing all my energy on being cool—I remember that, painfully.

I remember how dry my mouth was, how I wished I'd had

a beer or two or ten before she arrived, how long the wine took to come.

Finally, it did. I'd prepared a toast. It spoke of fate and friendship, and it was pretty darn good, if I do say so myself. Not the least bit corny or presumptuous.

And as I raised my glass, the words flew out of my head.

"Here's to...to...."

The label caught my eye. I'd ordered a 1991 Cherryblock Cabernet Sauvignon, from Sonoma Valley.

"California," I said.

"To Venice Beach!" Allison agreed.

Relief: Allison to the rescue.

We were sailing now! Off and running! I clinked my glass against hers.

It shattered.

Shards flew, wine showered the table, and Allison was left holding a stem.

I believe at this point the screenplay would be labeled farce.

"Oh, no," I said. "Let me clean this up."

I reached for a napkin—and knocked the bottle over. It fell to the floor, spewing its contents as it did.

"I'm so sorry," I said. "Are you OK? Did I get any on you? Jesus. What a stupid klutz."

The restaurant was silent, all eyes on us, as the maître d' approached our table.

He did not look forgiving. He looked like he'd taken retirement from the French Foreign Legion and still had some score to settle.

"Monsieur, you and the young lady must abandon the table so that we may clean the *mess*," he said, very loudly.

We stood.

"You may sit over *there*," he ordered, beckoning to the table closest to the kitchen.

"I can't believe this is happening," I said.

Allison was giggling.

"I love it," she said. "Did you catch the look on his face—he was ready to have a stroke, the old fart!"

You can't imagine how grateful I was to her for that—one sarcastic comment, one nasty little crack, and the whole evening would have been in the toilet. But she'd saved it.

I settled down then.

The waiter brought a new bottle of wine and Allison got a new glass, and she insisted I make a new toast, and before you knew it, we were conversing as freely as by keyboard and phone. We talked about the murderous O.J. Simpson, who was still in the news that fall. We talked computers. We talked licensing and royalties and VR, and I revealed more than I probably should have about the inner workings of my firm. We compared notes on Hollywood and we talked about Bud Robbins, an executive vice president these days at Paramount/ Viacom—"my very good friend," I called him, even though we hadn't spoken in over two years.

We talked about The Cranberries, Jewel, and The Wallflowers, and pondered the tragic cosmic thread linking Jim Morrison, Janis Joplin, Kurt Cobain, John Lennon and Jimi Hendrix. I told her I cried when I heard the news about Cobain, even though it wasn't true, and I told her I'd been depressed for days after Lennon was shot, which was true.

I complimented Allison's hair and she called my new glasses "a definite happening thing."

I told jokes too ridiculous to repeat here and Allison laughed at every one.

And it was all quite the rush, to use that hideous '70s phrase, to discover I hadn't lost the touch.

"Please do it," Allison said when I mentioned my Jack Nicholson imitation, a great crowd-pleaser once upon a time.

"It's been so long," I said.

How long exactly—fifteen years, during the first year of my marriage?

"So? I want you to do it."

"Not here," I said. "The maître d' would kill me."

"Fuck the maître d'."

"He'll throw us out."

"Not before we pay, he won't. Don't be a wuss. I want you to do it."

"I left my shades in the car," I said.

Allison reached into her purse and handed me hers.

"Here," she said. "Do it."

I put them on.

"Chinatown or Cuckoo's Nest?" I said.

"Cuckoo's Nest."

Dipping my fingers in the water glass, I slicked my hair back and launched into the scene early in the movie where Randall Patrick McMurphy is interviewed on admission to the institution. And I must say I was pretty darn good, for being so out of practice. Allison begged for more, but the maître d' was lurking suspiciously, ready to pounce again

"He loves you," Allison said, but I had to draw the line somewhere.

I forget just where we were when libido began to assert itself—probably after dessert, when we were lingering over Amaretto. I had a wicked buzz going and as we talked, I studied Allison the way a critic might contemplate fine art.

God, she was perfect. Julianne Moore in the flesh.

Gravity hadn't touched her yet, nor had sun taken a toll.

And her lips—I've mentioned how I was fixated on her lips.

What I haven't mentioned is how there were times I studied her pictures and clip and thought I saw a certain sadness, as if she harbored some disturbing secret. A look that might have raised a red flag. But there was no trace of that tonight—only a girlish sparkle I'd first seen the night Sally Martin and I lost our virginity in a tent on Blue Hill.

But I wasn't stuck on Sally. Sally had never dressed like Allison, who was wearing a black skirt, red belt, and white blouse opened three buttons down. Pearl by pearl, my eyes moved down her necklace until I determined she was, in fact, wearing a bra. What is it, anyway, with men and bras? No matter: This one was ivory-colored and lace, allowing a contour of nipple. The sight actually had me *wiggly*. No other word fits.

Allison caught me staring.

I turned away.

"It's okay," she said. "I don't mind."

"I don't ordinarily look at a woman like that," I said.

"I don't ordinarily allow a man."

"Guess that makes two of us."

"Is this how you imagined tonight would be?" she said.

"Yes."

"What would make it better?"

As she said that, she touched her leg to mine.

"I can't think of a thing," I said.

"Nothing?"

I sat dumbly as Allison leaned over and kissed my cheek. It wasn't anything like my awkward sisterly opener—this kiss was enticement.

"Nothing?" she repeated.

"Well, maybe something."

"Let's go," she said, "to your car."

I'd parked next to Boston Harbor.

The night was unseasonably warm and we sat with the windows down. Allison was flipping out over my Vette. She couldn't stop touching it: instrumentation, leather upholstery, stick shift. She kept proclaiming it the car she'd always wanted.

I was prattling on about how my childhood baseball hero had owned this very car when she took a mirror from her purse, poured cocaine from a glass vial, and formed two neat lines with a hundred-dollar bill. She rolled the bill and snorted twice, one line per nostril. She drew two more lines and gave the mirror to me.

"Enjoy," she said.

"No thanks," I said.

"You have to."

"I really shouldn't."

"For Venice Beach."

"I think I'll pass."

"Jack would do it. You know he would."

"I'd like to," I said, "it's just...."

I didn't finish. I was thinking: *We could get arrested.*

How things had changed. There'd been a time when I'd regularly done nose candy on the Santa Monica Pier and not been concerned about anything save for its purity.

"It'd be a shame to waste it," Allison said.

"Maybe next time," I said.

"Who says there'll be a next time?"

I must have looked hurt because she said, gently: "Of course there'll be a next time. I'll save yours."

Allison did the lines herself and settled back in her seat and then I thought she was going to pass out. Beads of perspiration appeared on her forehead and her breathing sped up—and not some incremental adjustment, but a power shift to the point of hyperventilation. The pupils of her eyes dilated and I was about to ask if she was all right when her breathing returned to normal and her face relaxed.

It was astonishing, how quick the transformation was. Allison got this dreamy look and I noticed she was fingering her pearls.

"Kiss me," she said.

That's when I succumbed completely to the madness, with those two words.

Our mouths met and I inhaled wine and Amaretto, and discovered her tongue, and felt her hair. I'd forgotten this part altogether: the intensity of anticipation.

Allison pulled away.

"Imagine if you could do that with a machine," she said.

She'd lost me.

"VR," she explained.

"Oh, right."

"This would be only the beginning."

"It's a hell of a beginning."

"Imagine how many people you could please with a machine like that. Imagine being a digital lover. You'd live forever."

"As long as the hard drive didn't crash," I said.

Allison laughed, and then she turned the ignition key.

The engine caught. I watched the tach settle in at 1,100.

"Drive," Allison said.

"Any particular destination?"

"Ten Revere Way."

That was corporate headquarters.

"Why don't you take the wheel."

"Twist my arm," Allison said.

We exchanged places. I was about to explain the shift pattern when Allison popped the clutch and we roared off, leaving rubber.

I showed Allison my office first.

She noticed my new poster right away. Like you could miss it—I'd hung it next to the arcade version of *Shuttle Saga*, which greeted you when you walked through the door.

"Julianne Moore," she said.

"I told you she was my favorite actress," I said.

"You really *do* think I look like her, don't you?" Allison said.

"If I didn't know better," I said, "I'd actually think you were Julianne Moore."

I figured Allison might want to sit at my computer or something, but she didn't.

Thinking she'd like to re-enact Charlie Goldman's great Nerf fight scene, I handed her a Ripsaw Blaster and took a Chainblazer for myself.

"I challenge thee to a duel!" I said.

"Get real," Allison said, "I'm twenty-seven years old."

Ouch.

Thank God she perked up in our games room, where we had fifty platforms with fifty different titles, ours and most of our major competitors'.

But what she really wanted to see was our VR lab.

"It's like the Pentagon," she said outside the door, which had a sign: RESTRICTED ACCESS.

"Only six people are permitted in here," I said.

It was a lie, just as the sign was a lie—even the janitor had the code—but I could tell by the look on Allison's face that it was the right thing to say.

I punched the numbers and the lock opened. We stepped into the lab, a cavernous room that had warehoused paper goods in Ten Revere Way's previous life.

"Awesome," Allison said, so spontaneous and child-like that I was reminded of Timmy.

If she's a spy, I thought, *she trained with the CIA.*

The lab was loaded with computers and related hardware, of course, but they were dwarfed by the set we'd hired a

Broadway designer to build: a life-size recreation of the Clue gameboard. Digital actor motion capture required an actual 3-D environment.

"It's like a sound stage," Allison said.

"In a lot of ways, it is."

"All you need is a chair with your name on it. I told you you could direct!"

"When you get right down to it," I said, "I suppose that's what I've really been doing all these years. Except we use bytes instead of actors, ha-ha."

"Dig it. Mind if I walk around?"

"Just watch out for the live wires. Two-hundred-twenty volts of line current behind this baby."

Allison froze.

"Are you serious?"

"Of course not!" I said. "We plug extension cords into wall outlets."

"Jerk!" Allison said, slapping me playfully. We were way cool now.

Starting in the ballroom, we proceeded through the conservatory, billiard room, library and study. Allison didn't say anything until we'd left the kitchen.

"Awesome," she said. "I have just one complaint."

"Shoot."

"There's no bedroom. Don't more murders take place in bedrooms than anywhere else?"

"It was a marketing call."

"I keep telling you: Your marketing's wrong."

"Well, I do have something else to show you," I said.

I led Allison to a custom-built lounge chair—The Throne, we called it. She sat and I strapped sensors to her arms and legs, gave her handgrips, and helped her into our prototype helmet.

"Bear in mind we're at least a year from introduction," I said. "What you'll see is very crude. Can't even dignify it by calling it beta."

"That's cool," Allison said.

I was at the master console now. I booted up and followed on the screen a two-dimensional image of what Allison was seeing through her headgear.

"You're Professor Plum," I said.

"Okay."

"You have arthritis and so you get around rather slowly. Go ahead. Move your feet."

"I'm walking!" Allison said.

"You're in the hall."

"Awesome!"

"It's the only room we're happy with so far. Now you're going to meet someone. She'll come out of the door on your left. Go on. Walk over to it. Okay. Stop. Wait a minute."

I worked the keyboard. The door opened and a character with Allison's face and body appeared. Working off her homepage, my engineer had enhanced them to the point of startling realism. I'd given my best guy the job, I should add.

"This could be the adult version," I said.

"It's me!" Allison said. "It's really me!"

"A rough version of you. Like I said, we've a ways to go."

"Who am I in the game?"

"Miss Scarlet, of course."

"I love it. It's so—corny!"

"I couldn't see you as Mrs. Peacock."

"Could another player touch me?" Allison said.

"Not yet. The coding on this is unbelievably slow."

"It's just as well," Allison said.

"Why?"

"Because we haven't rehearsed yet," she said, and I didn't care, didn't give a good goddamn hoot, if it was a line.

We left CreativeWare after that. I was going to suggest a drink when Allison said: "It's almost midnight."

"Do you turn into a pumpkin at midnight?"

It was one of my inane little comments, but Allison didn't laugh this time.

"I have to be back at my hotel," she said.

"But the night is young."

She didn't laugh at that, either.

"My father is going to call," she explained.

"Call him from here."

I had a cell phone, of course. A Motorola flip model, StarTAC, state-of-the art, naturally.

"He's overseas. I don't have the number."

That sounded like horseshit. I debated not asking the first question that sprang to mind, but decided I had to.

"Are you seeing someone?" I said. "I mean, it's okay if you are."

"Men," she chuckled. "You're all alike. No, I'm not seeing anyone. I honestly am going to call my dad."

"Okay."

"You don't believe me."

"I believe you."

"You're angry."

"I'm not angry."

"But you're hurt."

"I'm not," I lied.

"I really care for you, Mark," she said, kissing me.

"I care for you, too, Allison."

"I've never met anyone like you," she said. "Just being with you makes me feel all wiggly."

"Me, too," I said. I was brightening.

"I want you to come to New York. Before Christmas. Will you?"

"Is the Pope a Catholic?" I said. And she laughed, and I laughed, and as I watched her disappear into the hotel, I had the most exhilarating, and absurd, thought:

She's waited her whole life for me.

CHAPTER SIX

I was transferring files onto my laptop when Timmy came into my study.

I saw his face and knew immediately what he was thinking. It was Monday morning, the 19th of December.

"Why do you have to go to New York?" he said.

"You know why," I said. "I have a conference."

"But *why?*"

"Because that's how I make money."

"Don't we have enough money?"

I'd never been asked that question before, except by my father.

"I have everything I want," Timmy continued. "Except for the stuff Santa's gonna bring."

"It's not that simple," I said.

"Why not?"

"Because it isn't. Someday when you're older, I'll explain."

"Are you gonna be home for Christmas?" Timmy asked.

"Of course I'll be home for Christmas. Christmas isn't until Sunday. I'll be back Wednesday. That's only two days, Scooter."

"Oh," Timmy said. "Do they have mailboxes in New York?"

"All over the place."

"Goodie!" he said, brightening. "You can mail my list."

"I thought we already mailed your list."

"This is my *new* list."

"I see."

"I did it this morning. Come look."

I followed Timmy to his room. He went to his computer and made a printout. It had everything from before: a hamster, a

Michael Jordan T shirt, a baseball autographed by Mo Vaughn, Star Wars and Batman figures, Legos, Where in the Universe is Carmen San Diego, a Nerf Chainblazer, six neon tetras and an algae eater. Only the priorities had changed: the hamster and Jordan had displaced Vaughn at the top of the list.

"Santa knows about your asthma," I said.

"I know," Timmy said. "But maybe he'll forget."

"I doubt it. Santa wouldn't do anything that could make you sick."

Timmy pondered that a moment.

"But baseballs don't make you sick," he said, "so Santa can bring that, right?"

"You got it."

I know I've given you reason to suspect Timmy was a spoiled brat, but he wasn't. He asked for things and he got things, and on those rare occasions when he asked but didn't receive, he didn't whine or throw a tantrum: the most he did is ask again. His autographed baseball, for example, which had surfaced as a major request during the Red Sox playoffs. I'd visited a couple of shops and placed some calls, without success, and eventually, as baseball had faded to basketball, with Michael Jordan replacing Mo Vaughn, Timmy had stopped asking.

And as I reflected on it now, I felt like a shit. I didn't like the feeling that but for the madness, I'd have persisted until I'd gotten Timmy his baseball.

"Well, Scooter," I said a few minutes later. "It's time to take me to the train station."

"You sure I can't go with you to New York?"

"Someday," I said, "but not this time. Now let's get going. Mom's already in the car."

I usually nap on the way to the city, but not this time. My mind was stuck in free-association mode and sleep eluded me.

I thought about my conviction that computers were reconfiguring our brains, the way TV itself had. I pondered my theory that VR, once firmly established, would do no less than reconfigure our physical lives. I thought about Allison, of course. I thought about my mother, calculating how old she'd be were she alive: sixty-seven, nine years younger than my dad. I thought about Phil and wondered if he were bringing Lisa to New York or, more likely, would be on the prowl again. I thought about Christmas Eve—how it was the most exciting night of the year for Timmy, what with watching *How the Grinch Stole Christmas*, and building a fire, and hanging the stockings, and leaving cookies and milk for Santa and his reindeer. I thought about tucking Timmy into bed, and after he was asleep: wrapping presents with Ruth, drinking wine, and finally tiptoeing up to bed—how every Christmas Eve but one we'd made love.

Let me tell you about this brilliant idea I had at Venice Beach, when I was all of twenty-three.

In light of later events, I understand how contrived it will sound; how it will seem as believable as one of those transparent plot twists a struggling screenwriter might use to move his script along, a *deus ex machina* of the worst kind.

I understand, but I swear this is what happened.

The idea was a vasectomy. I would bullshit some urologist about being happily married with three kids and wanting no more, and he would snip me, and suddenly I would be liberated—remember, this was before AIDS. And by God, that's what I did. I even convinced myself how politically progressive I'd become, since I, the male, was willingly shouldering the entire burden of birth control. Women I became involved with and women I did not praised my contribution to sisterhood. *If only more guys were like you,* they said, and *aren't you cool,* and *if you ever want kids you can get it reversed,* and so forth and so on. I mean, I got such a great reaction that I actually began using vasectomy as a line—quite effectively, I should note.

I had no regrets, until six years into my marriage.

Ruth was looking at thirty by then. Her career was established, and the showers she was invited to were increasingly for babies, not brides, and her mother had started discreetly inquiring if there was a problem. Her father had outright declared there was, with my "plumbing," as he put crudely, if correctly, although unbeknownst to him.

Ruth wanted a family and no longer was willing to wait for some nebulous tomorrow, which is where I'd parked the issue.

Well, okay, I could be persuaded. What would delaying accomplish, really, except increasing the chance of birth defects? I wasn't experiencing any yearning like Ruth, I don't think most guys ever do, but I'd reached the conclusion there is no perfect time for a man to have a kid.

A woman fantasizes about how she'll dress her newborn, and a guy—well, the average guy wonders if she'll still want sex with him with baby on the way, not to be blunt about it.

My doctor referred me to a surgeon who reverses vasectomies and he put the odds of success at fifty percent—not bad, considering how much time had passed.

So, I was unsnipped.

I will not humiliate myself describing the post-operative mechanics—the bottom line is that three specimens brought three discouraging reports from the lab. Ruth turned thirty-one and then thirty-two and we remained childless. Our only hope before getting into the gruesome business of artificial insemination was for me to go under the knife again.

Which did not make for happy times at Marblehead-by-the-sea, I can assure you.

Do you have a clue (pardon the pun again) what it's like having surgery on that part of the anatomy? Let's just say if you drew up a list of the things you've always wanted to do, needle in eye would be ahead of vasovasostomy.

But prospective reoperation was not the worst nastiness in our lives that fall.

CreativeWare was.

How did Charlie Goldman put it? "Despite his vision, Gray's firm was a one-trick pony back then," something like that.

We had *Attack Ship* and it was doing quite fine, thank you, but Phil and I were hungry. We watched Nintendo and Sega and knew we could compete in their league.

Hometoons, I eventually convinced Phil, was the way to do it.

I won't duck this one: *Hometoons* was mine, and mine alone—a program that would let kids as young as three create their own short films by combining custom animation and live-action footage we would buy from the studios. Its roots were my NYU film, *Eating People*, the one the *Village Voice* had called "fascinating and fun."

So, I brought a new project director on board and Phil raised capital and Bud Robbins, who was producing for MTV by then, put us in touch with a Hollywood licensing agent. Phil warned me about the guy and his promises, but did I listen? He was talking Harrison Ford and Sly Stallone and, with any luck, Arnold Schwarzenegger, and I was getting religion. All we needed was for them to sign.

They never did. Nor did we break any development paradigms, as they say in the business, in what we accomplished in-house. Nine months after announcing *Hometoons* to the trade, we were left with a piece of shit our best engineer couldn't get to draw a halfway-decent stick figure. Good budding capitalist that I was, I fired my project director. If *Hometoons* was going to succeed, I concluded, I'd have to write the software myself.

God bless Goldman for glossing over *Hometoons* in his *Wired* piece. We hadn't bet the house on it, but damn near, and as the true dimensions of the disaster began to emerge, Phil did not let me forget for a moment the reservations he'd had.

Looking back, I see that period as what my father would have called a test of character. Superficially, I suppose, I passed. As *Hometoons* continued to crash and burn under my personal direction, I did not fire anyone else, argue with Phil, or blame the vicissitudes of software. At home, I did not scream, pout, or hit the bottle; I simply became a stone. The emotional meter dropped to zero and stuck there, starting at Halloween the year before Timmy was born.

Ruth sympathized, at first.

"I think you need Vermont," she said.

"I think I need to be left alone."

"I'm only thinking of you, Mark."

"I wish you wouldn't," I said. "The last thing I need now is pity."

It took only a couple of exchanges like that before Ruth gave up on the care and feeding of her husband. But she didn't let go of babies.

"I'm not getting any younger," she would say.

"Do you know anybody who is?" I would reply.

What a toad I was. If only I'd seen that then.

"You haven't scheduled your second operation."

"I can't think about that now Ruth," I said. "Maybe after *Hometoons* flies."

"Do you have any idea when might that be?"

"Do I look like I have a crystal ball?"

So, I was a stone, a smart-ass stone, except for one night the week before Christmas when I got home to find Ruth on fast boil.

I haven't mentioned that side of Ruth—how she held certain things inside until they reached critical mass. I'd seen her like that with her father, a true prick of a man, but only rarely with me: most notably early in our marriage when a friend from Venice Beach visited and we stayed up all night, doing cocaine and watching movies, just like the good old days, and the next morning she had to literally kick him out.

This time, the trigger was our Christmas tree.

Ruth had bought a beautiful blue spruce, and, leaving that morning, I'd promised to be home early to decorate it. The tree was in its stand, the ornaments and lights were ready to go, hot mulled cider was on the stove—and what had Mister Sensitivity done? Forgotten. I was two hours late and planning to work, at home, most of the night.

Ruth started on me at the door and before I got to my study, I was returning fire. Vile things were said, by both of us—accusations, and lies, and nasty truths. People must subconsciously stockpile these for use in all-out attack, because once engaged, we were at war. Ruth threw a book and I nearly punched a hole in a wall, and when it was over, Ruth was at her parents' for what turned out to be over a week.

I was damned if I was going to be first to apologize. What exactly was my crime—fighting to save CreativeWare, our bread and butter? Not producing babies on demand? I don't know what was going through Ruth's mind, for she could be a stone, too.

"We need to be apart," is all she said when I called the next morning.

I agreed. The pressure of *Hometoons* had really gotten to me, I said, and I was the sort of guy who best dealt with pressure alone, and it wouldn't be very long, anyway, because I could see light at the end of the tunnel, and blah-blah-blah.

"You're an asshole," Ruth said, and hung up.

For the next week, I put in 15-hour days at CreativeWare and when I got home, I watched movies until three or four in the morning. I didn't expect Christmas day to be as difficult as it was. I thought I would rise, fix breakfast, call Dad, and get right back into *Hometoons*. I wasn't bullshitting Ruth about light at the end of the tunnel: I'd decided if I could put up enough smoke and mirrors so the damn thing could make it through a formal presentation—I still believed we could—we'd be able to sell the concept and at least recoup our losses.

Which is how the first part of Christmas unfolded, me at the computer until late afternoon, when the setting sun bathed the undecorated tree, illuminating a solitary present: an expensive gold necklace I'd bought Ruth last night, minutes before the mall closed.

I tried to ignore that damn tree, unsuccessfully. Memory surfaced of the tree my family had in 1967, the year mom died, and how for the first Christmas ever the sound of her piano didn't fill our house.

I looked at Ruth's Steinway, next to the tree, and remembered last Christmas, when my father had been down—how Ruth had played every Christmas song she knew and still he wanted more, how Ruth had talked him into caroling for the first time since he'd retired.

I tried desperately to force these memories from my head but where I wound up was wondering how old folks without families passed Christmas—if anyone visited or called, and did they bother with wreaths or trees, and could it be possible they might not receive a single card or gift. I had a vision of them shuffling with their walkers along darkened corridors in concrete high-rises, into elevators and down to dining rooms with folding chairs and paper tablecloths for processed turkey and canned peas.

I felt like shit and if I hadn't forced myself to stop looking at that tree, I bet I'd have cried.

Instead, I had a beer and put my copy of *Miracle on 34th Street* into the VCR.

And after my fourth beer, I called Ruth.

Her father answered.

"Well if it isn't Prince Charming," he said. "To what do we owe the honor?"

God, how I hated this man.

Vincent Sydlowski was a bloated, cigar-smoking man whose one redeeming characteristic was he seemed a prime candidate for a stroke. He'd inherited his money from a father who'd made it in Cape Cod real estate, and he'd been raised believing everyone has his price. On Syd's ledger, I was a closeout—a commoner with a questionable past and dubious future who belonged with some free-spirited hippie chick, not his precious Ivy League-educated girl. He'd never gotten past how royally he believed his only child had screwed up marrying me and it galled him to think that if we stayed together, his money eventually could be mine; the only thing worse was knowing that when Ruth had her baby, half his first grandchild's genes would be mine. The horror of *Hometoons* was the first thing I'd done that gave him true joy. I couldn't imagine how many I-told-you-sos had been lobbed at his daughter in the last week—with Ruth, for once, not telling him to shove it.

"Is Ruth there?" I said.

"Well, she's certainly not at your place," he said. "God willing, she never will be again."

After a liberal dose of his crap, which I somehow managed to swallow, Syd put Ruth on.

I apologized, and Ruth did, too, and that evening, she came home. She adored her necklace, and I was thrilled with the case of wine she gave me, and she played "Silent Night" and "Hark the Herald Angels" on her piano and we lit a fire and held each other and fell asleep on the rug, too drained to make love.

Talk about timing. A week after Valentine's Day—on the very evening we signed the contract that finally rid us of

Hometoons—Ruth said there was something she had to tell me.

She did not look well. She hadn't looked well in days. That morning, I'd heard her in the bathroom, throwing up.

"What is it?" I said.

Her eyes scared me.

"I'm pregnant," she said.

As I replayed that scene in the weeks and months to come, I kept wondering if she'd rehearsed. I wondered if she'd searched desperately for words that might frame reality in softer tones, but there were none. The fact was, I was as sterile as a mule, had three certified lab reports to prove it. What else could Ruth say, but those two terrible words?

"If that's a joke," I said, "it's not funny."

"It's not a joke."

"It has to be."

"It's not. I'm so sorry, Mark."

"Who's the father?"

She took a breath and said: "You don't know him."

"Who is he?" I said, my voice rising.

"It doesn't matter now," Ruth said, and I knew this was something she'd given great thought to already.

I couldn't bring myself to press on, not then.

"How pregnant are you?" I said, as if numbers mattered.

"Six weeks."

I did the math. Fuck the herald angels: There was every chance she'd conceived on Christmas Eve or Christmas morning. I wasn't much of a God-fearing man, you've surely gathered that by now, but there was something sacrilegious about that.

Ruth started to cry.

"I feel worse than I've ever felt in my life," she said. "If there was any way I could turn back time...."

She didn't finish.

I was silent.

"Hug me? Please, Mark?"

I wouldn't.

Instead, I went for the Yellow Pages.

"You're getting an abortion," I said.

I heard myself speak, and I imagined I was reading a line

from *General Hospital*. A script from a really bad day in the writers' room.

Ruth did not answer.

"You *are* getting an abortion, aren't you, Ruth?"

"I can't," she said.

"What do you mean, you can't?"

"I can't."

"You have to."

"You don't know how much I've agonized over this."

She started to explain, but I didn't let her.

"Goddamn it, it's not mine!"

"It's not the baby's fault," Ruth said softly. She wasn't crying anymore.

You think of all the things that can go wrong in your life—you wreck the car, you lose your job in a downsizing, your house burns to the ground—but this one isn't on the list, not mine. I couldn't even sustain anger, I was so blown away.

"I'll understand if you leave," Ruth said, "or if you want, I will. Just tell me."

I didn't, not then. I said I needed time, but that was baloney; that was token retribution. The truth was, I knew I'd stay. Maybe not forever—but for now.

Once already in my life I'd treated a pregnant woman badly. I wasn't going to again, regardless of circumstances.

"It's not the baby's fault," Ruth repeated. "Whatever else you think, I'm begging you not to forget that."

"I won't forget that, Ruth," I said. "I won't forget that for the rest of my life."

It's funny, looking back. I guess I'd always believed if they ever made a movie of my adult life it would be directed by Kubrick or Scorsese, or, with any luck, Forman.

And here I was, suddenly living a soap opera.

From that night on, I reburied myself in my work. I joined a health club, and I watched a hell of a lot of movies, and I had a dream about Sally Martin that was so vivid that the next morning at work I called directory assistance, but her number was unlisted. I was so pitiful that I even started socializing with

Phil, who was going, rip-roaringly, through a divorce.

One Saturday evening in May I dropped by his Beacon Street condo to find him with a twenty-something waitress whose name escapes me.

She'd come over with her friend Kerri—a pretty, petite woman who radiated happiness like some sort of '50s Welcome Wagon lady. I don't mean to be snide—Kerri was genuinely pleasant, not a bit of saccharine about her at all, the kind of person the world could stand many more of. You got the impression nothing pleased Kerri more than whatever she happened to be doing at the moment.

What she was doing when Phil introduced us was playing the new version of *Attack Ship*, whose success was making it easy to forget *Hometoons*. I should note for the record that Phil did not mention I was married, or that Ruth and I had just signed up for Lamaze classes.

"It's really cool," Kerri said. "It's like flying your own plane."

"That's the basic idea," I said, not smugly. Kerri was too sweet for me to be smug.

"Phil told me you invented it."

"I did."

"How do you learn to *do* something like that?"

"He's a star," Phil said. "A regular fucking star."

"I guess so!" Kerri said.

"Here," Phil said, handing me a joint. "Live it up."

I inhaled as deeply as I always did on one of Bud Robbins's famous fat boys and passed it to Kerri. She took a toke, knocked back the last of her beer, and let out a giggle. Her friend giggled, too; evidently, the three of them had been going at it all afternoon. I had a beer myself, and then a second. And a third, at which point I decided to try to interest Kerri in a ride in my Corvette.

"I've never *been* in a Corvette," she said.

"It's a '67 Sting Ray."

"Wow!"

"I spent twenty-five grand to restore it," I said.

It was a shameless boast, but it was true.

"And I got us a tax deduction for it, every cent," Phil said.

Indeed he had, although how exactly, I didn't care to learn. As I've noted, Phil was the numbers guy. Presumably, he knew the IRS rules.

How wrong that turned out to be.

"I'd love to go for a ride," Kerri said.

"There's a cooler in the pantry," Phil said. "Take some Heinies. Go wild, Markie-boy."

We drove north from Boston, past Salem and Marblehead and on toward Gloucester. Seeing her play *Attack Ship*, you wouldn't have believed Kerri could get any happier, but she did. I was pretty damn fine myself. The night was warm and I had the top down and I didn't give a flying fuck if some conscientious citizen got the plate number as we blew past at 85 belting back Heinekens, the radio blasting WBCN, The Rock of Boston. Kerri played with the radar detector and, just for kicks, used my cell phone to call her mother, who was babysitting her two-year-old son for the weekend. Kerri was a clerk at Kmart—sales associate, she called it—but was studying to be a paralegal; school was the only way for a single mother to get ahead, she said. I liked her ambition. I liked her smile and her giggle. I liked a lot about Kerri. By the time we reached this little beach I knew about in Rockport, I wanted to bury my face in her breasts.

We parked by the ocean and sat listening to the surf and watching the moon creep across the water. I wasn't drunk, but I wouldn't have put money on passing a field sobriety test, either.

Kerri *was* drunk. Not slurring or falling-down drunk, but one look told you she was feeling no pain.

"You know what I'd like to do?" I said.

"What?"

"Kiss you."

Kerri giggled.

"But you're married!"

"Who says?"

"You're wearing a wedding ring."

By God, I was.

"I'm...separated," I said.

I know where my credibility stands on these matters, but God's truth: I was uncomfortable, telling that lie. Kerri was a good, decent, hard-working woman and all I was thinking of was whether the clasp of her bra was in front or in back.

"How long have you been separated?"

"Five months," I said.

"Oh."

"So, can I kiss you?"

"Are you really separated?"

"Honest to God."

"I don't know...."

"Just one kiss?"

"I really don't know...."

I pulled Kerri toward me.

Her body stiffened, and her lips were bloodless and cold.

I suppose I could have persisted—Phil would have. He would have trusted alcohol and insistence to sweep away inhibition, and if he didn't make Kerri tonight, he'd try again tomorrow. And if she resisted still, he'd toss her aside, because there was no shortage of Kerris out there.

Yes, I suppose I could have done that—but how different would I have been from the father of Ruth's baby? All the woman wanted was a ride in a damn Corvette.

"I don't know what came over me," I said. "I am so sorry."

"It's okay," she said, but you knew it wasn't. You knew this was how she'd been treated by too many men. And yet you knew she kept believing that somewhere out there, one—just one—had to be different than the rest.

"I'll take you back now," I said.

"Thank you," she said, managing a smile.

That night was a turning point for me.

In light of Allison, I know it sounds like more bullshit, but the truth was I didn't want to lead a double life. I didn't want to get into hiding expenses and washing off perfume and crossing my fingers I wouldn't get caught. I didn't want to manufacture a justification involving a pseudo-scientific theory whose essence was that sperm controlled your destiny. I didn't want to take advantage of the Kerris of the world, nor risk my own real-life version of *Fatal Attraction*: an entanglement with a woman who wasn't content with great sex but sought a piece of my soul. No bunny in a stew pot for me, thank you.

I expected to remain your basic married guy, a good father to my kid, a man who—admittedly more for practical than noble reasons—had no burning desire for revenge. And I'd been all of those people, until Allison.

I got to Penn Station on time, checked into the Waldorf and took a cab to the Javits Center, where the Gamers Convention had opened with a reception hosted by Nolan Bushnell, founder of Atari and patron saint of our industry.

I found our booth, a half-scale mockup of a space shuttle that had cost a cool fifty grand. Phil was there with Lisa, our PR person, and Charlie Goldman, who'd signed with some dweeb publisher hot on just what humanity needed: yet another a book about VR. Goldman wanted CreativeWare for the opening chapter and me as the thread throughout. I had no objections.

"Hey, Charlie," I said.

"Love the tie!" he said.

"It's a killer, isn't it?"

I'd forsaken my Spiderman tie for Superman—Allison's idea.

"And don't drop the John Lennon shades! They're way cool!"

"I wouldn't dream of it," I said.

In fact, I was going to wear them for my speech.

"Now if you'll excuse me, I have some last-minute details to go over with my PR guy."

I was hoping we could have dinner afterwards," Charlie said. "Maybe preview the convention."

He had that lap dog tone in his voice. Doing a book with him was going to require extreme self-control.

"I'd love to," I said, "but I'm afraid I can't."

"He's got plans," Phil said. He was wearing one of his shit-eating grins.

"I'm seeing a friend," I said quickly.

"A *good* friend," Phil elaborated.

I shot Phil a glance.

"My college roommate, in fact," I said. "I'm sure you'll meet him someday."

That satisfied Charlie.

"Well, break a leg," he said.

"I'm warning you," I whispered to Phil when he'd gone.

"Relax," he said. "That wonk wouldn't know a mistress if she sucked his dick."

Phil walked with me toward the stage.

"I don't see him," I said.

"Who?"

"Jack Nicholson."

Emboldened by his e-mail, I'd invited Nicholson to be my personal guest at the Gamers convention. Lo and behold, he was planning to be in New York this week anyway. Chances were good, his agent said, that he'd drop by.

"Probably crapping out on us," Phil said. "You know those Hollywood types."

"Let's wait a few minutes before we start," I said.

"No way," Phil said. "You're already late."

Judging by the applause—fourteen interruptions—my speech was a mega hit with our digital brethren. I was positively evangelical in the world I envisioned—a world in which every house had a computer, every computer a cable modem, every consumer an insatiable appetite for online services and games.

"After his loss to Deep Blue," I said, "Garry Kasparov said, and I quote: 'I'm a human being. When I see something that is well beyond my understanding, I'm afraid.' Well, Mister Kasparov, technology isn't our enemy..."

Wild applause.

"...nor is it our friend."

A hush in the auditorium.

"It's our *kindred spirit*! So, Garry, get a grip! Maybe it's a mystery to you, but to those of us here today, computers playing games are as natural as mothers' milk—and if *you* can't beat a microchip, at least don't be a spoilsport and try to ruin the fun for the rest of *us*!"

As the applause subsided, I compared the digital revolution to a movie: *The Greatest Story Ever Told.*

I even turned McLuhanesque.

"On one hand," I said, "our technology has divided us. We

now have the ability to lead lives without ever leaving home—couch potatoes with mice and pull-down menus!"

Big laughter, considering what a hopelessly confused metaphor it was.

"On the other hand, that very same technology has inextricably brought us together—African with Australian, Kansas farmer with New York broker, preschooler with grandmother, a fraternity of men, women and children glorying in their common humanity. Ladies and gentlemen, the global village has arrived, and we—we are its high priestesses and priests!"

I was on a roll. Name your cliché, and I whipped it: limitless horizons, rosy future, information superhighway. A good thing, too: The Discovery Channel was taping me and a crew we'd hired was getting footage for a CreativeWare infomercial. We needed great soundbites, and we'd gotten them, galore.

For the record: I have always had a soft spot for clichés, one of many reasons I favor writing software and screenplays over penning novels, as you will see as you read on.

For my closing, I brought the lights down. The screen behind me came to life with a shot of a somber, white-haired priest at his pulpit. If he bore any resemblance to my father, as some of the pundits would later declare, it was unintentional, I swear. I hadn't done the casting, only approved the storyboards and final cut.

"Introducing the game to beat all games—*Sermon*," I said. "The object is to keep the congregation awake. Succeed, and you get the gold chalice! Fail and the fires of hell!"

There was nervous laughter. Was this another of my celebrated practical jokes—or was I leading up to some ground-breaking new category?

The priest began droning on about how the meek shall inherit the earth. I clicked on my mouse. We cut to a shot of a woman in the front pew. She was nodding off.

"Looks like trouble for the Reverend Hunt," I said.

Click.

Father Hunt is scowling.

"But he knows where this woman's heart is…."

Click.

\The altar transforms into the set of "The Price Is Right."

"Shopping!"

Father Hunt morphs into Bud Barker who says: "Angela Heavens, come on down!"

"Well?" I said after about a minute of this, "do we have a hit or do we have a hit? Our sales V.P. will be taking orders on the way out the door."

The auditorium was stone dead.

"Not!" I said. "What's the matter with you folks—can't you take a joke?"

I had them eating from the palm of my hand.

Two beats and I continued.

"Well, there's no joke about what I'm about to show you. Ladies and gentlemen, children of all ages, presenting a never-before-seen sneak preview of the most ambitious and exciting project in the history of game software development, our lead title for next year...*Virtual Clue.*"

The lasers and smoke machines kicked in and we rolled the sizzle tape our ad agency had spent two weeks preparing. Publicly unveiling the game with so much engineering left was risky, no question, but Phil had agreed that with *Shuttle Saga*'s rocky start, we desperately needed a boost, particularly with our IPO coming up early next year.

I left the stage with a standing ovation. Thirty-five-hundred people on their feet. It was a major rush.

"Don't go anywhere," master of ceremonies Sam Spencer whispered as I took my seat in the front row. Spencer was president of the Video Gamers of America.

Spencer went to the dais and when the hall was finally silent, he said: "And now the other moment we've all been waiting for. The fifteenth annual Golden Gamer Award."

It was our industry's highest honor: often called a Wilbur, for Wilbur Von Esten, inventor of the joystick. Which is what the trophy was: a gold-plated joystick. Not exactly a work of art, but a fitting enough symbol.

Spencer paid tribute to Von Esten, who'd died of cancer since last year, and a hush descended on the hall.

"The envelope please," Spencer said.

He tore it open and announced: "And the winner is…Mark Gray!"

I was stunned—I had not expected this, had never imagined I might ever win a Wilbur, let alone at this stage of my career. Wilburs went to the young hotshots of the business—the shooting stars, some of them kids young enough to be my children. Of the old codgers, only Bushnell had won a Wilbur, and that was the first one, fifteen years ago.

So, I hadn't prepared a speech. Following instinct, I thanked Ruth, Timmy, Phil and all of our faithful employees and loyal customers.

Then I left the stage, to another standing ovation.

If I had any regret, it was that Allison wasn't here. I'd considered inviting her too risky.

"Incredible," was all Charlie Goldman could say when the ceremony was over and I made my way through the crowd, Wilbur in hand. His sentiments were echoed by everyone. I signed autographs and posed for pictures for close to an hour, and respectfully declined invitations to a bunch of parties. And if you must know the truth, I loved every minute of it. You narcissists out there know exactly what I mean.

"I wonder why he didn't come," I said to Phil as we waited for taxis outside the Javits Center. "It was my best performance ever."

"Who?"

"Nicholson."

"Get over it, will you?" Phil said. "You're like a goddamn kid."

"It would have been a nice touch for our infomercial, is all. A shot of a big-time movie star in the audience."

"Big-time, my ass," Phil said. "Jack Nicholson was washed up ten years ago."

"The hell he was."

"Would you get off this Jack Nicholson thing? You've got bigger fish to fry. Here."

Phil handed me a small bag.

"And don't give me that 'it's only dinner' line again."

"Well, it is only dinner."

This was beyond denial. I could have been one of Bill Clinton's lawyers. I could have handled the Paula Corbin Jones case with ease.

The bag contained a condom. I thought how condoms were as much a part of the culture now as Coca-Cola and realized I hadn't seen one since Venice Beach.

"The last thing you need is a disease," Phil said. "Trust me—I've been there. It's no picnic."

"Is there ever anything else on your mind besides sex?" I said.

"Money," he said. "but it's second."

"I don't want this."

"You don't need it," Phil said, forcing it into my pocket, "you throw it away. You need it, you can thank me tomorrow. Now go on, get outta here. You're going on a date."

CHAPTER SEVEN

We met at the appointed hour at Rockefeller Center. Allison was waiting by the rink, and as we watched the skaters, I thought how fabulous she'd look out there herself: a beautiful woman in jeans and black leather jacket, white scarf trailing behind her like the plume of an exotic bird.

I wasn't on edge this time. I hadn't prepared a corny toast and I wasn't thinking ahead to tonight, when Allison had invited me back to her place—the threshold I might be asked to cross. I was a man at peace. Maybe New York in December does that to you—messes, in a nice way, with your head. Or maybe the madness had spread through the cerebral cortex, leaving me a different, and hardly superior, man.

We'd planned to visit Strawberry Fields—since buying my new shades, I'd couldn't get John Lennon off my mind, go figure—but Allison had changed her mind. She wanted to shop. I hated shopping, but Allison had taken my hand and was gently squeezing it, and at that moment there was nothing on earth I desired more than to shop. She could have needed dish detergent and I would have gone breathlessly along.

We mostly worked Fifth Avenue. I mostly paid. Allison initially wouldn't hear of it, but her resistance withered at the sight of my American Express card. Allison knew her stores, knew precisely what she wanted: a necklace from Wempe, boots from Medici, perfume from Chanel. I didn't care; CreativeWare handled my charges. No bills would go to my house.

"I want a teddy bear," Allison said outside FAO Schwartz.

"It's yours."

"You don't think I'm too old?"

"You're never too old!"

"You're so wonderful," Allison said, kissing my cheek.

"A teddy bear would look perfect on your bed."

"How would you know? You've never seen my bed."

She giggled. I giggled. Life was good.

Allison had her eye on a Gund bear, and I bought it for her. On the way out of the store, we passed the radio-controlled car department. Damn, if they didn't have it—the very car, a Ricochet XRC, Santa had brought Timmy last year.

I guess my look gave me away because Allison said: "Is something wrong?"

"No," I said.

"You're thinking about Timmy," Allison said. "How he'd love it here."

"Not really."

"He doesn't have to know," she said. "This is our little secret. It's okay for grownups to have little secrets, you know."

I smiled, weakly. "Little Lies," the Fleetwood Mac tune, came into my head.

"Do you think so?" I said.

"I know so."

Allison kissed me on the lips.

"Come on—let's have dinner."

She'd chosen Novita, near Gramercy Park. I must've been starved, because once the food came, thoughts of Timmy disappeared.

We finished one bottle of wine and plunged right into another, and suddenly I began to get a whole new slant on Allison. I mean, the moral issues faded and I began to see tonight as practical opportunity, not temptation. How many men were in my position? How many could honestly say that fate, not philandering, had brought them an Allison? I hadn't gone looking for her. I hadn't sought her affection. I hadn't asked her to sleep with me, and wasn't planning to.

I hadn't done anything but answer her e-mail and tell her cheesy jokes and listen, as any self-respecting entrepreneurial creative star would, to her ideas about VR.

I looked across the table at this woman so obviously taken with me and was struck, again, by her looks. And only twenty-seven. *Twenty-seven.* Should age have been the linchpin? Perhaps not, but in this new moral framework that Chardonnay was helping to develop, it was. Phil was right on that point. Opportunity like this didn't knock every day; quite conceivably, it might never knock again. I was not a man who lived comfortably with regrets, as you may have surmised.

Sunday night, and Novita was filled with couples.

No kids, no families, no lonely out-of-town businessmen—only couples—straight, gay, young and old. It was like a Seinfeld segment, for heaven's sake. I wondered who amongst them was married, or on their first date, or together illicitly. How many would wind up in bed before the night was over? God, it seemed like everyone; I mean, apparently you weren't allowed in if you were chaste. So much wine, so many whispered conversations as hands encountered thighs under tables. In the candlelit intimacy of this place, libido was tangible.

Returning from the bathroom, I came up behind Allison and wrapped my arms around her.

"Remember what you said about secrets?" I whispered.

"Yes."

"I've got one of my own."

"Tell me."

"Promise to keep it to yourself?"

"Cross my heart and hope to die."

"I think I'm smitten."

I'd chosen that word carefully. It sounded so literary, and not the least bit presumptuous.

Allison smiled.

"Anyone I know?"

"I can't say—it's that kind of secret."

"She must be a very special woman."

"She is. And beautiful. And sexy, like a Greek goddess."

That would have been the time to put a gun to my head and pull the trigger—speaking those lines. Could they possibly have been more mawkish?

I say that now, but then—then, every word was poetry, my delivery straight from *Casablanca.*

My Greek goddess moved her hand up my thigh and then to my crotch, where she ran her finger, slowly, across my fly.

"The game would begin like this, in a cab," Allison said as we headed north on Lexington.

"What game?"

"The one you're going to put me in. Adult Clue. Virtual Clue. Whatever you call it."

"Oh, right."

I'd forgotten about that.

"Here's where the cocaine would come in," Allison said. We were at a stop light. Allison had her mirror out.

"You first," she said. "Remember? I saved them for you."

"What if I don't want any?"

"Then the game would end."

Allison drew two lines and handed me the mirror and a hundred-dollar bill.

"How could you ever do VR coke?" I said.

"We'll leave that to your genius," Allison said. "Go ahead. I won't take no for an answer this time."

I snorted. And when Allison offered two more lines, I did them too.

In light of the next three hours, I suppose I should plead temporary insanity from acute intoxication. Claim nascent substance-use disorder, to put it in DSM-IV terms.

Isn't that the thing to do when you're in it so deep, deny it's the real you? In the age of recovered memories, when truth has become a malleable and self-serving thing, aren't we all victims? Don't we all wrestle with traumas and demons traceable to childhood?

But I won't take that defense. I will accept responsibility for my actions and admit it's me in the scenes that follow, not some chemical imposter.

Still, it's important to note, if only for entertainment's sake, how profoundly dreamlike that night became from there on out. It was like flashing back to Venice Beach when we dropped acid and reality slowly slipped away, until it was impossible to

determine if you were a participant or a powerless bystander—
an on-screen character, or only some schmuck with his Jordan
Almonds in the back of the theater.

Allison did her four lines and then we were kissing and
her tongue was in my mouth and my hands were all over her
breasts and I rather think we would have screwed, right then
and there, if the cabbie hadn't stopped. I didn't recollect giving
him a destination; perhaps Allison had. A serious glitch seemed
to have developed in the short-term memory that night.

"We're here," Allison said. "The next level of the game."

She stepped out. I was about to follow when I realized I had
an erection, one seemingly in no hurry to go away.

You must be shitting me, I thought. *A fucking woodie!*

Yes, like Sebastian Dangerfield in J.P. Donleavy's *The Ginger
Man.*

"Are you okay?" Allison said.

"I have to zip my coat," I said.

"No need—we're going straight inside."

"My hand's asleep," I said.

"How could your hand be asleep? It was feeling me up."

"I mean my foot."

This was not working.

"Are you sure you're okay?" Allison said.

"I'm fine."

"Then perhaps you'd like to get out of the cab," said Allison,
unamused.

Think about Phil, I thought. *Think about pointcasting or RAM.
Anything but Allison.*

I crossed my legs and held my breath. With great effort, I
began to get results.

"See?" I said.

"See what?"

"I'm getting out of the cab."

The club was Michael Crichton's *Lost World*, and it was Allison's
set: actors, musicians, artists, twenty-something wannabes.
You walked in and were assaulted with sound and light. The
DJ's booth was suspended over a revolving dance floor next

to a 20-foot Tyrannosaurus Rex. The DJ himself was dressed like a member of *The Lost World: Jurassic Park* cast, as were the bartenders. A stadium-sized screen flashed live fast-cut views of the crowd.

"No Glove, No Love," was the current message on the neon board.

As a monument to mixed metaphors, something I knew a thing or two about, I guess the place worked.

And surely it was no coincidence that Allison had brought us here. Spielberg's movie, blockbuster of the year, had catapulted Julianne Moore to Hollywood's A-list.

"Excellent choice," I said.

"I love this place," Allison said. "It's the tackiest club in New York. Tacky is very in this winter, as you know."

"They're playing the Bee Gees," I said.

"It's '70s night. Weren't you into them?"

"No," I said, "I was into LSD."

It was true. Disco was for cultural lightweights, not budding apostles of the avant-garde.

"I absolutely *adore* disco," Allison said.

"Well maybe I was into it," I said. "A little."

"Did you have platform shoes?"

"Yes," I lied.

"Bell bottoms?"

"Three pair."

"Stop it! You *were* into it! Awesome!"

I suddenly realized I was clutching my Wilbur.

"What do I do with this?" I said.

"Check it," Allison said.

"Check it?"

"You think somebody's going to steal it? Get real. Nobody knows what the hell it is."

I checked my Wilbur. Allison pulled me to the bar and ordered us Velociraptors: half rum, half liquor I didn't recognize. They came with dinosaur-shaped swizzle sticks.

"The tie has got to go," Allison said.

"I thought my tie was a happening thing."

"It was," she said, "until we got here."

I took off my Superman tie.

"Now unbutton that button-down collar."

"I never do that."

In fact, it was a vital part of my look. Truth was, wacky ties notwithstanding, I was a modest, even conservative, dresser. Not since Venice Beach had I worn cut-offs or sandals. I'd brought a bureau full of tee shirts into my marriage and when Ruth, on one of her tidying jags, proposed giving them all to Salvation Army, I'd not protested a word. Charlie Goldman, God bless him again, hadn't figured out the true nature of my schtick.

"You do now," Allison said, unbuttoning my collar for me.

She drained her Velociraptor and admonished me to do likewise. Just what I needed, high-octane alcohol. But it sure tasted good. I wanted another already.

"Now we dance," Allison said.

"In penny loafers?"

I hear myself now and realize how incredibly asinine I sounded.

"Take them off," Allison said.

"I can't do that."

"Why not?"

"Germs."

"Germs?"

"Have you looked at a New York street lately?" I said. "All the...*fluids*."

"My God, you're a headcase!" Allison said. "Will it help if I take mine off?"

She tossed her Nikes into the crowd.

"There," she said. "Now off with the loafers. Hideous word, by the way, *loafers*. Ugh."

"Well they are L.L. Bean."

"I don't care if they're Gucci," Allison said. "Off with them."

I did as I was told.

When was the last time I'd danced? With Ruth at a friend's wedding years ago, I guess.

But dancing must be like bicycling: you never forget.

Because I was pretty darn good, or so I imagined. An image

of John Travolta came to mind and wouldn't leave. Not the has-been of Saturday Night Fever but the ultimate-cool Nineties Guy of Pulp Fiction. I'd seen that flick twice, plus endless clips on MTV, and I knew the dance scene well enough—or thought I did—to reenact it now.

The way Travolta came at Uma Thurman, his brilliant self-parody, the hypnotic music—that was me out there on the floor of Lost World now. You could tell Allison was with me, because whenever our eyes met, I saw witchery. The people around us must have seen it, too, because we were attracting an audience. First, a small circle, and then an expanding one, people cheering us on, and me and Allison going at each other like we would end up on the floor screwing. Soon, the whole damn place was intent on us. As I heard wolf whistles and whooping and clapping, what occurred to me was how deeply I was indebted to Quentin Tarantino.

"Are you all right?" Allison said on our first break.

"Sure. Why?"

"You're out of breath."

"Nah," I said, panting, "just into it."

"You're *good*," Allison said.

"You sound surprised."

"I am."

"That's not very nice."

"You know what attracted me," she said, kissing me. "It wasn't what you did on a dance floor."

"What was it then?"

"What's between your..."

"My?"

"...ears!" Allison said, giggling.

"Tease."

"Teasing makes the world go 'round," she said. "Now be a good little boy and get us another round."

I battled my way to the bar. When I returned, Allison had taken off her blouse, leaving only a black T-shirt, conspicuously without bra. She was engaged in animated conversation with two guys her age. One was a hacker I recognized from the convention—I'd autographed his copy of *Wired* and posed with him and my Wilbur for a picture. The other was a stranger: handsome, dressed like he read *GQ* or *Vanity Fair* and endowed with thick hair like what I'd once had.

As I watched, Allison kissed him. Briefly—but on the lips. A kiss! On the lips!

I stood, barefoot and frozen.

Allison spotted me.

"There you are!" she said.

I gave Allison her drink.

"Darling," she said, "I want you to meet my friends: Steve Ferreira and Paul Shaw. Guys, this is Mark Gray. He's only like America's biggest software game developer."

"I know," Shaw, the hacker, said. "We met at the convention. That Clue's cool stuff, dude."

"Thank you."

"The only thing I'd add is sex."

"See?" Allison said. "I rest my case!"

The other guy extended his hand.

"Steve Ferreira," he said.

I shook, reluctantly. I couldn't have warm feelings for this one—he was too good-looking, and not in a pretty-boy TV way. Ferreira was genuine hunk material, reminiscent of Matthew McConaughey, the kind who someday could light up a Hollywood screen.

"Steve's an actor," Allison said. "He's appearing in *Kiss of the Spider Woman*."

"As an understudy," Ferreira said.

"Semantics," Allison said. "Anyone who's anyone knows you're a star."

"Not yet," Ferreira said.

"But soon," Allison said. "I have complete confidence. Just don't forget those who knew you when."

"Like I could ever forget you," Ferreira said

I wonder how Jack Nicholson would handle this, I thought. *He'd be cool,* I decided.

"Well I'm thrilled to meet you," I said, with a phony smile. "Can I buy the two of you a drink?"

"Sure," Ferreira and Shaw agreed.

I slicked my hair back, put my sunglasses on, and said, in my best Nicholson voice, J.J. Gittes in Chinatown: "What'll it be—Shirley Temples? Or would you boys rather a Coke?"

Ferreira and Shaw looked flabbergasted.

"That's his Jack Nicholson imitation," Allison explained.

"Of course," Ferreira said.

"You don't like it?" I said.

"It was fine."

"Maybe doesn't meet your rigorous understudy standards?"

"Mark!"

Allison was pissed.

"I was just making a joke," I said.

"His software's better than his humor," she said. "Just ignore him."

And as I stood there, barefoot, I wondered what comeback Jack would have had to that.

The cab dropped us at a Park Avenue high rise. A doorman let us into the lobby, rich with brass and mahogany, then summoned the elevator. It stopped at the top floor, discharging us into an enormous foyer. No hall, no door with peephole and double deadbolt, just a grand entrance to an apartment.

"You have the whole floor?" I said.

"Plus the roof," Allison said. "There's a garden up there."

"That's where you shot your video."

"The one you've seen," Allison said, a sparkle in her eye.

I glanced around. This was serious money—original oils, Oriental rugs, twelve-foot ceilings, crystal chandelier, marble fireplace, all done in art-deco motif. I could imagine the place in a ten-page spread in *Town & Country*.

"Come on," Allison said, beckoning toward a doorway. "I'm down here."

We moved through a parlor and a dining room, past a kitchen and a library into a hall. I was starting to feel like I was on the set of *Virtual Clue*.

"What's that?" I asked, stopping at a closed door.

"My father's room."

"Is he here?"

"No," Allison said. "He's hardly ever here."

I wanted to open that door. I wanted to see bathrobes, slippers, reading glasses, leather bound books on a night table—the accouterments of a wealthy man nearing sixty.

"You don't believe it's my father, do you," Allison said. "Well, see for yourself."

She opened the door. It was a cavernous space, tastefully filled with bureaus, chairs, sofa, rolltop desk, and canopied bed. There were glasses on the night table, along with magazines, a phone, a pipe rack and decanter of tobacco.

If it was a ruse, it was a hell of an elaborate one...and for what?

"Satisfied?"

"I never doubted you."

It was no longer entirely clear why I'd been suspicious. My head was mushy from Velociraptors and cocaine.

Allison took my hand again.

"This is my wing," she said when we got to the end of the hall.

We stepped into Allison's study. Beyond was her bedroom and off that, a balcony with a view of Saint Bartholomew's Church, Episcopal equivalent of Saint Patrick's Cathedral. I knew about Saint Bart's: When I was at NYU, my father concelebrated service there one Sunday with the bishop. A tremendous honor for him, and I hadn't attended. I'd forgotten about it until now.

"Cool," I said.

"You like it?"

"It's awesome."

This was no Amy Grant aficionado, folks—decorating her walls were posters of Nine Inch Nails, Green Day, Jim Morrison, and two films: *Reservoir Dogs* and *Blue Velvet*. And Allison had a surround-sound stereo, wide-screen TV, VCR, and the arcade version of *Doom*. She had a Sega game system, a Pentium multimedia computer, a Netscape browser for her homepage, and a bookcase filled with software and documentation. On an end table, next to a lava lamp, I saw the dozen roses I'd sent her yesterday.

"This came, too," Allison said. "Anonymously."

She was unfolding a poster—that great *Lost World* movie poster of Julianne Moore cornered by the T-rex.

"Any idea who might have sent it?"

I smiled and said, with that bad pun again: "Not a clue."

Why had I sent it anonymously? A secret admirer kind of thing, I guess.

"Anyway," I went on, "you're so much prettier than her."

"You're sweet," Allison said. "Silly, but sweet."

She sounded the tiniest bit peeved.

And probably she was, it suddenly occurred to me.

It was dawning on me how badly I'd overdone the Julianne Moore thing. Who could blame Allison for being annoyed—or hurt? She was tired of not being appreciated for being *her*! So what if she'd planted the seed in my head in the first place? That had been nothing but an opening line, a casual come-on, not something she intended to become a building obsession. What an idiot I'd been! And to think I didn't even like much about Julianne Moore, past her looks. I vowed to myself never to mention her in Allison's presence again.

Something about Moore must have made me remember my Wilbur, for I exclaimed. "Shit! I left my Wilbur at the club!"

"You can get it tomorrow," Allison said.

"Shouldn't I call?"

"No," Allison said, "you should sit."

I did, and the Wilbur flew out of my mind.

"This is my concept for our game," Allison said, booting up. "It's not nearly as sophisticated as anything at Ten Revere Way, of course. It's more like a bunch of storyboards that are sort of in sequence."

"I'm sure it's awesome," I said.

How many times today had I used that word? Fifty? A hundred?

Allison called up a file. It had text and graphics—mostly 3-D-like renditions of me and her which she'd constructed from *Wired*'s website. Ingenious, how she'd cobbled it all together. The woman knew her stuff.

"Okay," Allison said. "You're on."

She handed me the mouse and I started through. It was like

walking through my life lately: Man meets woman through e-mail. Woman meets man for dinner. Man shows woman trophy car. Man and woman get high, make out, visit night club, dance, end up in woman's apartment. That's if man makes right choices—wrong moves brought penalties, such as discovery by spouse. The real-life penalty would be something far beyond my imagination.

I had to admit, the thing had potential. It made CreativeWare's titles look tame.

"Is this better than Clue or what?" Allison said.

"Infinitely better. What comes next?"

"Wine." Allison smiled. "Red or white?"

"Red," I said. Like I needed more alcohol.

"Don't go anywhere," Allison said, and left.

Did Allison intend for me to snoop? In hindsight, I have to believe she did. I have to believe she knew my curiosity would get the better of me, which it did. Clicking around, I found where the game was headed. Woman undresses man. Woman ties man four-corner to her bed. Woman straps on sexual device and...

...and she hadn't written the end.

How long had Allison been gone?

Seemingly forever.

I was about to look for her when some enterprising neuron emerged from its chemical bath and it occurred to me that Allison's computers might hold other interesting secrets.

So, I scrolled through the main directory.

BUSINESS stopped me—Allison had never mentioned any business but Daddy's bank.

I called up the directory. A folder called MADAM caught my eye. It contained the names of a dozen women with telephone numbers, rates, on- and off-duty hours, and lists of sexual specialties. They ran the gamut, from innocent naughtiness to Jimmy Swaggart-style masturbation to some sick shit you know all about if you've seen *Hard Copy* or read the tabloids.

"Oh shit," I said, audibly.

Allison was an East Coast Heidi Fleiss.

It got worse. Opening the ALLISON folder revealed a long list of files. I looked at the first: BATES. It had a photo of a well-dressed man, identified as Richard Bates, along with two dates and a location, one of the finest hotels in Philadelphia.

"Cash," was one line.

"Into enemas, YUCK!" the line after that. At least Allison didn't totally lack taste.

The second entry was Donald J. Dolan.

Donald J. Dolan... I knew a Don Dolan, by God—he was my Congressman! Mister Family Values, father of three, loving husband Dan Dolan! Allison had one entry for him: "November 29, 11:45 p.m., Copley Plaza Boston, cash and diamond earrings."

November 29—the night we'd had dinner—she'd porked my congressman!

"Quick," was her critique of Dolan. "Typical Republican."

Next was Stephen Ferreira. She'd had three liaisons with Steve, one as recently as a week ago yesterday.

"Dude's into Tantric. Cool," the notation read.

Tantric? I thought. *What's Tantric?* Some kind of Hindu sex thing, I seemed to recall.

I called up Ferreira's picture. It was him all right—Mister Understudy himself. She'd done Ferreira in her bed and filmed them with a digital motion camera. It was high-quality stuff—used lots of RAM. I watched a few seconds and couldn't take any more.

I pulled up the GRAY file, considerably longer than any other, and saw my picture, copies of our e-mail, the date and topic of our every phone call, a synopsis of our dinner, a memo to leave tonight open. She hadn't had an opportunity to personally film me yet, of course, but she'd fooled around some more with the *Wired* clips and footage of herself and managed to come up with something softly pornographic.

"Crude, isn't it? You can see why I need your help," Allison whispered into my ear.

I spun around.

"You're a—prostitute," I said.

"That sounds so mercenary," Allison replied. "I prefer to call myself an adventuress."

"Why didn't you tell me?"

"Would it have made a difference?"

"Yes."

"Really?"

"Really."

"If it helps," Allison said, kissing me. "Tonight's on me. I wouldn't dream of charging you—you're going to make me famous."

The bitch of it was, she was right.

I lay naked on Allison's brass bed, my arms and legs secured to the posts with clothesline. I was more or less blind: She'd taken my glasses, but I had sufficient residual vision to recognize the video camera, the doors to the balcony and what was visible beyond, the roof of Saint's. Like I needed some heavy-handed symbolism right now.

Allison was wearing her pearl necklace and panties, and nothing else, when she came out of her bathroom. She was carrying a whip, but I didn't focus on that. I focused on her body, extraordinary even viewed through myopia.

"How would you simulate being tied up?" Allison asked.

I didn't like her tone. It wasn't so playful anymore.

"Good question," I said.

"Your engineers would find a way."

"Sure."

And right here. She turned on her camera, not the security camera, but her own, private hi-def camera that would have caught her snorting the coke, having the convulsion, and falling off the bed.

"Do you have to?" I said.

"It turns me on."

"I think it might, you know, affect me the other way."

"Once we start," Allison said, "you'll forget it's there. Trust me."

I'd never been into bondage or submission, not even on Venice Beach.

The closest I'd come was when Ruth—Ruth!—early in our marriage had begged to tie my ankles and wrists. We'd drunk too much wine already and after another few glasses, the idea degenerated into the good old time-honored missionary position. But bondage was never brought up again. There was a good reason for this. I am profoundly claustrophobic, the result, my father has conjectured, of locking myself inside one of those old-fashioned refrigerators when I was a young boy, a trauma I can still recall. To this day, I cannot watch a Mafia film, not even one of the *Godfather* flicks, masterpieces all, without a sense of horror. Snitches in those movies are always winding up in Dumpsters and trunks of cars.

Not to get graphic, but there was no sign Allison was going to help me work through my inhibitions tonight. I needed testosterone…and what I had was a feeling of impending doom.

Allison opened her night table drawer.

She had—cocaine.

"You first," she said. It didn't sound like an offer.

"No, thanks."

"Bad boys get punished," she said.

She bent over, so that her nipples were in my face.

"They certainly don't get these," she said, withdrawing her breasts.

"Maybe just a little," I said.

Maybe I could be coaxed into this, after all.

"Bad boy," she said, spanking my rump—not lightly. "You didn't say please."

"Please?"

"Pretty please."

"Pretty please."

"Pretty please with sugar on it."

"Pretty please with sugar on it."

Allison spanked me again and said: "I go first."

She drew a line and snorted it.

"A big line for me," I said.

"You naughty boy. You forgot something."

"Pretty please with sugar on it."

Allison was licking the plate.

"The bigger the better," I insisted.

Allison did not respond.

Her breathing was suddenly labored, like that night in my Corvette. She was coughing, and not some throat-clearing but a violent paroxysm involving her whole body. Her eyes rolled like Linda Blair in *The Exorcist* and spittle appeared at the corners of her mouth.

"Allison. Allison!"

She was in full convulsion now, her skin suddenly sweaty and blue. And then her muscles went limp and she fell backwards, hitting her head on the floor with a *thwump*. That's exactly what it sounded like—even now, I can hear it, painfully clear. *Thwump.*

You fucking moron! I thought. *Why didn't you see it coming?*

Why hadn't the episode in the Vette set off alarm bells?

Because I was thinking with what was between my legs, that's why. I knew about overdosing on cocaine—after Len Bias and Reggie Lewis, what Bostonian didn't? We knew about things like arrhythmia and full-blown cardiac arrest, in great medical detail, from our very own *Boston Globe*.

"Don't!" I said. "Please Allison don't!"

I had to administer CPR. I didn't know CPR, but surely I could come close—slap her on the back, start mouth-to-mouth resuscitation, do Heimlich, something, anything.

I was tied. I thrashed, futilely at first.

Allison did not appear to be breathing.

Near-sighted as I was, I could see blood flowing from the back of her head. It sounds like more baloney, but the truth is I wasn't thinking of consequences then. Not Ruth, or Timmy, or the police, or the media circus, only saving a life.

Whatever else Allison deserved, she did not deserve to die.

I freed my right foot. More wriggling and I had my left hand clear.

I untied myself and rushed, buck-naked, to Allison.

"Son of a fucking bitch," I said. "Goddamn it!"

I had her by the shoulders and was shaking her. I slapped her face and thumped her back and tried mouth-to mouth resuscitation, and nothing. No breathing. No pulse that I could detect.

"Allison can you hear me? Oh God, what have I done?"

The camera would have caught all this, too. I desperately wanted to revive her, but having failed to, I did the only think I could think of: I dialed 9-1-1.

I didn't have the address so the operator told me to stay on the line, but I couldn't do that. The operator was asking me who I was and what had happened and so on and so forth but I couldn't get into any of that just then. I was freaking out—more scared than I'd ever been, a man reduced to primal instinct, all flight, no fight.

I put the phone down and found my glasses and clothes and got dressed and tried to find a pulse again on Allison, and when I couldn't, I squeezed her hand and said: "I'm sorry, Allison. I tried my best to save you."

In the background, I heard the 9-1-1 operator, asking if anybody was there, help was on the way, please answer if there's anybody still there. I heard a siren fifteen stories down, but it could have been any siren, going anywhere. On my way through her study, I saw Allison's backup tape and thought: *This would make a hell of a screenplay.*

Honest to God, that's what I really thought as I pocketed it.

The bigger irony, of course, was yet to be revealed:

I had just embarked on my biggest production ever, and while I had the starring role, it came without creative control.

CHAPTER EIGHT

It was nearly two a.m. when I got back to the Waldorf. The red light on my phone was blinking. The first message had come in at five p.m. It was Allison.

"Thought I might catch you," she said. "Just wanted to say thinking about tonight has me *wiggly*! By the time you get this, who knows what will have happened. I think *I* know—do you? Well, see ya at Rockefeller Center!"

The other message was from Phil.

"No, I'm not calling to check on you Markie-boy, you devil," he said. "Calling about your friend, Jack. Sources having informed me he'll be at the Knicks tomorrow night—and considering what a crybaby you were when he dissed your speech—your old Uncle Phil figured seats directly behind him might shut you up! I got us tickets—four of 'em—you can thank me now. You ought to bring your girl—unless you're afraid Jack might steal her away. Ha! Ha! Ha! See you in the morning."

I tuned the TV to New York 1, the 24-hour news station.

I can't say what I expected to find—a live shot of Allison's draped body being loaded into the meat wagon? A detective announcing an all-points bulletin for a man fitting my description? Allison's tearful father, mourning the loss of his only child?

I found nothing. There was plenty of death and dying in Gotham tonight, as every night, but none involving Allison and me.

I wasn't relieved.

Nor was I tense, frightened, or remorseful. I was numb. That window of clear thinking that inspired me to call 9-1-1 had closed, leaving chemicals free to roam my brain again. This did not encourage formulation of a plan, even a half-baked plan, but that was okay; something eventually would occur and until it did, there was time to fill.

So, I brushed and flossed my teeth.

I shaved, showered, and had room service bring three bottles of Perrier, which I drank one after the other.

I turned on my laptop and checked my e-mail. I sorted my dirty laundry. I packed my bags, unpacked them, then repacked them a different way. I imagined the police knocking and me slipping onto the fire escape as they battered down the door, and then my mind flew completely into fantasy. There I was: descending, cat-like, story after story, the cops in hot pursuit, shouting for me to stop, firing warning shots over my head, sirens and searchlights ripping the night. I made it, just in the nick of time and found—a black '30s roadster, idling, driverless, by the curb. Where had I seen that car? What movie? What star behind the wheel?

I hopped in. Tires squealing, I tore off down Park Avenue...

In the real world, I went back to New York 1.

Still finding nothing, I surfed through the pre-dawn TV, a place, for all my media savvy, I'd never been. Newt Minow was right—what a wasteland. I mean, if this was the best we Americans could do, we were one bunch of losers.

Weren't we the ones who'd cured polio and put man on the moon? How had we come to this—the Psychic Friends Network and informercials for mops? I wondered what anthropologists would make of it all a hundred years from now and then I wondered if the world would last that long, and finally I found salvation, in the form of sleep.

When I came to, it was seven-thirty a.m. New York 1 still had nothing about the late Allison Manchester and the man last seen in her company, nor did AP or Reuters when I went online. Allison's homepage was still up and running, and unchanged, although I now saw it for what it was: a slick marketing tool.

My head didn't hurt anymore but my stomach was woozy and I wanted to blow off breakfast with Phil.

I didn't. I dressed and met him downstairs in Peacock Alley. "OK, slugger," he said over coffee. "Did you hit one out of the park?"

"You could say that," I said.

"All right!"

Phil slapped me five.

"I knew you could do it, Markie-boy! Tell me," he said. "Was it everything you imagined?"

"And more."

"You dirty dog! Now maybe you'll listen to your old Uncle Phil. Was I right or was I right?"

"You were right."

"Are you seeing her again tonight?"

Sure, I thought. *On my way out of booking, they'll bring me by the morgue. And then to my cell, bail denied.*

"We kind of left that up in the air," I said.

"Don't be a fool," Phil said. "She's yours, Markie-boy. Make hay while the sun shines!"

I figured Phil would want the play-by-play, but he had a list of convention issues requiring immediate attention. He went down the list and I nodded my assent and gave one- and two-word answers and even our waiter, I bet, could have sensed I didn't give a shit about it.

"Say, are you okay?" Phil asked.

"Sure," I said. "I'm fine."

"Then how come you're not eating? You're usually a pig at the trough when it's on the old expense account."

"I'm just worn out," I said.

Phil brightened.

"Didn't I tell you it would be the time of your life?" he said.

"You certainly did."

"I think what you need is sleep," Phil said. "Recharge the batteries. For tonight. It's not every day you get to go to the Knicks with your all-time favorite movie star. And with your mistress, no less!"

"I'm okay."

"I insist. I can handle things by myself."

"A couple of aspirin, and I'll be fine," I said.

Phil shrugged.

"Do what you want," he said.

We parted at the elevator.

"See you at ten," I said, but I wouldn't.

The next time I would see Phil, he would be on national TV.

I went back to my room, showered again, took four aspirin—not baby strength, mind you—checked New York 1, put my coat on and left the Waldorf.

The temperature had dropped sharply overnight and the morning air felt good on my face.

I walked south, to the Port Authority bus terminal, where I knew I would find pay phones. Would the cops trace my call? Probably. But by the time they got somebody over there, I'd be long gone.

"Name of the person you're reporting missing?" the police dispatcher asked.

"Allison Manchester."

I heard fingers on keys and the dispatcher said: "Who's calling?"

"John," I said. "John...Manchester. Her brother. I'm calling from Los Angeles."

"You say you've been trying to reach her and there's been no answer?"

"Yes."

"For how long?"

"A week."

"And what is the address?"

I gave it.

"One moment please," the dispatcher said.

I was put on hold and then a different voice came on. It was soothing, a voice that wanted to be my friend.

"Mister Manchester?"

"Yes?"

"This is Detective Brian Malloy. I understand you're calling regarding your sister."

"Yes. I'm worried about her."

"I'm sure you are."

I'm sure you are—what did that mean?

I said nothing.

"Mister Manchester, are you there?"

"I'm here," I said.

"Is there are a particular reason why you're worried about your sister?"

"I haven't been able to reach her in a week. I already told the dispatcher all that."

Malloy's tone suddenly sharpened.

"We're not getting testy, are we, Mister Manchester?"

"Of course not," I said.

"Good. Because that would be a mistake."

This guy was starting to give me the creeps.

"Now tell me what your sister looks like," Malloy went on.

I described Allison.

"Any distinctive clothing?"

"I don't know—she dresses hip, I guess. The Gen-X look—tee-shirts, jeans, leather jacket."

"Does she wear a watch?"

"A ladies Rolex," I said.

This was getting awfully detailed.

"Jewelry?"

"Pearls," I said. "She wears a pearl necklace."

"Real pearls, I bet, fancy address like that. And what about her undergarments?" Malloy said. "Does she wear panties or is she one of those free-spirited types who likes to feel the breeze down there? You know, like Sharon Stone in *Basic Instinct*—you *did* see *that* movie, didn't you?"

Excuse me?

"That was a joke," the detective continued. "Do you lack a sense of humor, Mister Manchester?"

"Look," I said, "I'm worried about my sister. I just want to know if there have been any reports."

"My dispatcher informs me that you are calling from Los Angeles," Malloy said.

"That's right. I'm in my office."

"Do you work for Greyhound, Mister Manchester?"

"Excuse me?"

"According to our system, you're actually at an NYNEX pay phone on the second floor of the Port Authority bus terminal. That's mid-town Manhattan, last I checked."

Oh, God—it hadn't taken two minutes. For all I knew, I was already under surveillance.

"Mister Manchester? Hello? Are you there?"

I hung up, and was quickly swallowed by the crowd, another harmless nobody headed to the daily grind.

Undercover, I thought. *They could be tailing you. This could be Hitchcock.*

Evasive maneuvers were in order.

I headed south on Eighth Avenue, darting across Thirty-ninth after the light had turned green and anyone following me would have been flattened. You know that cut-throat New York traffic.

Then I doubled back to Times Square, where, I couldn't help but notice, hookers were already plying their trade. I went into the subway, bought a token and waited at the turnstile for the next train. At the very last second, I dashed through and onto a car.

I was the final one aboard. The doors closed and we headed north, toward Central Park.

I could not bear the thought of returning to my room. I needed space. I needed time, and not the sort measured by station breaks on TV.

Funny—much as I should have been, I wasn't preoccupied with Ruth. She was there on the fringes of consciousness with Timmy and Phil, but Allison still had the largest claim on my thoughts. I couldn't erase her image—those glazed-over eyes, her desperate struggle for breath, her sweaty blue skin, *please God do not let her die.* And me—naked and tied to the bed like some porno Willy Loman in one of Forty-second Street's hourly rooms.

I left the subway at Central Park, confident of one thing: I wasn't being tailed. Or if I was, the operation was so seamless there was nothing I could do about it anyway.

It was starting to snow—a light dusting that was painting the park white. I found Strawberry Fields and stood in silent reflection until the only other person there, a woman with dyed hair and a disposable camera, turned to me and said:

"We'll never know what he would have done."

"No," I said, "we won't, will we."

"I was at their Wrigley Field concert in 1965," the woman continued. "I was twelve. All my friends loved Paul. I was the only one who dug John."

I got interested after he left the Beatles, I could have said. *Not to be condescending, but you were caught up in the teeny-bop craze.*

How completely and arrogantly condescending, but please cut me some slack. This was not my shining moment.

"I cried when they broke up," the woman went on. "To this day, I blame Yoko. It sounds funny, but it's true. By the way, I'm Sue Partington. Pleased to meet you."

"John Manchester," I said.

"Isn't that something! You even have his first name!"

She prattled on—one of those friendly Midwesterners who's compelled to share her life's story on first meeting. She told me about her three children, her first grandchild, the three female friends who'd traveled east from Milwaukee with her. She was depressing the living crap out of me, to be honest. But at that moment, at least, I obliged her.

"Would you join me for coffee?" she asked when I said I must be on my way.

"I'd like to but I'm late," I said.

"What for?" she said.

"A funeral."

"I'm sorry. Was it someone special?"

"No," I said, "just a casual business partner."

"Could you do me a favor before you go?" the woman said.

"Sure."

"Could you take my picture?"

"It'll have to be fast," I said.

I'd spotted a remote-broadcast TV van heading our way.

I snapped the picture and ran, deeper into Central Park.

I spoke to no one and no one spoke to me for the remainder of the day. No one was following me, I was sure—I'd gotten a grip on that. Cops didn't give me a second look, newspapers weren't publishing my mugshot, and TV crews weren't jumping out from behind bushes.

I can't say my spirits rose, but they didn't sink deeper. I stopped for coffee and gave in to the temptation of a bagel and lox, and then I went to the top of the Empire State Building, which I hadn't visited since college, when the heaven tops of Manhattan still thrilled.

The borough was mostly hidden in white and I tried, unsuccessfully, to pick out Allison's apartment. From the Empire State Building, I went to the New York Public Library, where I sat for three hours thumbing through books about the films of Forman and Scorsese, who were atop my personal A-list. At three-thirty, I left the library and went to Michael Crichton's Lost World, where a janitor let me into the coat room. My trophy was there, untouched, and I claimed it without even being asked for an ID; it could have been a lost mitten, for all the janitor cared.

"Wilbur, huh?" he said. "I thought some chick left her dildo. Weird one it would have been, but I've seen worse."

Then I walked past Allison's, on the opposite side of Park Avenue. There was no yellow crime tape, no sawhorses, no mobile command center or cruisers with lights flashing.

Night was falling when I reached Rockefeller Center.

The rink was crowded with skaters again, and I heard blades, and laughter of young couples, and Christmas carols over the PA. Oh, to be innocent again.

And when I closed my eyes, I could almost see myself down there, with Sally Martin, the person who, save for my mother, had held sacred ground for the longest time.

We grew up together, Sally and I did.

Pick up an old Blue Hill High Record, and you'll see photos of us together everywhere: the senior prom, spirit week, homecoming, the film club, which Bud Robbins and I chaired. Judging by our yearbook, you'd think Sally and I were going to last forever, and I guess I believed that then. I know Sally did.

We graduated and had the most amazing summer and September came and she stayed in Maine to enroll in a nursing assistant program at Bangor Community College. Against the advice of my father, who hated Hollywood almost as much as the Pentagon, I went off to NYU to take up filmmaking. And at first, Sally and I were crazier than ever for each other. We exchanged letters daily and ran up big phone bills and over Columbus Day weekend, she made her first visit to New York. I was in Blue Hill for Thanksgiving, and before Christmas, Sally took the bus again to New York. Classes had ended and for three days we had the dorm room I shared with Bud to ourselves. We listened to records and got drunk and smoked marijuana and made love—more amazing, if that were possible, than that glorious summer. I couldn't wait to give Sally her Christmas gift.

On a night not unlike tonight—here, at Rockefeller Center— snow falling—the same carols playing—I gave her the opal ring I'd financed by selling my silver dollar collection, a childhood inheritance from Mom. With the ring, I gave her a white rose, her favorite flower.

Things cooled not long after that.

Not for Sally—I don't believe Sally ever cooled, not completely. I mean, even in her reunion note you could sense it: an ember still burning, as she herself might have described it.

I returned to New York after the holidays and soon became friendly with Doris Wong, an exotically beautiful classmate from San Francisco, and while it wasn't love or anything, I wanted to ask her to a screening of Bunuel's classic *Discreet Charm of the Bourgeoisie* without having to get into a long explanation with Sally.

So, I didn't tell Sally.

I didn't tell her about Bunuel, or the party Doris and I went to after, or how very near we came to fucking after our host had passed out and everyone else had left and the possibility of seeing another woman unclothed was too much to bear.

Thanks to Doris, I got a measure of relief.

"Take them off," she said when I'd slid my hand down to the crotch of her jeans.

I obliged. She was not wearing underwear. She parted her legs.

"You like that?" she said, and I acknowledged that I did.

"Maybe someday you can have it," she said, putting her jeans back on. "But it will be on my terms, not yours."

Doris was like that: impetuous and independent-minded, nothing at all like that girl from Maine. Or so I thought then.

I won't get into every little detail of the next three years, for much of my life (not to mention Sally's) was mundane, even though at the time I rather fancied it was material for a great movie if not the great American novel, which even in my most far-fetched fantasies I never believed I could write. That thing for clichés and many more handicaps would have killed me.

Sally and I were like characters in some country-and-western song: breaking up, making up, breaking up again. We were back together the summer she graduated from Bangor Community—the summer after my junior year. That fall, she moved to New York and took a studio apartment and put her retailing degree to fabulous use on the perfume counter at Macy's.

Sally was no classic beauty—rather, she was possessed of what you'd call a fresh look, very girl-next-door, like someone in a J.C. Penney catalogue. She enrolled in Barbizon School of Modeling and a so-called drama academy, I forget the name, and never mind that her lone performance was at talent night, which didn't draw an audience to fill the church basement where it was held. I was going to be a Hollywood director and she was going to be my star.

By senior year, I was pretty damn cocky.

I'd directed six films, and one had been favorably reviewed in *The Village Voice* and another praised in a wrap-up of student artists in *The New York Times*. I'd been contacted by a couple of New York ad firms regarding employment after graduation, but I'd told them to take a hike. I was an artist—so said *The Times*—not a corporate suit. Bud was heading to L.A. and I was going with him and Sally was going, too…or so she believed.

I can't pinpoint when I became derisive of the woman for whom I'd sold the only thing of material value my mother had left me.

I suspect it was after September, when I declined to live with her, using some pathetically lame argument about space and freedom, and I know for certain it was before she got knocked up. My guess is late October. I was running the first annual NYU Jack Nicholson film fest and on this particular night we'd screened *Cuckoo's Nest* for a sellout audience of 300, including John Lennon—John Lennon!—who'd arrived, unannounced, with Yoko and Sean.

During the discussion period, which I moderated, Sally raised her hand and said: "If Chief could talk all that time, why'd he wait so long to say something?"

Utter silence in the auditorium.

Bud rolled his eyes and *The Voice's* film critic looked pained and if Lennon hadn't been fussing over his son, I bet he would have had some sharp-tongued barb.

I did not let on that I knew Sally.

"Thank you, Miss," I said, "now would anyone care to pick up on Professor Pagliano's observations on Nurse Ratched as a metaphor for neo-capitalist authoritarianism?"

Lennon did, and his remarks were printed in the next edition of *The Village Voice*, along with a photo of me handing him the mic.

Later that evening, alone with Sally, I said: "If you have to be so stupid, can you at least not do it in public?"

"Why was that stupid?" Sally said.

"Oh my God," I said, with blustering intellectual indignation, "now you want me to *explain* your stupidity. It's like the Bunuel subtitles again."

"Well, I hate subtitles," Sally said. "If I want to read, I'll get a book."

She had a point, a good one in fact, but I didn't see it then. There was a lot I didn't see then.

If I hadn't gone home that Christmas, I suppose our relationship would have been over, finally, by year's end. But I did go home, and Sally did too, and Christmas Eve found us together and it was like the calendar had been turned back.

I told Sally I loved her and somehow we'd make things work and we should consider tonight a fresh start—all the sweet talk a twenty-one-year-old guy who hasn't been laid in a month can muster. We made love that night, and every night for the remainder of the holidays, and we went back to New York together, and several weeks later, when Doris Wong began strongly hinting that my day was soon to come, I told Sally it was over—this time, for good.

She didn't plead.

She didn't ask for explanations and she didn't call or come by, and when two weeks had passed and Doris hadn't moved past hinting, I called her.

She didn't want to talk over the phone.

"Meet me at Rockefeller Center," she said, and hung up.

The funny thing was, the second I saw Sally, I wanted to kiss her.

Go figure—I can't wait for her to be out of my life and once she is, all I can think is *I want to kiss her. Kiss her and take her clothes off and spend a week in bed with her. Like Yoko and John, except no peace-in, but sex non-stop.*

I swear, no one had ever looked better: her lips redder than I remembered, her hair so long and silky and brown, her skin so rosy. I mean, she was like Barbara Hershey, another actress I had a thing for then. And I did kiss her—this clumsy thing involving contact with her cheek. We exchanged pleasantries and then we skated and after, as we drank hot chocolates, she told me she was two months pregnant. Given how we'd spent the holiday—together virtually 24/7—there was no shred of doubt about paternity.

I look back on that moment of revelation for my emotional response—and I find none, no clue that Sally's feelings counted or we were confronting something weightier than whether we'd have another hot chocolate.

I remember telling Sally I didn't give a shit about the particulars—that's a direct quote, "I don't give a shit about the particulars"—whether she'd forgotten to use her diaphragm, or whether it had failed, or she'd planned this the way I'd heard some women did, or it was the sequel to the Immaculate Fucking Conception.

"The sooner you get it taken care of," I said, "the better off we'll all be."

Those, too, were my exact words, delivered with a detachment that echoes eerily, horrifyingly, and coldly in my head even now. "You don't understand," Sally said. "I'm having the baby." I was stunned.

Abortion was automatic in these circumstances, wasn't it? You screwed up, you got it taken care of. There was no dilemma, no debate, nothing but consulting the Yellow Pages for the nearest clinic and hoping insurance would cover the cost.

Sally presented her case: Abortion now increased the chances of miscarriage later. Abortion was unsafe. Abortion was immoral.

Like after growing up with my father, that was going to get her anywhere with me.

What if the baby—that's what she kept calling it, the *baby*, not "fetus"—was destined for greatness? What about you, Mark— what if your parents had decided on abortion—we wouldn't be having this conversation now—maybe look at it that way?

I'd never heard her so impassioned and eloquent, although those were not words I would have used that day. That day, I saw Sally as one of those crazies who hand out photos of dead fetuses outside Planned Parenthood clinics.

"This is ridiculous," I said.

"It's bigger than us," Sally said.

"It's fucked-up, is what it is."

"I want to marry you," she said. "I love you."

Before I could respond, she launched into how she would do the diapering, the baths, and the midnight feedings—she would do all that, and still she'd be a movie star, just like Barbara Hershey, who'd had a kid and still made it to the top. The limo on Academy Awards night would need to have room for nanny, is all.

I got furious after that, my voice rising to a level where heads turned.

And before the night was over, Sally relented.

She insisted I not go with her the morning she had it done and I didn't. I was shooting the last scenes of my honors thesis, *Eating People*, a 30-minute film influenced not by any premonition of heavy-handed irony, but by a longstanding infatuation with Jack Nicholson and, more recently, Luis Bunuel, whose films were all subtitled.

The day I graduated from NYU, Dad tried one last time to dissuade me from going west.

"You don't belong there," he said, but it was a half-hearted attempt. We both knew his days of influence were over.

Everything Bud and I owned fit into Bud's van—with room for Doris Wong, who was making the trip with us. We took a southern route: through the Carolinas, Georgia, Alabama, and Texas, smoking weed and goofing on rednecks. We arrived on the Fourth of July in Venice Beach, a destination that appealed to Bud because he'd read that Jim Morrison, a musician he hoped someday to make a movie about, had founded The Doors there with Ray Manzarek on one of his LSD trips. Bud was really into Morrison at the time. Doris came from money and she had the cash for a down payment on a pretty decent three-bedroom apartment a block from the Pacific. We unpacked our stereos and moved in.

Doris was the second woman I ever slept with.

It happened the first week we lived together, and it happened pretty much the way it did with the women who followed in Venice Beach: we put Steely Dan on the stereo, lit the bong, and screwed. "Told you someday you could have it," Doris said in that first occasion.

I realize I am not painting a romantic picture here, but this was not poetry or art—this was getting your share, all of us, me, them, everyone. When Doris confessed she was sleeping with someone else, that was cool; when she said that someone else was a woman she was leaving Bud and me for, that was cool, too. I'd taken up with another woman myself. Her name is lost in time: all I remember is she was bleach-blonde and her previous boyfriend, of precisely two week's standing, was Bud.

That first summer, Bud and I hung out on the beach and in the bars and movie houses and it seemed everyone was the same age, into the same thing, namely, partying.

And films. And video games, which were starting to take off.

I remember going with Bud to the bank for rolls of quarters, which would take us through an afternoon of *Pong*, *Indy 8* or *Donkey Kong*, the big titles back then. Strange: The names of women I slept with have vanished from memory, but I recall with absolute clarity the time, day and place I met Chris McCauley.

Chris was older than our crowd—he was pushing thirty—but he wore his hair in a ponytail and favored tie-dye shirts and sandals, and you wouldn't have guessed, until he began to talk, that he'd been a Marine helicopter pilot who'd returned from Vietnam with a box full of medals and a brain that was wildly creative, and totally fucked-up from PTSD.

I met Chris Labor Day weekend in Sonny's, coolest bar in Venice Beach.

He was playing *Tank* and he was blowing his opponent away. He blew Bud away, then me, then a succession of other wide-eyed young men who waited in line. We bought him a beer and listened while he talked about the job he'd just left, with a firm I'd never heard of—Atari, it was called. Chris was a games designer who wanted to be a movie animator. When Doris moved out, Bud and I asked him to live with us.

I remember the day he moved in not only because he was such a vivid character but also because it was the day Sally called—a Sunday in late September, when the ocean air carried the first tang of autumn wafting down from the Santa Monica Mountains.

Bud answered the phone.

"Who is it?" I said.

"Sally," Bud said.

"Tell her I'm out," I whispered.

"Sorry. Already said you were here."

I've mentioned Sally's abortion, but not how I saw Sally only once, and that only for a few minutes, after she had it.

She didn't call after that, or attend the NYU film festival, or come to my graduation. She wrote one letter, in April, saying she was moving to her cousin's house back home in Maine, sorry but the number was unlisted, and she was sad how things had worked out, and it was best to remember the good times and try to forget the bad. She wished me luck in Hollywood and said she was sure that someday, quite possibly in the Blue Hill

Nickelodeon, where together we'd seen so many flicks, she'd watch my first feature film.

I stuffed that letter with all of her others and a few other mementoes in a giant manilla envelope, thinking someday they might form the basis for a screenplay. I was a shit, I really was. In my next lifetime, if I get one, I hope I do better.

"Hello, Sally," I said that Sunday in September.

"How are you, Mark?"

"I'm fine."

"I was sitting here thinking of you and I thought I'd call," Sally said.

I didn't respond.

"You don't mind, do you?"

"I guess not."

"Your father gave me the number. He said it would be okay."

Wait'll I talk to him, I thought, but I doubted I would again soon: at graduation, Dad had given me an earful of how badly I'd treated Sally. And he didn't even know about her abortion.

Or so I thought then.

"Good old Dad," I said.

"He says hi."

"That's very nice of him," I said.

"So, have you directed your first movie yet?" Sally said.

I laughed, uneasily.

"No, but I have my first job."

"Tell me."

"I just got hired as a production assistant."

It was a lie.

I'd schlepped my films around Burbank and Universal City and a couple of junior producer types had told me to stay in touch, but my phone hadn't exactly been ringing off the hook. In fact, it hadn't rung once. Lately, I'd been sneaking peeks at the classifieds.

"You're kidding!"

"Nope. Major film, too."

"Who's the director?"

"Milos Forman," I said.

"He did *Cuckoo's Nest!*"

"You remember."

"I remember a lot," Sally said.

Neither of us spoke for a moment. I could feel it, the heaviness on both ends of the line.

"Mark?"

"Yes?"

"There's something I need to tell you. Something that goes back to us being together."

"I don't want to get into that," I said.

"It would mean so much to me."

"What's past is past."

"Just give me five minutes. I promise no longer."

"No, Sally."

"Please. I'll never ask again.

"No."

"For me? For us—for what we used to be?"

I thought I heard crying, but as I replay that conversation in my head now, I'm not sure I still do. I hear a quiet sort of anger.

"I can't get into all that again," I said.

"Please. It's not what you think."

"I'm sorry, Sally."

"Please, Mark, I'm begging you."

"I have to go now."

"Please don't hang up on me. Say anything...say nothing... just don't hang up."

But I did.

"Who was that?" Chris asked.

"No one," I said.

"Do you always take the phone off the hook after talking to no one?" he said.

"This was an especially annoying no one," I said, and Chris nodded, in manly understanding.

This all took place, I should add, before I began to ponder an issue my father had long wrestled with, which was: Do people quite literally burn in hell, or is fire only a metaphor for something worse, unending regret and shame in the here and now?

Or is the truth what he preached from the pulpit every Holy Week: Crucifixion is required before redemption.

Don't ask why it had taken so long, but somewhere in the time I was at Rockefeller Center, it occurred to me:

Maybe Allison's not dead! Maybe the EMTs miraculously got there in time! Maybe she's lying in a hospital bed, taking her first liquids and awaiting get-well cards, bouquets, and edible panties from her many concerned clients! Maybe this whole cop trip is nothing but paranoia, a powerful imagination gone temporarily awry!

I found a pay phone and dialed Detective Malloy.

"I was hoping you'd call again," he said.

"I just wanted to explain about this morning," I said. "Saying I was in L.A. when I really was in New York."

"I'd love an explanation," he said.

"It's simple—I was confused."

"Is it a regular practice of yours to confuse opposite sides of the continent?"

"I travel a lot," I said. "The jet lag's a real killer."

"Interesting turn of phrase, 'real killer.'"

Jesus, this guy gave me the willies. I could feel a headache drilling back into my skull.

"Have you found my sister?"

Malloy sighed.

"Mister Gray—Mister Mark A. Gray, age 42, of 16 Ocean Drive, Marblehead, Massachusetts, Social Security Number 111-22-3333—don't you think it's time we dispensed with the bullshit?"

So, they'd made the ID.

"Is she alive?" I blurted out. "Please. I have to know."

"What would make you suspect she *wasn't* alive? The fact that you left her unconscious and bleeding?" His voice was rising. "You know what I'd like to know, Gray? Did you have a hard-on while you were strangling her, you sick fucking creep?"

"But—" I kept trying to say, "But—"

"But? Butt? How's we strap your naked butt to the electric chair, Romeo?"

He was screaming now—screaming!

I was about to hang up—should have hung up—when his tone did an abrupt one-eighty and he apologized, profusely. It had been a long day, he said, a very long and frustrating day, and he had some problems at home, and, well...man-to-man, surely I could understand.

"May I call you Mark?" he said.

"Please."

"Look, Mark—you're in trouble, right? It's the kind of trouble that could happen to any guy. Babe that hot—hey, I hear you. You figure here's your chance to get a little frisky in a way you can't with the old lady, maybe spank her cute rump—maybe *whip* and ride it like a cowboy!—believe me, I understand! And before you know it, you're carried away. You know, like someone in *A Clockwork Orange*."

"It wasn't like that."

"Anything you say, Mark," he said. "What you need to focus on now is getting out of this. Let me help you. Please. That's what public servants are for."

"How could you help me?"

"Let's meet. Nothing heavy-duty, no sheriffs, no lawyers, just two guys talking over drinks. You know where Novita is?"

My God, he even knew the restaurant.

"No," I managed. "I've never heard of it."

"Oh, you'll like it," he said. "It's a quiet little place. We can talk in peace."

He gave me the address and said, hopefully: "Meet me in half an hour."

I heard sirens—could a cruiser be on scene that fast?

"I'll think about it," I said, and hung up.

Ducking into an alley, I watched flashing blue lights soar by.

Three messages awaited me at the Waldorf. Charlie Goldman wanted to know where I was, please call ASAP. Phil wanted to inform me that he couldn't make the Knicks game after all, but be sure to say hello to Jack for him.

The last was Timmy.

"Hi Daddy, it's me, I miss you," he said. "My angelfish died.

That makes me sad. Mom says call. I love you. Come home soon. See you in Dreamland."

I turned the TV on, but New York 1 still was unaware. Damn. Didn't reporters sniff twenty-four hours a day for sensationalism like this? Wasn't this the Digital Age, when news travels at the speed of electrons? Maybe they'd had trouble notifying Allison's father. Maybe cops needed time to build their case—what did I know about police protocol? Maybe Malloy would have the TV minicams waiting at Novita. Ultimately, it was academic. I was on borrowed time, and the only issue was whether it would be measured in hours or days.

What's to stop you from going to the Knicks? I thought. *May as well live it up, your last moments as a free man.*

For a few mad minutes, I actually believed I could pull it off.

"So, *you're* Mark Gray," I imagined Nicholson would say when I sat down behind him.

"That's me," I would beam. "I'll bet the tie gave me away!"

"You're a genius, Mark, a creative *genius*. A star in your own movie."

Nicholson would not remember, of course, that we'd already met, about a million years ago, in Malibu.

"I'm flattered," I would say.

"I mean it. *Tomcat* is awesome. The only game I've ever liked more is *Shuttle Saga!*"

"Gosh."

"And this *Virtual Clue* deal that's generating this buzz—sign me up now!"

"Consider it done."

"You know, I've never done this before with anyone," Nicholson would say as he pulled a pen from his pocket. "It's always been the other way. But could I have your autograph?"

"Only if I can have yours!" I would retort.

"Dude!" Nicholson would say as we high-fived, and photographers from the *Post* and *Daily News* snapped our picture.

But I couldn't be seen in Madison Square Garden, or anywhere public.

I thought of Malloy, and was suddenly sober.

Meet him, I thought. *Turn yourself in.*

Except I couldn't do that, either. Maybe tomorrow, or the next day, or the day after that, when things had settled down I would. Tonight, it was too much to bear: the thought of the headlines, the mugshots, the cameras and pretty-boy TV reporters as I was led in handcuffs into the cruiser. This was New York, where the media beheld humanity and saw raw meat.

What I needed was advice—but from whom? Phil? I'd had enough of Phil's advice. My lawyer? This creative fucking star didn't have one, and the last thing I wanted was to drag in corporate counsel. My dad? Syd? Please. I'd fare better with the *Post*.

That left Ruth. During the time it took to dial, I almost convinced myself I could come clean.

The sound of her voice put that notion to rest.

"I was getting worried," she said. "You haven't called since you arrived."

"It's this damn convention," I said. "I swear it's the last one I ever do."

"When have I heard that before? Like, a million times?"

"This time I'm serious."

I wondered if she could sense the artifice in my voice. I was trying so hard to sound normal, or what passes for it.

"I'm serious, too," Ruth said. "I do not enjoy going this long without you calling."

"I'm sorry," I said. "Here's the hammer. Nail me to a cross."

Ruth allowed herself a small chuckle.

"Have you been taking to your dad?" she said. "You know how his sense of humor has changed in retirement."

"No, I haven't talked to him," I said.

"Please don't wait so long to call when you're out of town," she said.

"Scout's honor," I said.

I told Ruth about my Wilbur, and she congratulated me, and then I had her bring me up to speed on her work, and then she said: "You'll get a kick out of this."

She launched into a story about Pierpont, who'd escaped, treed a cat, then been scooped by the dog officer. On their way to fetch their pet, the Morgans had crashed up their Jaguar.

"Is that poetic justice or what?" Ruth said.

"It's poetic justice," I said.

"Is something wrong?"

"No, why?"

"You seem—I don't know, distant."

"I'm tired, that's all," I said.

"I definitely see Vermont in the not-too-distant future."

"I think so."

"Speaking of tired," Ruth said, "somebody's still up. Want to say hello?"

"Of course."

A small voice came on the line.

"Isn't it past your bedtime, Scooter?"

"Mommy let me watch *Home Alone 2.*"

"Are you being good?"

"Very good. Daddy?"

"What, Scooter?"

"Do fish go to heaven?"

"If they're good."

Timmy laughed.

"Angelfish must be good 'cause they have that name," he said.

"You're right."

We chit-chatted some more, and I didn't want to hang up, didn't want to have to contemplate our next conversation, which for all I knew would take place in the visiting room of a jail.

But I have to tell you: Hearing my son's voice might have been the only thing that prevented me from slitting my wrists. We said our goodbyes and eventually I fell into a terrible sleep. Malloy's voice rumbled through my head as I drifted off.

I was totally screwed now, no way around it.

CHAPTER NINE

The TV was still on when I awoke—morning aerobics, so perky and full of the promise of the brand-new day that I wanted to puke. I switched to New York 1.

"In the top of the news at eight," the anchor woman was saying, "police are investigating the attempted murder of socialite Allison Manchester, found unconscious early yesterday morning in her Park Avenue penthouse."

Attempted. I couldn't believe it—she was alive!

"Miss Manchester is the only child of George W. Manchester Jr., senior vice president at World Bank and co-owner of the New York Knicks," the anchor woman continued. "We take you live to Precinct 57 and reporter Doug Fenning. Doug?"

"Mary, police say Manchester was nude when EMTs found her in her apartment shortly after midnight. Bruises on her neck and shoulders indicate a life-and-death struggle."

"I was trying to save her life!" I shouted at the TV.

"Police are awaiting the results of tests before speculating on the motive for this brutal attack. We spoke a short while ago with Detective Brian Malloy, who said there are no suspects at this time."

Malloy came on.

He was younger than me, tall, ruggedly handsome, well-dressed. In my mind's eye, he'd been fiftyish and frumpy—Columbo, if you needed the TV analog.

This guy had presence. You could tell the camera was his friend. This was a bad omen.

"We're working on some promising leads," Malloy said,

"but nothing I can disclose at the moment. All I can say is, we'll get our man."

He sounded calm, collected, no trace of the psycho I'd talked to yesterday. Maybe it was some cutting-edge criminal investigation technique: good cop/bad cop, all in one person.

"Doug," Mary said, "what is her condition?"

"We spoke to the hospital a few minutes ago and she remains in critical condition in intensive care. She has not regained consciousness."

"What hospital?" I shouted.

But Doug didn't say.

And Mary was on to the next story, a warmed-over rumor that the surviving Beatles were reuniting for a Central Park concert next spring—with Sean Lennon filling in for his dad. One of the women she'd interviewed for reaction was a certain Sue Partington, a middle-age woman who was visiting from Decatur, Illinois.

"I'd go in a second," Sue said. "I'd pay two hundred dollars a ticket, if that's what it took!"

I rode the elevator to the lobby, convinced, given how my luck was lately, that I would run into Lisa or Phil.

I did not.

I saw Allison, at the newsstand—her mugshot was on the front page of the *Post*. My God, she was the lead story! In their collective wisdom, the editors of one of America's largest newspapers had decreed Allison's misfortune the single most important development on the planet in the last twenty-four hours! The headline read:

SOCIALITE
IN SICKO
SNUFF SNAFU

And I could not but think: *Damn good headline, ghouls.* I really was jealous of such creativity.

But I said: "Oh, shit."

"Excuse me?" the clerk said.

"I'll take the *Post*, please," I said.

She handed one over.

"It had to be robbery," she said. "What else could it have been?"

"Sex."

"Do you think so?"

"Isn't everything about sex these days?" I said.

"I suppose so. Terrible thing."

"Horrible. You know what I think?" I said. "I think she was a prostitute."

"No! A pretty girl like that?"

"Wasn't that Heidi Fleiss a looker?"

"But this girl is *rich!*" the clerk said.

"So was the Mayflower Madam."

"Goodness—I'd forgotten about her! What is the world coming to?"

I waited until I was safely outside before opening the paper. The story was worse than the headline—far worse. It read:

NEW YORK—*Sultry socialite Allison Manchester struggles for life this morning after a vicious attack by a sex-crazed sadist in her ritzy Park Avenue penthouse.*

Her unknown assailant is being sought in a nationwide manhunt today.

Manchester, 27, is the daughter of George W. Manchester, Jr., aging playboy and wealthy co-owner of the New York Knicks.

The glamorous socialite, a regular on the Manhattan club scene, was found nude and bleeding on the bedroom floor of her posh apartment. Sources said her assailant broke in bearing ropes and a whip which he used in the attack.

"*She* had the ropes and whip," I said. "Her fingerprints were all over them. How could they miss that?"

The article continued:

Manchester this morning remained comatose in the intensive care unit of Beth Israel Hospital. A doctor who asked not to be named said she was on a ventilator.

"It's a minute-by-minute proposition," the doctor said.

Reached as he boarded a plane home from Turkey, where he'd been on extended World Bank business, a teary Manchester said: "Why would anyone want to kill my Allison? She's a sweet girl who never harmed anyone."

Detective Brian Malloy said police are still combing the Manchester penthouse for clues. Malloy said they have no motive and no suspect at this time, but sources said Manchester was seen in the company of a fortyish white male wearing a Superman tie and penny loafers the night of the attack. And there were reports the man was carrying a gold-plated sexual device.

"All indications are that it was a premeditated assault," the source said. The source said the assailant will be charged with attempted murder and felony assault. Malloy would not comment on possible charges.

"All I can say is we will get our man," Malloy said. "Of that, I am confident."

The detective, one of the force's most highly decorated, would not elaborate, nor comment on reports that a psychological profile of the would-be killer matches that of Ted Bundy.

"You've got to be shitting me!" I said. "Ted Bundy?"

The Post wasn't done. The story continued:

The elder Manchester, heir to the Manchester & Abraham securities fortune, was a notorious playboy during the 1960s and early '70s. His second marriage, to starlet Libby O'Reilly, Allison's mother, lasted less than a year, as did his third marriage, to heiress Charlotte Browning. Manchester has recently been seen in the company of Faye Dunaway and Mia Farrow at Lost World and other hot spots.

Allison graduated from Miss Potter's School, the exclusive boarding school in swanky Farmington, Conn., and attended Bennington College, a favorite for children of the ultra-rich. Reliable sources say she left the Vermont school in a scandal involving cocaine and a middle-aged dean who subsequently was canned. Details were not immediately available.

"It's a real tragedy," said Kiss of the Spiderwoman star Stephen Ferreira, a close friend of Manchester.

I folded the paper and went south, toward Fleet Bank.

Whatever was about to go down, I needed money.

I knew that as instinctively as it was time to leave New York. And it had to be cash—credit cards left trails an enterprising fellow like Malloy would be only too happy to follow. I went into the lobby of a Fleet Bank branch, found an ATM machine, and attempted to withdraw $5,000. The machine whirred and clicked and posted a message: "Limit: $1,000."

I tried again, with the same result. It was like *Maximum Overdrive*, that stupid movie Stephen King never should have directed and probably wouldn't have if he hadn't been snorting cocaine. The damn thing was refusing me my money! Like I was in the mood for this now.

"There's something wrong with this ATM," I told a man who was seated behind a desk, his face in a computer screen.

"And just what does the trouble seem to be?" he said.

I related what had happened.

"Our machines are not authorized to dispense such large amounts," said the junior officer, an impeccably groomed young thing who had the pale, doughy look of a Grade-A nerd.

"What if I have a gun?" I said.

"Excuse me?"

"Nothing."

"Suppose our machines *were* able to dispense such amounts," the officer said. "Can you imagine how quickly we would run out over a long holiday weekend? Or an *ordinary* weekend, for that matter?"

You could tell he'd actually given this intense consideration.

"But I would be *happy* to access your account for more," he went on, smiling. "May I please see an ID?"

I balked until I realized: What did it matter? Malloy would get to the bank sooner or later.

I handed over my driver's license and Junior got right to work.

"Goodness!" he said, after a few taps on his keyboard.

"There *is* a slight problem. On this account, withdrawals of any kind over $1,000 require a co-signature."

"From?"

"Another executive officer. This is a corporate account for CreativeWare."

"Thank you for enlightening me," I said, "about my own company."

"And a marvelous company it is, Mister Gray. Would you believe I personally own *Tomcat* and *Stealth Striker*—and that *Shuttle Saga* is on my Christmas list? It's true!"

What was it with this dweeb—was he a Dale Carnegie graduate or what?

"I assume you know a Mr. Phil Grace," Junior said.

"He's my partner."

"Well then, getting his John Hancock should be easy as... as...reaching the second level of *Stealth Striker*! After sufficient practice, that is!"

"Shut up," I said.

"Excuse me?"

"Shut up and listen to me."

"Yes, sir," he said, deflated.

"What if my partner was in Africa?"

"I'm afraid you'd be out of luck."

"The hell with luck. It's my money."

"I'm sorry, Mister Gray," the banker said. "I'm only doing my job."

"Well, your job sucks," I said. "And you suck."

Co-signature—it sounded awfully fishy, but what did I know? I hadn't opened the account. I'd never tried to get more than a few hundred bucks now and again from it. Finances were Phil's baby. He attracted the investments, balanced the books, posted the profits, dealt with the IRS, had his bean-counters pay the bills. I'd entrusted him and his boys to handle my mortgage, my taxes, my investment portfolio, my retirement plan...you get the picture.

Me? I struggled with a simple sales forecast. I was the Creative Fucking Star—hadn't *Wired* officially anointed me? There was no need for me to dirty my gifted little hands with something so mundane as money.

"If you'd like me to call the branch manager..." junior said.

It occurred to me that perhaps this was not a brilliant idea. And what if he had a panic button, as he almost certainly did?

"No need," I said. "I'll take a cash advance from my Visa account."

I handed him a gold card. It was another of CreativeWare's accounts.

"And sorry for the grief," I said. "Ever have one of those days?"

"All the time, Mr. Gray!" he said, brightening.

He entered the account into his computer—and looked pained again.

"I'm so sorry," he said, "but there's a thousand-dollar limit on cash advances on this account as well."

"Fine," I said, forcing a smile. "Give me the thousand."

"You're such a splendid sport," Junior said. "Mind if I bother you with just one more thing?"

"Of course not," I said.

"May I have your autograph?"

"Patient condition," I said to the Beth Israel operator.

I was back at the Waldorf.

"Name?" the voice said.

"Allison Manchester."

"I'm not allowed to give that out," the voice said.

"I'm her brother," I said, "John Manchester. Calling from Los Angeles."

"Still critical," the voice said. "Anything more you'll have to get from her doctors."

Call it instinct, but I knew Allison was going to make it.

She was going to make a full recovery and she was going to explain everything to Malloy, leaving me to deal only with Ruth. Not that that would be a walk in the park, but it sure beat a murder rap. For the first time in two days, I was almost happy. I mean, I was actually humming as I turned on my TV for a last loving look before I blew town.

"In the rest of the news at noon," Mary the anchor woman was saying, "New York 1 has learned the identity of the man police believe tried to kill socialite Allison Manchester. He is Mark Gray, 42, president of CreativeWare, a Boston-based maker of a popular line of video games. At this hour, Gray remains at large."

They showed a still photo of me receiving my Wilbur at the

Gamers convention, and the angle of the shot combined with the way I held the trophy—a gold-plated joystick, remember— lent credence to the sexual device scenario alluded to in the Post. Those ghouls were good.

"New York 1 has also obtained an exclusive copy of a videotape police seized from Manchester's penthouse apartment shortly after the attempted murder," Mary said.

"Oh, no," I said. I'd forgotten about Allison's camera.

"For the full report, we bring you to Doug Fenning. Doug?"

Doug had joined Mary at the anchor desk.

"Mary, police on the record have no comment about how the tape was made. Sources say, however, that it was a secret security camera Manchester had installed."

"So Gray, the alleged attempted murderer, didn't know he was being taped," Mary said.

"That's right," Fenning said. "Detectives now are confident that simple sexual assault wasn't the suspect's intent, but rather something darker related to a sadistic psycho-sexual personality defect."

"Like Jeffrey Dahmer," Mary said.

"Right, except Dahmer was into boys."

"The way Andrew Cunanan was into men."

"Exactly. The important difference being that Gray appears to be straight."

"In other words, more like Ted Bundy."

"Or John Wayne Gacy."

"Or Richard Speck. You remember him: he killed all those nurses, in 1967. In their beds."

"But not before he raped them," Doug said.

"I thought he raped them *after* he killed them," Mary said. "I thought he was a necrophiliac serial killer."

"The worst kind. Perhaps you're right."

"In any event," Mary said, "once you get past the details, it's all the same animal."

"And animal is exactly what we're dealing with here, Mary," Doug said.

I couldn't believe what I was hearing. Did an "alleged" every now and then save them from libel? Or did they understand how weak my case would be, if it ever went to trial—that they could take whatever license they wanted from here on out?

I was beginning to hate the First Amendment.

"We're going to show some of that tape," Mary said.

"Please, no," I begged. "Have mercy."

"Because of its graphic nature, viewer discretion is advised. Doug, tell us what we're seeing as we roll."

They picked it up at the point where I had just freed myself from Allison's bed. For an instant, we had a frontal shot of me, black bar across my penis. I knew where that would wind up: the cover of the National Enquirer.

"Mary, here's the suspect at the moment something inside him snaps. Notice the barely contained anger."

"That's not anger—that's terror," I said.

The tape rolled on.

Now my back was to the camera as I bent over Allison, collapsed on the floor. You couldn't see her—only me. Specifically, my naked ass, without benefit of a black bar.

"Son of a [bleep] [bleep]," the tape me proclaimed.

"Hear that hostility?" Doug said.

"Scary," Mary said. "It's like a Stephen King movie."

"Except this is all-too-real."

"Are any of Gray's video games this violent?"

"Apparently," Doug said. "Now watch this. Studies of serial killers show a rush of adrenalin at the moment of attack. The suspect is super-charged. Only a miracle now can save Manchester."

"This is almost too much to watch," Mary said.

"But it's important we do in order to understand just what police are up against," said Doug. "Listen carefully. You can actually hear strangulation sounds."

"Chilling," Mary said.

"Just as suddenly, whatever snapped inside of the suspect unsnaps. In a second, you'll hear remorse for what's been done. Police say that's all that saved Allison Manchester's life: a quirk or fluke, whatever you call it, inside the twisted mind of a killer."

Sure enough, the tape me said: "Allison can you hear me? Oh God, what have I done?"

The tape ended and Mary and Doug reappeared.

"The rest of the tape," Doug said, "is the suspect leaving followed very shortly by the EMTs arriving."

"Because I called them!" I said. "What kind of killer calls 911?"

"If there's anything encouraging," Mary said, "police say it's that this tape should allow them to make a positive identification of the suspect once he's apprehended."

Sure, I thought. *An ass print. Or maybe just pick my butt out of a police lineup.*

"Sort of like Paula Corbin Jones and what she claims is a distinguishing mark on Bill Clinton's you-know-what," Doug said.

"Exactly," Mary said.

This is now officially absurd, I thought. I'd officially joined the ranks of Frank Gifford and Marv Albert, not to mention the philandering president.

They cut to Malloy again. He was telling them everything they wanted to hear.

"My feeling is we're dealing with one of the most vicious criminals in the history of New York," Malloy said.

Sure, same league as Son of Sam, I thought.

I was beyond sick of this clown. If Allison's daddy hadn't been who he was, you could be damn sure he wouldn't be wasting time on me. What was Malloy after—season tickets to the Knicks?

Sports was next on the noon broadcast. The lead story was last night's Knick's game. Sure enough, as the camera panned the crowd, there was Jack Nicholson, sitting behind the bench. With him was Pat Riley, former Knicks' and Lakers' coach and now coach of the Miami Heat, New York's opponent.

I watched through to the weather, then shut off the TV, booted up my laptop and went online, into America Online's travel service. In half a minute, I'd made a reservation, in my name, for a one-way seat to Zurich. If Malloy was as savvy as he seemed, JFK would be crawling with cops the day of my supposed departure.

Jack would appreciate that, I thought as the reservation was

confirmed. *He'd think that had real class.*
I looked through the peephole: the corridor was empty.
Closing the door quietly behind me, I started toward the elevator. I hadn't gotten more than a few steps when the doors opened and five policemen stepped off. Four were uniformed; the fifth was our boy Malloy. All had their automatics drawn.
I turned the other direction and saw an Exit sign. Blessed with something I was sure had run out as I lay hog-tied to Allison's bed—luck—I opened the door and stepped into the stairway. As I started down, I heard Malloy banging on my door with orders to open up.

I needed a disguise. So, I bought a Yankees ballcap and clip-on shades. I bought a sweatshirt, sweat pants, socks and Nikes. I bought black hair dye and self-acting tanning creme, and when I got to Grand Central Station, I ducked into the men's room.
It was morning ablutions—a dozen homeless men washing and combing their hair, one even brushing his teeth. Another guy was fixing his tie. A tie! For what? For whom? I followed the directions on the rinse, then rubbed tanning creme onto my face, neck and arms. I examined myself in the mirror and found, to my satisfaction, that I was a generic American white male, the kind the cops don't stop and frisk. An insurance salesman, say, with a wife and two kids, a neatly trimmed lawn, and a Chrysler mini-van.
Once my tan developed, in two to four hours according to the label, I'd be in clover.
"Here," I said to one guy.
I handed him my shopping bag. It had my khakis, button-down collar shirt, penny loafers and Superman tie.
"Geez, thanks!" he said, opening the bag. "How'd you know it was my birthday?"
"I just did," I said.
"My mother must have told you!"
"She did. Tell her I said hello, will you?"
"Who are you, anyway?" the homeless guy said.
"Name's Stochher," I replied. "Steve Stochher, that's Steve S-T-O-C-H-H-E-R. You have a nice day, okay?"

I bought pliers and a screwdriver at a hardware store, then rented an Oldsmobile at Avis. I drove into an underground garage, stopping at the first car I found with Connecticut plates. I had them on in under five minutes.

Then I left New York City and headed toward Connecticut, in no hurry.

I was now a wanted man—Public Enemy Number One.

Big deal.

How critical could apprehending me really be? The media circus would have a limited life cycle; soon, it would fade, especially outside New York. Something better would come along, and my sordid little saga would become barely remembered titillation, a *Hard Copy* rerun, a minor if titillating footnote to life in America at millennium's end.

On the law-enforcement agenda, I already was small potatoes.

Malloy had put on a good show because of who Allison's father was—I mean, you don't further your career dissing World Bank VPs—but Malloy knew and his superiors knew and every two-bit local cop who happened to stumble onto my name in a national data base knew I was no natural born killer; I was, at worst, just another idiot who'd made too many bad decisions. There would be no roadblocks, no helicopters, no manhunts or mobilizations of SWAT teams. As long as I was careful and Allison's heart continued to beat, my fate was my own.

The road—the glorious freedom of the open road!

Not since I'd gotten my license had driving felt so good.

My fellow motorists—what did they know? Or care? Out here, I wasn't a software guru, or a happily married man with a wonderful wife and beautiful little boy, or a fugitive from justice. I was a nobody. I was an anybody. I was Jack Kerouac, on the great American road.

I was Joe Sixpack in a baseball cap, a guy with no past and only a blurry sort of present.

But the future—the future, neighbors and friends, was wide-open. Like the Internet itself, asphalt simultaneously connected and divided a nation—provided anonymity, while promising limitless opportunity. It was like the ultimate virtual reality game, one that could deliver you to endless universes, each more tantalizing than the one before.

Okay, so I was getting seriously carried away—I realized that soon enough.

But then, those first miles out of New York—I felt unchained. I was thinking of the men in the Grand Central restroom, how bleeding hearts got all torn-up over them but if you got inside their heads you'd probably find that lice and hunger and panhandling and taking your craps in a communal underground outhouse were a small price to pay for a rare freedom they willingly chose. I was thinking of John Lennon, after he left the Beatles, and J.D. Salinger, who disappeared into New Hampshire after *Catcher in the Rye,* and about the stereotypical good family man, I forget his name, I once read about who dropped off the face of the earth only to resurface, years later, with a new wife and kids in some Pennsylvania hamlet.

I was thinking of the legendary D.B. Cooper, who parachuted from a jetliner at 22,000 feet with a bagful of cash, never to be heard from again. But you had to believe he made it, and lives now in comfortable solitude in remote woods, on his own blessed terms.

When you got right down to it, the list of people who'd had enough of being themselves was surprisingly long. I was into it, I really was.

I was off on one of my absurdist software fantasies, thinking:

It'd be a hell of a game.
New Man, you could call it.
Stealth Snuffer.
My Adult Life.
1997.
Or maybe, simply, Blue Hill.

I can't say exactly how seriously I contemplated this—for an hour or two at least, I suppose, pretty damn seriously.

As it unfolded in my mind, the fantasy grew ever more elaborate: How I would wait until midnight, then park my car at the base of the Tobin Bridge, highest span in Boston. Engine running, I would leave a note heavy with disgrace and shame that ended with anguished apologies to Timmy and Ruth.

Then I would take the subway to South Station, where I would board the late train for Baltimore, where I would take an early-morning flight to Dallas, where I would rent an apartment in a neighborhood where no one asked questions. I would read the obituaries every day until I found a man my age who'd died without offspring, spouse, siblings or distinction; someone named Bob or Joe would do just fine.

Somehow, I'd bullshit the funeral home into disclosing his social security number—claim to be his long-lost brother or something, how tough could it be? Armed with it, I'd go to the Registry of Motor Vehicles and request a replacement license. A new person now, I'd continue to L.A., where I'd have a plastic surgeon rearrange my face. I'd become a reclusive inventor, selling absurdist software ideas to Hollywood dream-makers. It would be a living—in time, perhaps, a lucrative one. The past would have no claim on me; eventually, it would cease to exist. With effort, with the mere passage of the days, I'd be able to forget.

Eventually, I'd experience a freedom rarely known to the living.

What a self-pitying mess I was becoming—a true caricature.

I didn't even have the pathetic depth of a Richard Ford character.

But the sobering truth was: Who *would* give a shit if Mark Gray disappeared off the face of the earth? Not Malloy, provided Allison didn't croak. Not the media, certainly. Dad believed he'd lost me years ago. Phil could cash out his CreativeWare chips and be set for life. Syd would have enough I-told-you-sos to last him the rest of his life. Ruth would mourn, but her grief would pass—at a speed, I suspected, directly correlated to how frequently the naked ass clip came to mind. Who else was there?

Only Timmy.

But Timmy was young.

Sure, he would be anguished, but Ruth would reassure him, would make everything better, she was a good mom indeed, and with each passing day I would grow fuzzier. Eventually, a day would come when I wouldn't cross Timmy's mind, just as the day had come when I no longer dwelled on my own departed mother.

Timmy would be okay.

Sooner or later, they'd all be okay.

It was three o'clock when I pulled off the Massachusetts Turnpike. I was in Framingham. WABC was still carrying Allison's story but it had slipped to five seconds at the end of the news. I was fading, faster than I'd dared hope.

Behind a motel, I stole a new set of license plates just to keep Malloy on his toes and continued down Route 9, quite possibly the most garishly overdeveloped strip of highway in all of New England.

I was starved.

I could give a rat's ass about cholesterol—after what I'd been through, I deserved an overdose of saturated fat. I started at McDonald's with a Big Mac, Coke, and fries. Then I had burritos and nachos at Taco Bell. Next was a Baskin-Robbins hot-fudge sundae, extra whipped cream and nuts. At Famous Amos, I had two chocolate-chip cookies and another Coke.

I was like the cartoon fat man in my student film, *Eating People*—bloated, but feeling fine, on my way to becoming anonymous blimp man.

I was almost to Boston when I spotted the sign for Newton Cinema, one of those small arts theaters specializing in foreign films and American classics. I couldn't believe my luck— *Badlands*, Terrence Malick's greatest, and number four on my all-time Top Ten list, was playing. When had I seen it last on the big screen—Venice Beach? Could it have been as long ago as the Blue Hill Nickelodeon? I only remembered watching it on videocassette, part of my private collection, and thinking how much was lost on a TV screen, how sad it was that Malick had disappeared from directing, at least for the time being.

I bought Jordan Almonds—when had I last had those?—a root beer and the five-dollar mega-popcorn and took a seat in the back row. There were all of a dozen people with me.

When I emerged into the December evening, the sky was

clear and I had no trouble picking out the Big and Little Dippers, just as Dad had taught me so many summers ago, when mom was still alive. In the distance I saw the Boston skyline, shimmering like some enchanted city on a Medieval horizon. I thought I could pick out the lights atop the Tobin Bridge.

CHAPTER TEN

I checked into the Boston Sheraton under the name Steve Stochher—no second look from the clerk—definitely not a card-carrying member of the Bad Pun Club, of which I was president—and awoke the next day to discover that the tanning creme had done its job.

I didn't look like I'd been in the sun—I looked like I'd been reengineered, from WASP to Sicilian. An unnecessary precaution, it now appeared: there wasn't a mention of me on CNN, MSNBC, New York 1 or anywhere else. I worked out at the health club, saunaed, showered but didn't shave, put on my sweats and walked to Copley Place, a high-rent mall near Ten Revere Way. I found a pay phone and dialed Beth Israel Hospital in New York.

"Serious," the spokesperson said.

Allison had been upgraded.

My next call was to the Javits Center. I asked the operator to page Phil.

"Hello?" he said a moment later.

"Phil."

"Oh my God, it's you, Mark. Are you okay?"

"I'm hanging in there."

"I've been sick with worry. Are you sure you're okay? Where are you? I'll drop everything and come."

"And then what?"

"We'll call the lawyers," Phil said.

"You want me to turn myself in."

"I'll stick by you, Markie-boy, I swear I will. Whatever happens, I'll be there."

"Did Malloy tell you to say that?"

"Who?"

"Don't tell me the good detective hasn't paid you a visit."

"Oh—Malloy. Well, yes, but I didn't tell him anything."

"Of course not. Nothing about where I was Monday night, for example."

"No way."

"Or about somebody I happened to meet through e-mail."

"I wouldn't do that to you, Mark," Phil said, and an independent observer, someone who didn't know him, might have been convinced he was sincere.

"Look," he went on, "you're in deep shit. I can help."

"I didn't call for help, Phil," I said. "I called to clear up a mystery."

I related the shenanigans with the CreativeWare accounts at Fleet Bank.

Phil had an explanation—something about standard business practices, and accounting procedures, and security in a high-tech trust-nobody world, and IRS end-of-year reporting requirements, and blah blah blah. It might have been legitimate, but I didn't like his tone, which struck me as defensive, even rattled. I didn't like the sudden feeling I had that Malloy was listening in, and getting everything on legally admissible tape.

"You're under a lot of pressure, Mark," Phil said. "Tell me where you are. I'll come immediately."

"You want to know where I am?" I said.

"Please."

"I'm at Kennedy Airport. I leave for Switzerland in twenty minutes," I said, and hung up.

Copley Place was crackling with upscale consumerism. I swear you could feel it: the intensity of shoppers who lack for nothing yet are insatiable for more. I got swept up—I mean, I wasn't about to let traitor Phil get me down.

I bought a Red Sox cap to replace my Yankees one, a Batman pen, a Spiderman lighter, a new guide to videogames, the latest book on the Internet and another on the films of Kubrick. I bought a five-dollar cigar, which I smoked strolling through the crowd, tickled by the knowledge that no one knew that Steve Stochher, a.k.a. the Society Stalker, was in their midst. I hadn't intended to go into CompUSA, but there it was, too tempting to pass up.

I walked the aisles, past scanners, monitors, servers—the icons of the new age.

Technically, my first computer had been a slide rule; I wondered if you could even buy one anymore, let alone if I'd remember how to use it. But the true revolution hadn't been hardware, I knew that better than anyone. By themselves, computers were dumb brutes, no more or less a force than the toaster-ovens seeking a consumer's affection at Sears. The revolution was software—the vaporous nothingness of binary code, of which I was lord and master.

I was standing, a dumb look on my face, when I became aware of two adolescent boys.

"Look, they got it!" said the tall, skinny one with blond hair. *"Ultra Bloodfest!"*

"Awesome!"

"Your mother will let you have it?"

"Shit—you think I'm gonna tell her?"

"It's forty bucks."

"That's cool. I got it."

No one was looking at any of CreativeWare's titles. I picked up a copy of *Shuttle Saga* and discovered that since my last not-so-friendly chat with CompUSA's buyer, they'd made good on their threat and marked it down, savagely—I mean, they'd slashed that mother in half. You could get it for $19.95, the price of Mr. Potato Head, like, how lame was *that*. Phil was right: *Shuttle Saga* was rapidly becoming *Hometoons* 2.

"Hey, guys, seen this?" I said, waving *Shuttle Saga*.

"Yeah," the tall skinny kid said. "It sucks."

"Have you ever played it?" I said, and I could feel a sudden stab of anger. You may have gathered by now that I was not exactly an emotional Rock of Gibraltar by this point.

"Yeah—my cousin has it. Like, his 4,000-year-old grandfather bought it for him. It's boring."

"Boring?" I said.

"Wicked boring."

"Well, take a bite out of my naked ass."

I hadn't intended to say that. It just sort of slipped out.

"What's that?" the kid said.

"I said take a bite out of my naked ass. Your friend can take a bite, too."

The kid didn't know what to do. Alone, he probably would have walked away. But he had an audience.

"Take it easy, old man," he said.

"Listen," I said, "I made this. Not only that, I own the frigging company."

The kids looked at me oddly.

"And not only *that*," I went on, "I just won the Wilbur! So, I know a thing or two about games. And this one is crap."

I threw the tall kid's copy of *Ultra Bloodfest* onto the floor.

"So's *Shuttle Saga*," he said.

"So are you," I said.

"Yeah?"

"Yeah."

"Shithead."

"Asshole."

"Fuck you."

"Fuck your mother."

The kid had to do something now. His hand shot out for *Shuttle Saga*, but I'd anticipated him. He swiped empty air.

"You're buying *Shuttle Saga*, goddamn it!" I shouted.

I thrust the package at him, but he wouldn't take it.

He threw a wild punch, and I ducked, and I threw one that missed, and he came at me with a head-butt, and I got my arms around him and we were wrestling—wrestling! I had seventy-five pounds on the kid, easy, and I was going at him like Goro in *Mortal Kombat III*.

God knows what pathetic primal instinct he'd activated, but all I could think was: *It's a fight to the finish!*

He went for my face, ripping my glasses off and scraping my face with a fingernail.

Bring the bastard down! I thought, and after a few more seconds of American Gladiators, I did. We landed on my glasses, but I didn't give a naked rat's ass, if you'll pardon another pun.

He was down, squirming like a bug pinned to a board and nothing he could do about it.

A clerk was running toward us.

"Sir? Is everything okay? Oh, goodness, there's blood! Someone call the police!"

I froze. The kid froze. The kid's friend froze.

"No—don't!" I said. "I can explain."

I figured I had maybe five seconds before the cops were on their way.

So, I stood and helped the kid to his feet.

"This is my, ah...son," I said, lovingly brushing the dirt off his clothes. "And he knows he's not supposed to buy that game and I'm terribly sorry about this and so is..."

"Adam," the kid said.

"And so is Adam. Let me pay for this," I said, meaning *Shuttle Saga*, which had gotten smashed, along with my glasses. "Adam, you run along. I'll deal with you later."

"Later, dad," the kid said.

"Later, son."

The kid and his friend dashed off. If I'd had time, I would have slipped him a twenty. More time and written a thank-you note.

"You're bleeding, sir," the clerk said. "From the nose."

There was blood, all right, but not much. I was more interested in my glasses. I dropped to hands and knees and felt along the floor until I found them. The frame was bent, the allegedly shatter-proof lenses shattered.

"Here," I said, handing the clerk a fifty. "That should cover *Shuttle Saga*."

He returned one of the bills.

"It's on markdown," he said.

That hurt.

"Right," I said, "markdown."

I made my way out of the store, slowly.

OK, hotshot, I thought, *now what?*

I was not merely myopic—technically, I was legally blind. All I could see was moving shapes, presumably shoppers, and lots of blurry colors.

I lucked out: the mall had an Hour Optical, which I found after wandering fifteen minutes in fog.

"You look like you were mugged," the clerk said.

"I was."

"Maybe we should call the police."

"No need to," I said, "I already did. "What I need is new glasses. Better yet, I'll take contacts."

Contacts were definitely the new me.

I couldn't see the clerk's face well, but I caught her change in tone.

"You have to pay, you know," she said.

"I understand that is how capitalism works," I said.

"You have to pay now."

"But I haven't bought anything."

"I'm sorry, it's store policy," the clerk said.

"What kind of policy is that?"

"Look, sir, perhaps I should get the manager—"

It dawned on me—she thought I was no different than my buddies at Grand Central!

"No need for that," I said, pulling out my wallet.

I counted my remaining twenties. I had ten of them.

"Will two hundred cover contacts and an exam?"

"Yes, thank you."

She instructed me to put my chin up to the machine.

"I'd like blue-tinted ones, if you have them," I said.

My eyes were naturally brown.

As she examined me, I drifted back to the day Officer Bill, Blue Hill safety cop, Lions Club president, Citizen of the Year, came to school to conduct the annual eye test, which consisted of reading one of those charts from that Norman Rockwell painting.

I was panicked, because over the last year, during fifth grade, my vision had deteriorated.

Not glasses! The only kid I knew with glasses was Donald

Collins, a shy, stuttering boy who still wet his pants. At my school, Donald was the biggest loser of them all. In the different self that followed all this, I would wish him only the best, wherever he was. I never did learn. Real-life people can become ghosts quickly.

But there was no way around it: my eyes were going bad.

I'd noticed it first at the beginning of the year, when I was assigned a seat at the back of the class—how sentences on the board were blurry, unless I squinted. By spring, I'd asked Mrs. Remington to move me to the front.

She asked why.

"To be first in lunch line," I lied.

My request was denied. Except for Sally Martin, whose vision was perfect and who sat within whispering distance, I'd have been dead.

One day, I sought Donald out at recess. He was doing what he always did—desperately trying not to be noticed.

"Can I ask you something?" I said.

He looked scared. He looked like he figured he was being set up again—that I was going to try to extort his milk money, or his yoyo, or maybe just give him a smack, the way seventh- and eighth-grade bullies sometimes did to liven up their day.

That look still haunts me, thirty-plus years later.

"I don't have any milk money," he said quickly, softly.

"I don't care about your milk money," I said. "I want to know about your glasses."

"What about 'em?"

"When did you get them?"

He hesitated—trying to determine, I suspect, whether it was to his advantage to lie or speak truth.

"Kindergarten," he finally said.

"How'd you know you needed them?"

"I couldn't see the ball."

"What kind of ball?"

"A basketball."

"You couldn't see a *basketball*?"

"Sure I could."

You could tell he was backpedaling now.

"Then why'd you get glasses?"

"'Cause my dad made me. He said I'd hit foul shots better that way."

"Are you used to them?"

"No. And they break real easy. Say, why do you want to know, anyway? Do *you* need glasses?"

Donald was suddenly animated.

"An All-Star like you?"

"Oh, no," I said. "I don't need glasses. I was just wondering, is all."

I sure wasn't going to tell him that this spring, I was having trouble getting around on a fastball.

"'Cause they come with straps, if you do," Donald said.

"I told you: I don't need glasses," I said. "And don't you go telling anyone I do."

"Geez, you don't have to get all sore about it," he said.

I don't believe I ever had another word with Donald Collins. I wish now that I could. Empathy doesn't develop in grammar school, does it?

When they announced Officer Bill was here to test our eyes, I was terrified.

As I moved up in line, I kept hoping the bottom row of letters would come into focus. They didn't. I felt dizzy and my mouth was dry. Sally was in front of me, and I made her swear she'd memorize the lines on the chart and whisper them on her way back, just like in class.

She tried, but Officer Bill was wise to such tricks:

"Move right along, young lady," he said. "An all-star Little Leaguer doesn't need any help from you."

So, I did what any enterprising fifth-grader would have done—I fainted. When I came to, I was in the nurse's office. My mother was there and Officer Bill was gone and I figured I had a whole year to find an eye chart and commit it to memory.

And I probably would have, if it hadn't been 1967.

"Well, it appears you have presbyopia," the Hour Optical clerk said. "It's when the eyes have trouble changing focus between near and far. It comes with age. Have you had any problems going from close to far—trying to read the instrument panel of your car, say?"

"No," I said.

I was lying. I had exactly that problem. My ophthalmologist had picked up on it, too, as I've mentioned.

"Well, you will. I'd recommend bifocals. They come in contacts. And it might not be a bad idea to have your hearing checked, too. We have a complimentary test this week."

"No, thanks," I said.

"Are you sure? It's free."

"I'm sure."

"No bifocals?"

"No bifocals."

"Well, you're the boss. But I wouldn't go much longer without them."

The clerk selected my new contacts and I put them in my eyes. She handed me a mirror. They were blue, all right, but they hurt, like she'd sprinkled sand in them.

"Give them a few minutes," she said. "Sometimes it takes a while to adjust."

"And if they don't?"

"We'll try another pair."

"I'd like sunglasses, too," I said.

She led me to the display.

"These are non-prescription," she said. "Take your time."

She disappeared into the back room.

I sat, looking across the mall to Circuit City, where TVs were stacked floor to ceiling. All were tuned to the same local station.

A "FIVE AT FIVE" logo appeared and a pretty blond anchor woman kicked off the early newscast. From this distance, I couldn't hear what she was saying, but I didn't need to: The images said it all. The first shot was of a body bag being carried out of a brownstone; the second of an ornately furnished living room with a chalk outline on the floor. A still photo of a young woman identified as Hannah Gregory was next, followed by a policeman at a press conference. He was holding a plastic bag with a necktie that had some sort of cartoon print on it.

Jesus, I thought. *What kind of sick fuck would do that?*

I got my answer on the next shot. It was the Wilbur photo of me they'd aired in New York, with the caption:

SOCIETY STALKER STRIKES AGAIN

I knew what was next.

And it was: the naked-ass clip.

A crowd was gathering at Circuit City. I adjusted my new sunglasses, pulled my cap lower on my face, and left Hour Optical, taking a position at the rear of the crowd.

"Channel Five takes you now live to JFK Airport in New York, where police believe Gray was attempting to leave the country," the anchor woman was saying.

They cut to the tarmac, where Doug Fenning had his microphone in Malloy's face. In the background, you could see German shepherds and a SWAT team surrounding a Swissair 747 whose escape chutes were deployed. Malloy was not a happy camper.

"Score one for Gray!" I said.

"We understand he wasn't on it," Fenning said to Malloy.

"That is correct."

"Is it possible he got away on another flight?"

"I have no comment at this point."

"Can you tell us what tipped you off?"

"No," Malloy said.

Boy, was he a testy sort!

"What I will say is that with this latest attack in Boston, we now have police in two states as well as the FBI after him. If necessary, we will involve Interpol. We will get our man."

"Perhaps," said the anchor woman, cutting away, "but he won't be the first suspect they arrest in this chilling and increasingly bizarre case. That distinction goes to a homeless man detained less than an hour ago at New York's Grand Central Station. We switch now to Matt Lewis, of affiliate New York 1. Matt?"

The camera brought us to Grand Central, where Lewis was standing outside a men's room. Yup, I recognized it.

"Ginger," Lewis said, "police are not saying if a man now identified as Henry Tolhurst was in league with Gray, or somehow, perhaps due to some mental condition, came to believe he was him. All we know is that based on anonymous tips about a homeless man wearing polished penny loafers and a Superman tie, police arrested Tolhurst where I'm standing now. I'm told that Tolhurst insisted he was Gray—even mooning passersby, apparently in imitation of the so-called naked-ass clip that's gotten so much airplay."

I was flattered, in a perverse sort of way.

"But he is not—repeat, *not*—the Society Stalker."

"Thank you, Matt," Ginger said. "Doug, we understand Detective Malloy has something else to say."

"That's right, Ginger."

We returned to JFK, where Malloy was relating how his guys had followed a trail of purchases: baseball cap, clip-on sunglasses, tanning creme, hair dye and jogging outfit. Putting it together, a police consultant working with a computer and a custom program called Suspect had been able to create an image of what I probably looked like now.

Fenning cut to a shot of the industrious consultant at work. I couldn't believe it—it was the same guy we'd snookered into buying *Hometoons* so many years ago! Using my own technology to help nail me! And offering his services for free, according to Malloy!

They cut to his computer, then what was on his screen. As the Copley Place crowd watched, transfixed, I saw the Wilbur me morph into the Society Stalker. Except for my new Red Sox cap, there I was. It was an extraordinary performance for a program based on that piece of crud, *Hometoons*. What magic had the consultant found that I hadn't?

An 800-number appeared and the public was urged to call with tips.

"Gray is considered armed and dangerous," Malloy said. "If you see him, do not attempt to detain him yourself. Please call the FBI or your local police."

The crowd was hushed. You could see them glancing around, nervously, a case of mass suspicion. I looked at them looking and saw—my number-one fan, the tall skinny kid who'd wanted *Ultra Bloodfest*.

"It's him!" he shouted, pointing at me.

"The crazy old guy!" his friend added.

"HE'S THE SOCIETY STALKER!"

The boys looked terrified. They looked like I was about to eat their livers, here in view of two hundred people—and then they ran, screaming as they ripped through the crowd.

In an instant, the place was bedlam. Kids shrieked as mothers tried to get them to safety. Elders fainted. And when I bolted, a blue-uniformed security guard decided it was his moment to become a hero. You know the type—a twenty-something high-school dropout entrusted with a loaded sidearm and carrying a boatload of attitude.

"Stop!" he shouted.

I plowed into the scattering crowd.

"Stop or I shoot!"

That only happens in movies, I thought.

I didn't stop.

It didn't happen only in movies: Our intrepid hero fired a warning shot over my head.

And then another, and another, until his magazine was empty.

The bullets must have hit a power line because bulbs blew and the ceiling started smoking and the mall went dark. Alarms were ringing and people were crying and screaming and Christ knows why, but the fire sprinklers were sprinkling—and I kept on going, past stores, down a stopped escalator, outdistancing the guard, across a promenade and into the enclosed walkway that connects Copley Place with the Prudential Center, which is next to the Sheraton, where I was staying.

I was being pursued.

Not by the guard—that slug had fallen by the wayside—but by a young man with a fancy camera. I never did learn if he was an off-duty news photographer, or an intrepid freelancer, or just some feckless passerby. Whoever, he wanted my picture. Wanted dozens of them! A paparazzi, of all things! And an athlete, to boot—a sinewy young man in Nikes who surely ran marathons! He was gaining quickly on me when, as impulsively as I'd done anything in that season of impulse, I stopped and dropped my trousers. Mooned him as he clicked away.

"Is that what you wanted?" I said.

Before he could answer, I snatched the camera from him, opened it and exposed the film. Then I threw his camera onto the floor. It shattered and the flash exploded.

I ran into the Prudential Center and ducked into an elevator. The doors closed.

I was going down.

"Shit," I said.

My room was on the twenty-third floor.

The elevator stopped at the parking garage. I was about to hit the button for my floor when I noticed a magnificent black '30s roadster. A distinctive-looking man dressed in a white three-piece suit and wearing a tan fedora was behind the wheel, smoking an unfiltered cigarette.

By God, it was Jack Nicholson! Driving the car he drove in *Chinatown*! He smiled when he saw me. Evidently, he'd been waiting for my arrival.

"Take a load off your feet, kid," he said, opening the passenger door.

I got in.

"What *happened* to you?" he said, examining my face. "Don't tell me the old liver's giving out."

The creme had created a tan in streaks, as was evident on inspection. Close on, the overall impression was jaundice.

"It's a long story," I said.

"Don't I know," Nicholson said. "I've been following you on TV."

"Then you know why I couldn't make the Knicks."

"Disappointed as I was, I understood."

I noticed Nicholson had a flask cradled between his legs.

"Johnnie Walker Red," he said. "Good for what ails you."

He offered me the bottle. I took a swig and thanked him.

"Don't mention it," he said. "Cigarette?"

He opened a silver case and I took one. He lit it. I hadn't had a cigarette since Venice Beach.

"I'm lucky I made it out of there alive," I said, inhaling deeply.

It was a Camel. It tasted wonderful.

"Tough audience," Nicholson agreed, "but aren't they all? They love you when you're up—and when you're down, you might as well be wind from a duck's ass."

It was J.J. Gittes' best line in *Chinatown*.

"Look how they crucified Roman Polanski," Nicholson said.

"Or Randall Patrick McMurphy."

"Exactly. All I can say, kid, is your story'd make a hell of a movie."

"I suppose it would," I said, modestly.

"Call it *My Adult Life* or *Blue Hill* or *Deep Blue*, something darkly ironic like that. Or *1997*, if you want to capture the zeitgeist of the era and quite an era it is. You'd have the critics eating out of the palm of your hand."

I said: "The only issue is: Would it be a comedy or a tragedy?"

"Neither," Nicholson said. "It would be a farce. What a silly ass you've become, if you'll pardon the pun."

I was crestfallen.

My face must have given me away, because Nicholson added:

"You haven't lost your sense of humor, have you, kid? That was a joke! As for tragedy or comedy, it would be both. You're talking Hollywood. Nuance means nothing out there. Think Oscar. We'd go for the big lights and forget the rest."

He took a long, loving swallow of Johnnie Walker.

"Only one person," he said, "would do justice directing: Robert Altman."

"Not me?"

"You're too close to it, kid. Not that you don't have what it takes, 'cause you do. Your day will come."

"Thanks." I smiled.

"Know who'd have to play you?" Nicholson continued.

"Sure I do," I said. "You."

"A gentleman you are," Nicholson said with that shit-eating grin I adored, "a casting agent you are not. I'm a little past that now, kid."

"No, you're not. You look the same as you did in *Cuckoo's Nest.*"

But he didn't. Off screen, up close, in the unforgiving fluorescent light of an underground garage, you could see gray roots and what probably were scars from plug transplants. I saw his eyes, the flesh around them especially, and I knew why he always went out in shades. Surgery may have ameliorated all those years in Hollywood, but it couldn't erase them.

And if I'd had a time-travel machine, I would have seen the sad last chapter of his life, when he suffered from Alzheimer's disease, his memories and long career achievements scrubbed from his mind, as if they had never happened.

"God bless you," Nicholson said. "I was thinking more along the lines of Tom Hanks."

"I'm flattered."

"The big question is who'd do justice to Allison. I kind of have Julianne Moore in mind."

"She'd be perfect," I said. "Perfect! They even look alike."

"Don't think I haven't noticed. You saw *Lost World*, I'm sure."

"Three times."

"Only thing wrong with that picture was Moore kept her clothes on. I ask you: What the hell would have been wrong with a little skin—say, one of those velociraptors ripping off her shirt just before she escapes into that building?"

"Nothing at all!" I said.

"I'm not talking sex—just give me a second or two of tit!" Nicholson said. "Use a body double if Moore's not the type—but give me *something* to hang a fantasy on, for Chrissakes! Well, that's Spielberg for you. Damn prude. Only skin he's ever given us was in Schindler's List, of all fucking flicks! What are your thoughts on who'd play Ruth?"

"Faye Dunaway?"

Nicholson looked over his sunglasses at me.

"Have you seen ole Faye lately?" he said. "I think Glenn

Close is more what I have in mind."

"Or Rene Russo.

"Better yet. Good middle-aged women are so hard to find."

We were relating now. I could feel it. Destined for each other over the miles and the years, our souls had finally, irreversibly connected.

Nicholson took another hit of whiskey and checked his watch.

"Sorry to cut out on you," he said, "but I've got a Celtics-Lakers game to catch. It's not the same without Magic and Larry, but that's life in the big city. Things change."

"Not you, Jack."

"Even me, Mark."

He started the car.

"Take me with you?" I asked.

Nicholson was puzzled.

"To Boston Garden?"

"To anywhere."

"I'm afraid you're on your own now, my man. Just watch out for that Malloy: There's something not quite right about him."

"Everything's so fucked-up," I said. "I need help."

"What you need," Nicholson said, "is a golf club!"

He grinned, and then he was cackling, and before long he was wheezing, he was so amused with himself. Apparently, he still wasn't over his freeway encounter.

"That's not funny," I said.

"Not funny? You really have lost your sense of humor. The shit you're in, my friend, you need one. I wasn't kidding about the golf club. They're all bastards. Have a little fun at their expense. You're good at that kind of stuff. I laughed myself silly at the Sermon put-on at the convention."

I was stunned.

"You were there?" I said.

"Hell, yes," Nicholson said. "Snuck in at the last minute and had to run out before you got your Wilbur—congratulations on that, by the way. I figured I'd see you at the Knicks. Now if you don't mind, I've got to go."

"Please don't," I begged.

"Don't make me do something I'll regret," Nicholson said. "We've been friends too long."

"We could go to the movies," I said. "I'll pay."

Nicholson took off his sunglasses and our eyes met.

"You just don't get it, do you, kid?" he said.

He was not a man to mess with now. I stepped out of his car and slowly closed the door. He put the transmission in gear and roared off.

Of course, none of that really happened, except in my head, a script I might have written to begin some new VR game -- "Close Encounters with Celebrities" you could call it. Imagination is a two-edgeds word.Tough to shut off sometimes.

What really happened was I ordered room-service pizza. It sucked. TV sucked. The Sheraton sucked. My contact lenses really sucked. I turned on my laptop and tried to access Allison's website, but couldn't; Malloy must have seized the server. I signed onto CreativeLine and found 173 e-mails awaiting me. A hundred-and-seventy-three! I hadn't received that many after the *Wired* piece, or ever.

"You sick fuck, I hope they fry you," the first one, from a guy in Toronto, read.

Someone in London personally offered to pull the switch: "I would of course be willing to pay my own expenses," he wrote.

"Lorena Bobbit had the right idea," a woman from San Francisco wrote.

And on and on and on. I read every one—like I had anything better to do. Most were in the vigilante mode, but several were outright depraved. Claiming membership in Necrophiliacs Anonymous, Loves Cold Sex asked if I had any tips. Another sicko wanted Allison's hospital room phone number. Someone else had superimposed a still from the naked-ass clip over the opening frame of *Attack Ship* and changed the logo to *ATTACK SHIT*: "A guaranteed bestselling video game concept," he wrote. Another e-mail suggested that if I had any balls, I'd make an appearance in the newly created SOCIETY STALKER forum. More sophisticated hackers had already constructed websites, including one that featured the naked-ass shot married to footage from the *Wired* website and called INTERVIEW WITH THE VAMPIRE.

Only one person was on my side: Charlie Goldman.

God love him, he didn't believe what the cops were saying. "Sounds like a classic frameup," he wrote in an e-mail. "Wherever you are, let me know if I can help. My brother-in-law's a captain with the N.Y.P.D."

Call me naive, but I was crushed by all the others.

These weren't media ghouls—these were my digital brethren, the folks who'd given me two standing ovations just three days ago, soulmates in a sacred cause. I'd busted my butt for almost two decades helping to enhance their empty lives and this was the thanks I got? I felt like Ted Kennedy and Chappaquiddick: One tragic indiscretion and it was open season forever.

What trifling consolation there was came from the AP Wire, which elaborated on the Channel Five broadcast.

"While Gray is wanted for questioning in connection with the death of Hannah Gregory," a paragraph buried three-quarters down the story said, "Boston police say he is not a suspect at this time."

But consolation was fleeting. In terms of the safety of my celebrated ass, it was doubtful a caveat would make a difference at this stage. We lived in an age of trigger-happy cops and citizen vigilantes.

If I'd had any sense, I wouldn't have dropped in on the SOCIETY STALKER forum. I would have shut my laptop off, maybe thrown it out my twenty-third-story window. But I was insane with curiosity. Sure enough, they were overheating their modems:

"Where do you think he'll strike next?" Bossboy was saying.

"We could place bets," said L.A. Momma. "I'll set up a betting forum. Let's call it STALKER LINE."

"Cool!"

"Know what's amazing?" said Self. "This guy's got a record a mile long. There's a story in www.murdersrapesandotherawfulstuff. com that lays it all out."

So it went, lies and fabrications tossed into cyberspace with lynch-mob zeal. Why wait for the next *Weekly World News* when you could string the bastard up now?

I signed on.

"Hello friends," I typed. "It's me, the Stalker."

"Mark Gray? *The* Mark Gray?" said L.A. Momma.

"Who's to say it's really you?" said Bossboy.

"How about I post a GIF of my naked ass?" I said. "You could compare it to the clip and see if it matches."

"Such wit."

"I wonder if he'll be as funny at the trial."

"Or strapping him into the chair."

"Hey Mark," said Cyberdude, "You gonna eat your next one?"

"You mean cannibalism?" L.A. Momma wanted to know.

"I do," said Cyberdude. "Cops aren't saying it yet, but he tried to eat that socialite, and not the way your dirty little mind would think."

"I'm not surprised," said Bossboy. "You know what pops up in *Attack Ship* if you hit Ctrl-Q during the seventh level, don't you? A man chasing a woman with a chainsaw."

"And don't forget his college film: *Eating People*," said JeanT. "It was a documentary on cannibalism."

"No, it was a snuff film."

"Not to let facts get in the way of a good story," I said, "but my film was a spoof on dining. Specifically, a satire derived from the eating scenes in *Discreet Charm of the Bourgeoisie* and *The Last Detail*."

"Bunuel and Nicholson in the same flick? Sure, Mark," said L.A. Momma. "We know how that goes."

"Well, he is into movies."

"Yeah—I heard he's got *Silence of the Lambs* memorized."

"Know what his motto is?" said Cyberdude. "Eat or be eaten!"

"LOL," wrote a dozen people.

"So where are you striking next, Mark?" said Cyberdude.

"Maybe he already has," said BillyBoy. "Maybe he's there with the body now. Are you, Mark?"

"Not fair! If he answers, he'll throw the odds off on STALKER LINE."

"You're all a bunch of losers. I have better things to do," I said, and signed off.

I put on my coat, went down to my car, and drove in darkness toward Marblehead.

CHAPTER ELEVEN

I parked at the Atlantic Country Club and crept across the fourteenth hole toward my house, stopping behind my garage for a cigarette—I'd bought a carton of Camels. I drew the smoke in and felt nicotine filling my body, relaxing me, leaving me pleasantly light-headed. I heard breaking waves, barely: The ocean was content tonight.

The house looked stunning with its brick chimneys, white clapboards, and slate roof, and framed by evergreens and Chinese maples and gas lanterns along a red-brick walk. Ruth's gardens were hidden by snow, but I pictured them in my mind's eye: carnations, Sweet Williams, Johnny Jump-Ups, delphinium, and roses, each plant lovingly tended.

All so perfect, I thought. *A cover shot for* Martha Stewart Living.

The thing was, we hadn't set out to make a statement—certainly not that kind. I know how this sounds, but it's true. I could rationalize every detail—and had, more than once, to my father. Knowing swimming was one of the few exercises allowed my son, who would have denied him a pool? With our time so limited, were underground sprinklers, a landscaping service, and cleaning ladies really extravagant? Were reliable, safe, long-lasting cars really a luxury just because such a machine could not be built for under thirty grand?

What about the ballfield and bleachers I'd had constructed when Timmy was one, before we knew how severely his activities would be curtailed? Was I guilty of "mindless consumerism," my father's phrase, or only doing what any good hard-working husband and father would, given the means...and we were fortunate to have the means?

You could go straight down the list, through the monogrammed towels, the wine cellar, and gym, and construct a credible rationale for everything. I had, and I was comfortable with it, no matter what my father thought or what inquiring minds might conclude, now that I was media prey.

I finished my cigarette and went into the garage. Our Volvos were there, and the John Deere tractor, and my Corvette. Oh, that Vette! I remembered the day (Ruth was newly pregnant) that I heard Tony C. was dead at the age of 45, almost my age now, after eight years as a helpless invalid—how I wanted to explain my feelings to Ruth but couldn't find the words.

How, a few months later, when I read his estate was being sold to pay the medical bills, I toyed with the idea of buying one of his gloves, or one of his balls that had cleared the left-field wall, the Green Monster—how at the auction, a couple of months before Timmy was born, I found myself successfully bidding on the car, which I promptly had restored for a price my father had called obscene.

"There's an expression for this," he'd said. "Sports-car menopause."

I expected that from him—he'd driven Volkswagen Beetles his whole life. But he was my only critic. I mean, this was a *car*. Zero to 60 in under six seconds, top end past 140, rated at 435 British horsepower. CreativeWare's clients loved that car and Phil coveted it so badly he bought a similar model for himself. Even Syd, the old fuck, swallowed his pride and asked to take it for a spin. I respectfully declined, as you might have guessed.

Sometimes, you know, it's the little things.

I got in and ran my hand along the seat.

They'd used the finest leather for the restoration—goatskin, soft as a velvet glove. Everyone but Dad was compelled to touch it, and touching it, was moved to highest praise.

I lit another Camel.

Damn him.

Hadn't he ever desired things? One secret longing for a car, a boat, a new chalice (for Christ's sake, literally)? Or had it always been principle with him, even as a kid?

"You're too hard on him," Ruth always said when I started in on Dad.

"He didn't raise you," I'd reply, but that never impressed her, the daughter of Syd.

Enough of the self-pity, I thought, crushing out my smoke. I disarmed the burglar alarm and stepped inside my house. The living room TV was on, loud enough to mask my footsteps as I crept through the kitchen to the front hall. Ruth was asleep on the couch, the portable phone in her lap. I tiptoed upstairs to my study, where I traded my contacts, which still hurt like hell, for a spare set of glasses. There were no messages on my private-line machine, but I noticed the red light was lit on Ruth's when I passed her study. Closing the door behind me, I hit the play button and heard—the voice of Phil, of all people. He'd called at four this afternoon, minutes after I'd spoken to him.

"Ruth, it's me," he said. "Called to make sure you're okay. It's pretty awful, but look at it this way. Things could be much worse. He could be—"

The message ended; she must have picked up there. The only other message was from my father, who wanted my wife, of whom he'd always been fond, to know his prayers were with us all.

I left Ruth's study and checked on Timmy. He was asleep, but his breathing had that roiling sound that warned of trouble ahead.

I pulled a chair up to his bed and sat. Closing my eyes, I saw this room as it was almost seven years ago, before Nintendo, before Power Rangers and Nerf—when we were converting it into a nursery. I remembered painting, papering, hanging the curtains and buying the furniture...and thinking, every step of the way, no matter how hard I tried not to: *All for someone else's kid.*

I don't care how sensitive or insightful or forgiving you fancy yourself to be—I mean, you could be Mother Theresa, but unless you've been there, you can't comprehend what a dark place the mind becomes when you've been put in my position.

The day Ruth announced she was pregnant, I seized on one thing—learning her baby father's identity—and refused, for far too long, to let go. I was propelling myself toward neurosis if not something worse—I willingly admit that—with elaborate fantasies about hiring detectives, getting court orders for blood samples, somehow enlisting Ruth's mother or even Syd to get at the truth. I mean, I was a head case, except I didn't see it that way then.

I believed myself justified, even righteous.

I believed if I were going to stay in this marriage, that's the least I was owed: a name.

Ruth did not relent, but as her pregnancy progressed, she weakened. For the sake of the baby she vowed never to disclose his identity, but eventually she decided I could know the broad outline of the circumstances in order to be reassured—she actually used that word, *reassured*—that Timmy's conception had been a horrible mistake, one she'd regret to her dying day.

And so, one night in this very room, as we were assembling a crib, she had told me:

The father of my son was an old friend who'd only ever been a friend, and a casual one at that, at least as far as Ruth was concerned (although, she had to admit, he'd probably carried a quiet flame for her since they'd met, in college). He'd called her at work just to say hello (as he did no more than once or twice a year) and she'd mentioned our separation, how torn up over it she was, and he called again and again in the name of comfort until one night—Christmas Eve—my math had been correct— she agreed to meet him for a drink. One thing led to another, and before you knew it they were in a cab, and then they were at his place, listening to the stereo and doing shots of tequila like the college kids they once were and then she was crying, and he was consoling her, and…I cut her off there. I wanted basic facts, not true-confessional color.

Did knowing this help?

I suppose an old friend was better than the alternatives: a pickup in a bar, for example, or an old lover she'd never gotten over, or a long-running affair that might, for all I knew, still continue. But on another level, Ruth's story made everything worse, because my imagination had been primed. What was playing on the stereo as they moved toward fucking? Were they on a couch? His bed? Did they kiss? Whisper words of love? Or was my wife too drunk to even remember the details? My wife—whose idea of imbibing, except for Christmas Eve (don't think I didn't see the irony there) was a shot of Glenfiddich.

I did not get into any of that. I asked only one question, again: "What's his name?"

"Think of the baby," Ruth said.

"Don't you get it?" I said. "I can't think of the baby without thinking of him."

Ruth was stunned by my anger; I guess she thought we were starting to move on.

"Did you get any of your father's goodness?" she said. "His belief in forgiveness?"

To that, I had no ready answer.

A month after he was born, I carried Timmy from the hospital to our car. Ruth followed with medications, a cylinder of oxygen, and an infant-sized mask. Timmy was still sleeping when we laid him in his crib, set the monitor, and went downstairs for a glass of champagne, which we drank, after a perfunctory toast, in silence.

The early going was tough.

Timmy was colicky, and often, like tonight, his breathing sounded like the inside of a jetliner. I remember Phil bitching about the ambulance bills, which were over ten grand, and the tab for the visiting nurse, considerably more, until he figured out a way to write everything off.

Ruth, who'd intended to take a six-month leave of absence, took a year. I was loving and warm with our son, but the fact was I couldn't hold him without studying his features to see who they brought to mind. He had his mother's chin, eyes, and ears, but the angle of his nose—that endearing little crook—it wasn't hers, and it wasn't mine, or Syd's, or my mother-in-law's. It was the biological father's—the *sperm donor's*—and he was out there somewhere. So, I studied noses: CreativeWare noses, Harvard Development Office noses, noses in restaurants and noses on the street. Eventually, I gave up on noses and moved toward Ruth's point of view:

You couldn't blame Timmy. It wasn't the kid's fault that a sperm and an egg that never should have met had...or that maybe in the grand scheme of things they had been destined to, if you wanted to pursue cosmic meaning.

Which had currency, as you will see.

And the truth was, the older Timmy got, the easier it was to forget.

From the nothingness of early infancy, personality emerged. Sick as he was, the kid was a charmer. Strangers couldn't keep their hands off him and his nanny was in love. Even Syd had a soft spot for his first grandchild. Grounded again, optimistic, I bought a video camera and an editing machine and began making movies again for the first time since NYU.

And this was the thing: Timmy gave love without condition, and in your sappier moments, you had to wonder why couldn't every member of the species be like him?

Yes, we were starting to sail again—all of us—as if the wheel that had ground us down had turned, bringing us back to the light again.

Hometoons was history and CreativeWare's next title, *Tomcat*, had generated twenty-seven million dollars in advance orders. My father visited from Maine and we passed an entire weekend without criticizing each other. We celebrated Timmy's first birthday and not long after, Ruth's folks took him for three days so we could get away. At Ruth's insistence, we went to Cape Cod, and one afternoon, an unseasonably warm afternoon that found us alone in the dunes, we made love, for the first time since she'd announced she was pregnant.

And I'd like to say it was wonderful and healing, a new start on that part of our relationship, but that would be a lie. The terrible truth was: He was in my head with us in those dunes.

I was leaving Timmy's room when he whipped off his covers, took aim, and shot me with his Nerf Razorbeast—a half dozen soft-tipped darts, bouncing off my back.

"Gotcha!" he shrieked.

"Timmy! I thought you were asleep."

"Nope," he said. "I woke up. I had a bad dream."

"About what, Scooter?"

I sat down and put my arm around him.

"About you going to jail."

He wasn't so light-hearted anymore.

"I'm not going to jail, sweetheart," I said.

"But they said on TV you killed somebody. They said when they catch you, they're going to put you in jail."

"They're wrong," I said. "Sometimes grownups make mistakes, even on TV."

"That's what I told my friends. They didn't believe me."

"Well, you tell them it's the truth, Scout's honor on your grandfather's Bible. Okay?"

"Okay."

Timmy was silent. I thought he was falling asleep when he turned his head and his eyes locked on mine.

"Dad?"

"What, Scooter?"

"If you didn't kill someone, how come the police are trying to catch you?"

"They made a mistake, too."

"Police can make mistakes?"

"Sure. They're human, like everyone else."

"But if they made a mistake," Timmy said, "how come you were trying to go away on that airplane?"

"I wasn't."

"That's what they said on TV."

"That's wrong, too," I said.

"That's a lot of stuff wrong," Timmy said. "Can't you make it right?"

"I can, Scooter. And I will, real soon."

"By Christmas?"

"I promise."

"Not promise like my ball."

"Not promise like your ball," I said, so racked with guilt that I would gladly have gone to confession there and then, for the first time since I was a boy.

"Promise like I've never promised anything before."

"You're the best dad in the world," Timmy said.

He started to giggle.

"What's so funny?"

"You know," he said.

"No, I don't."

"Your bum. It was on TV."

"It wasn't really my bum. It was…a *computer-generated* bum. Like in a video game."

"Honest?"

"Honest," I said.

"Goodie! That's what I told my friends!'

"Did they believe you?"

"Yup. They said it had to be a computer bum, 'cause only someone on Jerry Springer would really show their bum."

Since when did he know about Jerry Springer? But now wasn't the time to inquire.

Timmy yawned and snuggled tighter. I wanted to hold him all night. I wanted to take him away, just me and him, to a place where no one ever hurt.

"You need your sleep, Scooter," I said. "Come on. I'll tuck you in."

"Check under the bed for monsters?"

"Of course."

I got on my hands and knees.

"No monsters," I said.

"The closet?"

I opened the closet and pronounced it safe.

"I love you, Dad."

"I love you too, Timmy. More than anything."

And that, ladies and gentlemen, was the God's honest truth.

Timmy was soon asleep. I kissed his forehead, arranged his covers, and tiptoed to the door.

Ruth was in the hall.

"Jesus!" I exclaimed. "How long have you been there?"

"Long enough," she whispered.

She put her arms around me.

"Thank God you're all right."

That threw me. I wouldn't have expected her first reaction to be relief.

"I'm not sure I'd call it all right," I said.

"Let's go downstairs," Ruth said.

She took my hand and led me to the living room, where the light allowed her a good look at me. She touched my face and smiled.

"Been to the beach?"

"It's tanning creme."

"And the hair?"

"You don't like jet-black hair?"

Ruth laughed.

"You look like *My Cousin Vinny* does bowling!"

"Short of plastic surgery, it's the best I could do. It obviously wasn't good enough."

"When this is over, I promise we'll do Vermont," Ruth said. "Meanwhile, there's Glenfiddich. Sit."

She poured two glasses of scotch and handed me one. She set the bottle down on her baby grand and somehow an image of Barbara Hershey came to mind.

"How about you just give it to me through an IV," I said.

"You've started smoking again," Ruth said. "So have I."

"Would you like a Camel?"

"I'd love one."

"Let's open a window first. Timmy, you know."

"Of course. I'll get a fan going, too."

Ruth put a fan in the window to exhaust the smoke. I lit our cigarettes and said: "Just like old times."

"You know what my first thought was when the shit hit the fan?" Ruth said. "That it was another of your practical jokes."

"Some joke."

"Then the cops knocked on my door. They wanted to go through everything. I told them they'd need a warrant. They said they'd be back tomorrow morning with one."

"I didn't kill her," I said, "the one in Boston."

"Thanks for setting the record straight," Ruth said. "I was

beginning to think I'd been living with Hannibal Lecter all these years."

"And the one in New York—it's not what they're making it out to be. She was someone I met on the Internet and—"

"You decided you needed a dominatrix. Perhaps you'd forgotten my offer."

Ruth laughed—laughed!

"I wasn't myself," I said, "I know how lame that sounds but the fact is...."

Ruth put a finger to my lips.

"I don't want to hear any more," she said, "not tonight. What's important is you're okay. I've been worried to death about you, Mark."

"I guess you couldn't fuck up worse than I have."

"Well, yes, it could have been a sheep."

I smiled, weakly.

"I'm sorry, Ruth," I said. "I don't know how yet, but I'll make it up to you. I promise I will."

I knew what she had to be thinking. *Mid-life crisis, the poor bastard, I guess most men go through it. But couldn't he have been discreet? I'll never live this down. I can just imagine how it will play at the Development Office. I can just imagine Syd....*

So why did she seem so—was blasé the word? Did Allison somehow even the score: she gets knocked up by another guy, I get caught with my naked ass on TV, let's call it even-Stephen? I didn't want to believe that, but what else could it be? Surely marital duty did not run so deep. Surely no love could be so forgiving. Ruth was no Kathie Lee Gifford (thank God), mindlessly standing by her man.

"Now comes the hard part," Ruth said.

"Yeah," I said. "Keeping my ass out of jail."

Ruth laughed again.

"So, you haven't lost your sense of humor! If it helps, you do have a great ass."

"Thanks. I feel better already."

"The first thing we have to do is call Paul Lawrence."

Lawrence was Harvard's chief legal counsel. He had friends in high places.

"Don't," I said.

"What do you mean?"

"I'm not ready to talk to a lawyer."

"Morning will be too late. The cops will be here."

"I'm not staying," I said. "Not yet."

Ruth had no idea what I meant. I'm not sure I did myself. All I knew was my mood had done another of those sudden one-eighties.

"You've lost me," Ruth said.

"I can't face the cameras and reporters and all that tonight."

"At the risk of sounding insensitive, I don't believe there is an optimal time."

"You're right. So, what's another few hours?"

Ruth pondered that, her face darkening.

"You're not suicidal, are you?" she finally said.

"Don't be ridiculous."

"It's not ridiculous. People have gone to the top of a bridge for less."

"I'm not suicidal."

"Swear?"

"I swear."

"Because Timmy couldn't handle that," Ruth said, and for the first time there was an edge to her voice. "He's been through enough already, Mark."

"I know. I just need a little more time, is all."

Timmy—so much revolved around Timmy, didn't it?

I've mentioned how soon enough I loved, not blamed, him... but Ruth...Ruth was something else. The delicate dynamics that keep a relationship functioning had been tampered with, and I lacked the desire, never mind the expertise, to perform the necessary repairs, initially. In those early days, I couldn't take a letter to Ruth from the mailbox without scrutinizing the return address. I eavesdropped on her telephone calls and clandestinely checked her messages. Nights she worked late, I made certain to check on her.

Was I an asshole for behaving like this? I like to think not.

I can't say I'd never suspected Phil, because I had.

He was my first suspect, but I'd quickly discounted him, for what seemed good reason. Phil had a new babe that Christmas season and they were headed toward the altar. Phil would never risk his business for a woman like Ruth, for she was far too brainy—and "old"—for his infantile tastes. Phil's nose was perfectly straight. And forget Ruth—her kindest description of my partner was "smarmy." That she could screw him—after no-matter-how-much tequila—it was contrary to the laws of nature.

But now—I guess I was exhuming everything again, not a bone undisturbed.

"I played his message," I said to Ruth. "Upstairs, on your machine."

"Whose message?"

"Phil's."

"He's been frantic—calling here three, four times a day."

"He didn't identify himself," I said. "He said only, 'Ruth, it's me.'"

Ruth didn't get it.

"So?" she said.

"How would he know you'd recognize his voice?"

"Because you've been his business partner for almost twenty years?" Ruth said.

"He said, and I quote, 'Things could be much worse. He could be—'"

"'Dead.' He said you could be dead. He was relieved you weren't."

We were silent. I couldn't imagine what was going through Ruth's mind.

"I don't see where you're going with this, Mark," she said.

"I don't either," I said, walking to the door. "All I know is I need a little more time."

I paused, waiting for Ruth to say something.

And when she didn't, I left.

A TV van was in the driveway, its remote-broadcast dish thrust into the air. A cameraman was arranging floodlights and a reporter was dolling himself up in a mirror. Before I could react, he had a microphone in my face.

"Excuse me," he said. "Aren't you Mark Gray?"

From the same part of my brain that gave birth to my absurdist software fantasies came a burst of inspiration.

"If I were Mark Gray," I said, "do you think I'd be leaving by the front door? I'm his brother. Mack Gray. That's Mack, M-A-C-K."

The reporter almost salivated.

"You could be his twin," he said.

"As a matter of fact," I said, "I am. Mack and Mark—fraternal twins, I would note for the record. Born nine minutes apart. I'm older. And one hundred-percent crime-free."

"How's it feel, having a serial killer for a brother?"

How's it feel? Can't you do any better than that? I thought.

"It sucks dead penises," I said. It was a line Howard Stern would have appreciated.

Air that, I thought.

The reporter tittered nervously.

"I'll tell you one thing," I went on. "Twin brother or no twin brother, if the bastard were here now, there wouldn't be any need for a trial. What he's done to our family…."

"Were you surprised when you found out he was wanted for murder?"

"Want to know the truth? No, I wasn't."

"But he was such a respectable member of the community."

"To the public, maybe. But there was a whole other side no one ever saw."

"Like what?"

Obviously, this guy had some pyscho-sexual thing about news. His eyes had widened and he was breathing faster.

"I remember one day—we must have been six or seven—I found him behind the garage, pulling the wings off butterflies. *Monarch* butterflies. Most beautiful creature there is. How it gets down to Mexico and back every year is a true miracle. I would imagine Hannibal Lecter's youth was spent mutilating the poor things."

"Terrible."

"Oh, that was nothing. I can't tell you how many fires he used to set. But the worst was what he did to his first girlfriend after she dumped him."

"What?"

"It's too horrible to describe."

"Please?"

"He kidnapped her cat."

"Frightful!"

"That was only the beginning. He brought it home and boiled the poor thing alive—right there in our kitchen, on our dear mother's stove, God rest her soul."

"Like *Fatal Attraction*!" the pretty boy said.

"Exactly."

He was hyperventilating now.

"Our Internet sources say he was involved in cannibalism!" the reporter said. "Even did a snuff movie! Is it true?"

"Just between me and you?" I said.

"Just between me and you."

I whispered: "I used to tell my poor sister-in-law: 'You married Dahmer. It's only a matter of time. Get out while you can.'"

The pretty boy's jaw dropped—actually dropped. Until that moment, I thought that was only a bad metaphor.

"You're kidding," he said.

"I swear to God. I can't tell you the number of times she called me in tears. Of course, he denied everything, but *I* knew. Especially after the dog."

"The *dog*?"

"Snuffy was his name. Cute little cocker spaniel. My nephew came across its corpse in the cellar—minus the head and internal organs. Never did find those."

"You don't think he *ate* them?"

"Our stove always had a funny smell after that—what other conclusion could you draw? I'm telling you, this was Dahmer. Know what his favorite saying was?"

"No, what?"

"'Eat or be eaten.'"

Even that absurdity did not elicit a hint of skepticism.

"My God. Why didn't someone go to the police?"

"We did, but he paid them off. You know how it is—enough money, you can buy anyone. The Fat Cat rule of life. And he had tons of money, as you can see for yourself."

I gestured toward the house and garage.

"Two million, easy, this place is worth," I said.

"He certainly was a success."

"But not where it counted. Not in his heart," I said. "I'll tell you something else," I continued. "He wasn't in this alone."

"Who else was there?"

"His partner. Guy by the name of Phil Grace. You ought to do a little digging."

"You mean he was a cannibal, too?"

"I can't divulge any more. Remember what detective Malloy said: This guy's still out there, armed and dangerous. No telling where he or his partner will show up next."

So now this airhead thinks it's in the can: The Scoop of the Century. You could see him first thing tomorrow morning, asking the station manager for a raise.

"Now if you'll excuse me," I said, "I must go." I started toward the garage, and the darkness of the golf course beyond.

"Where's your car?" the pretty boy said.

"I came by snowmobile," I said.

"Oh. Well, thanks."

"My pleasure," I said.

If I do say so myself, it had been an Academy Award-winning performance. I wondered what I would do for a sequel. I didn't have to wait long.

CHAPTER TWELVE

Only screensavers—winged toasters, flapping toward mindless eternity—whoever thought they would be cool?— were there to greet me at Ten Revere Way. Tonight was our Christmas party, in New York this year to coincide with the convention. What I would have given to be a fly on the wall. I wondered if anyone would be defending me, or if my own people, like the online community, had jumped ship too.

I suppose the final outcome depends on this, I thought, entering our VR project room. *Sell a million copies of Clue and they'll have your face on a stamp. Another Hometoons and it's your head on the block.*

I sat at the master console, booted up, and got into *Virtual Clue*: specifically, my engineer's work on Allison. I toyed with her image—moving her nose off-center, putting an arrow through her head, sophomoric stuff like that, and then I erased every one of her files. I found the backup tape and erased that, too.

And I felt better, I honestly did. Sometimes it really is the little things.

After rifling the petty cash drawer in the business office (I got all of $75), I stopped at Phil's office. I don't think I'd ever sat at his desk. I knew for sure I'd never gone through his drawers and I guess he believed no one ever would because they were unlocked.

His top drawer had the usual paper clips, rubber bands, and pens, all carefully arranged, as befits a bean counter. His second drawer had a bound set of our catalogues and annual reports. His black book—it really was black—was in his bottom drawer. I read every page: Lisa, Patti, Erica, and so on, a history of philandering well over a decade long. Ruth's name wasn't there. But what did that prove? If anything, only that Phil was no fool.

The digital record might be another story, so I logged onto Phil's computer and began rummaging through his files. Some were documents prepared by our marketing people: sales forecasts, advertising budgets, production costs, with which I was familiar. The rest was crap I'd never bothered to learn. In retrospect, it sounds stupid and naive, but I honestly never cared about amortization, depreciation, accrued liabilities, and all that. I honestly wanted nothing but to create great games—to provide the same entertainment as great movies.

So, I couldn't explain the multitude of transfers between and out of accounts that had been made in a ten-minute flurry starting at about four-thirty this afternoon, shortly after I'd hung up on Phil. I couldn't say for sure this wasn't the ordinary course of business. In light of my experience at Fleet Bank, all I knew is things were starting to smell fishy.

I made a backup tape of Phil's hard drive, pocketed it, and went into my office. It was eleven o'clock. I turned the TV on.

"A city waits in fear!" the anchor boy was saying. "Tonight, a special hour edition of the eleven o'clock news."

A lower third appeared: SOCIETY STALKER: WHO'S NEXT?

They cut to an exclusive neighborhood on Beacon Hill, just below the Statehouse. Cruisers filled the street. Lights flashed and the scene was thick with bystanders. We were live.

"Steve," said Karen Adams, the on-scene reporter, "police are tight-lipped about the shocking murder of Maggie Marceil, 22, found dead in her apartment here by her roommate less than an hour ago. Channel Five has learned, however, that clues at the scene point to the man who has come to be called the Society Stalker—the man who, police confirm, warned he would strike again in a message posted on the Internet. Hold on, Steve. Here they come with her now!"

The camera zoomed in on the front steps, where the boys from the meat wagon were in action. We got a nice closeup of the body bag, and then we went close on Karen's powdered face.

Fresh corpses didn't seem to affect her.

"Maggie was the daughter of Walter Marceil, president of the First Federal Bank of Boston," she said in the same sing-song voice as before.

"The woman he allegedly attacked in New York was a banker's daughter as well," Steve said.

"Correct. Sources say his taste runs to the rich and young."

"Thank you, Karen."

We were back in the studio with Steve.

"And grisly as it sounds, taste just might be the right word. Channel Five has learned exclusively that the stalker's purpose may not have been only sex, as originally believed. We bring you now to Frank Falvo, live outside the Mark Gray home in Marblehead."

There was Frank, on my snow-covered lawn.

"Looking at this lovely home, no one would ever guess its owner was anything other than the mild-mannered family man he appeared to be," Frank began. "To the outside world, Mark Gray was a minister's son, husband of a top official at Harvard, father of a six-year-old boy—and an international software guru whose computer games your kids might be playing even now. But according to Gray's twin brother, Mack, family members had long been concerned about what they describe as his violent tendencies, especially after he allegedly ate the family dog, Snuffy."

"*Ate?*" Steve said.

"Ate."

They rolled a few seconds of Frank's interview with me.

"Does that mean the motive was *cannibalism*?" Doug said.

"Police aren't commenting and it's too early for autopsy results," Frank said, "but our sources confirm that bite marks were indeed found all over both Marceil and Hannah Gregory, whose strangled nude body was found earlier today."

"Were any pieces, well, no way to put this delicately, so, ah...*missing*?"

"We just don't know yet, Steve. Whatever the outcome, authorities are urging all residents of greater Boston, women especially, to take precautions."

"What specifically?" Steve said.

"Lock your doors, of course," Frank said. "Don't travel out after dark alone. Don't answer your door without first confirming who's there. And at the slightest suspicion, dial 9-1-1. Gray is considered armed and dangerous. Do not—we repeat, *do not*—attempt to subdue or arrest him yourself. This is a job for the police."

"Thank you, Frank," Steve said. "Channel Five will have more on precautions later in the broadcast. But first, we take you to Boston Common."

They cut to the manger scene, strangely deserted.

"In this most joyous of holiday seasons," Steve said, "cheer has turned to fear as a region worries: who next? Not since the Boston Strangler have people been so concerned in the capital city."

This report was about paranoia: gun sales up, nightclub admissions down, silver-haired ladies and college girls barricading themselves behind double-deadbolted doors. Who knows if any of it was true? The only person who seemed to be enjoying himself was a college kid selling COED NAKED ASS T-shirts.

"Already sold enough to pay for spring break!" he told the roving reporter. "Tomorrow, I'll have caps and watches."

Phil will want a royalty, I thought, and the very idea was so ludicrous, and so right-on, that I laughed out loud. Literally, lol.

By this point, I figured there couldn't possibly be anything more to say, but there was. An hour was a lot to kill.

"Those who know Gray best say they have been concerned about him in recent weeks," anchor boy Steve said. "Joining us live again from New York is reporter Doug Fenning, of New York 1. Good evening, Doug."

"Good evening, Steve. As you know, Gray's company is in New York for the annual Video Gamers of America convention. Earlier tonight, we went to the Waldorf, where the company party was being held, and spoke to his partner, Phil Grace."

They cut to a banquet room at the hotel. Doug had a microphone in Phil's face.

"How's he been acting lately?" Doug asked.

"Like he was under a lot of stress," Phil said.

"Any idea why?" Doug asked.

"Two things," Phil said, with great assurance. "First is our new title, *Shuttle Saga*. It's dying at retail, just like I predicted. If only he'd listened."

"Liar," I said. "Until test market, you were as hot for it as anyone."

"He had so much of himself invested in it," Phil went on. "These creative types are like that, you know. I guess the best word is 'fragile.' It's like that artist—what's his name?—who cut off his ear to spite his girlfriend."

"Van Gogh," Doug said.

"Right, him. Highly unpredictable."

"What's the other thing?"

"His homelife, sadly," Phil said.

"You bastard," I said.

"Can you be more specific?" Doug asked.

"I'd rather not. All I can say is things have been bad for some time. Can I make a public appeal?"

"Certainly."

"Mark, if you're listening, please turn yourself in. We'll be there for you, I promise."

And then we were back to Steve, who noted that my father-in-law was offering a $100,000 reward for any information leading to my arrest and conviction. But not a word about Phil's financial shenanigans. Maybe that would come later. Or maybe in our brave new tabloid world, where everything is surface, corporate ethics no longer had currency.

"Assholes," I said.

I picked up my Nerf Chainblazer and blasted the TV.

Like I said, it really is the little things.

What time was it in L.A.?

Eight-thirty. I wondered if I could catch Bud Robbins at his office, and then I wondered what I would say if I did. I knew what Bud's reaction would have been—something about this being the best of my practical jokes, but wasn't it time to come clean? I wondered if Chris McCauley, a bigwig now at

Buena Vista Pictures, would take my call. I wondered whatever happened to Doris Wong, and all the rest of the Venice Beach crowd.

It was curious, realizing they all probably knew about the new me... and didn't really know anything at all.

Then I opened the drawer where I kept my Tony C. scrapbook and rooted around until I found an overstuffed manilla envelope I hadn't opened in years.

How had Goldman put it in his piece? Exactly as I gave it to him—those little white lies, you know.

"Hollywood lacked the exciting opportunities Gray craved," he wrote. "Creatively, the system had grown too rigid. It was only natural that Gray, whose imagination has always refused to be contained, would decide to abandon movie-making and plunge heart and soul into a field only a visionary—a brilliant star, as yet unblazing—could see was heading anywhere."

The truth? The truth was something else.

I wasn't honest the last time I talked to Sally, either.

As I have related, I told her I'd been hired as a production assistant on a Milos Forman film, but the truth was that Forman wasn't in the country in 1979.

The truth was, I'd blown my graduation money, and, with rent due, I'd taken a job at Musso & Frank Grill on Hollywood Boulevard. Real-live Hollywood stars hung out there, and for a while, I believed waiting tables was opportunity, not economic survival. Heck—hadn't Jack Nicholson started out in the mailroom of MGM?

The truth was, I was becoming the classic wannabe.

Nobody in L.A. gave a shit about the so-called ground my college films had broken, or the reviews I'd gotten in *The Village Voice* and *The New York Times*, or the unqualified success of the first NYU Jack Nicholson film fest, attended by none other than John Lennon.

Truth was, I was living my generation's version of *Reality Bites*.

With this difference: we weren't all in the same boat. I turned up my nose at commercials, but Bud didn't. Armed with an introduction from Robert Altman, his father's friend, Bud got a job at Ogilvy & Mather writing Barbie copy for Mattel. We teased the living crap out of him, but within a year, he was directing commercials; another year, and he'd left advertising to produce documentaries for rock bands, and I don't mean the type that practice in garages. His first music video aired the day MTV began broadcasting and last we talked, some two years ago, he was an executive V.P. at Paramount—a real suit, with chauffeur and access to the corporate jet.

"Any time you want a new challenge," he'd said in our last conversation, "there's a place for you here."

Sure, I thought. *In your next naked-ass music video.*

Chris McCauley lived with us only six months; long enough, I guess, to exorcise the Vietnam demons and get his head back on straight. I mean, Chris was the most intense person I ever met. The way he told stories, played video games, ate a sandwich—really, anything—you watched and you saw him in his Huey, flying support for some operation deep across Viet Cong lines. Chris would hole up in his room for days, and when he emerged, he had storyboards—wild, crazy animation storyboards of jungle creatures that blew us all away.

If you've seen *Lion King* or *Hercules*, you've seen some of Chris's recent work.

And me?

One year became three, and I refused to accept the truth.

A succession of roommates, Musso & Frank's, Sonny's— God knows the clues were there, big as the letters in the Hollywood sign. So, what did the aspiring director do? Took acting classes, instruction in directing not being readily available to someone unable to afford graduate school. I even landed a part: as the voice of Ken in one of Bud's commercials. God, I was pitiful, not a gram of talent and looks that were not, shall we say, in highest demand—but I didn't want to see that then, either. I scraped together the cash for a portfolio and brought the Ken commercial to casting calls and offered my Jack Nicholson imitation. I began to believe that my true calling transcended mere directing—that I would make my mark both in front of and behind the camera, that I would be the Orson Welles of my generation.

I was, as is painfully clear to me now, in the wrong place. Not to mention deluded. My father had been right.

I would be remiss if I did not mention my evening at the home of Bob Rafelson, who'd directed Jack Nicholson in *The Postman Always Rings Twice*. Rafelson's cousin was the lead guitarist for a band Bud had filmed, and through him, Bud had gotten to schmooze the director. Knowing my thing for Jack, Bud finagled an invitation to Rafelson's Christmas party. You would think that with all my groveling, I would have been to at least a dozen Hollywood bashes after more than two years, but I hadn't been to one. This was the real thing—in Malibu, no less, with limos, bodyguards and a champagne fountain.

And the man himself, Jack Nicholson.

He was holding court with Stanley Kubrick near a Santa Claus ice sculpture when we walked in. He looked exactly as he did in Kubrick's *The Shining*, his latest film: manic, playful, charismatic where it counted most, which was with the ladies. Lots of folks wore sunglasses that night, but Jack was the only one on whom they belonged.

"I have to meet him," I said to Bud.

"Be cool."

"You don't understand. I *have* to meet him."

"I do understand—just be cool, okay?"

Bud promised he'd ask Rafelson for an introduction. I went for a beer.

What would my opening line be? *"I've loved you ever since Chinatown?"*

Too lame.

"Would you believe I can remember where and when I saw every one of your films?"

Too big a suck-up.

I needed something with teeth in it, something to connect with the artist inside him, but after another beer, I concluded this was not the right venue for intelligent discussion of high filmic art. My best bet would be to start with small talk and see where it went.

Rafelson introduced Bud to Jack—and ignored me completely.

I stood dumbly while the three of them chatted.

"By the way, this is my friend, Mark Gray," Bud finally said.

"My pleasure, Mark," Nicholson said.

"Hi."

That was it: a monosyllable.

"Mark's a huge fan of yours," Bud went on. "At NYU, he put on the first annual Jack Nicholson film fest. It got written up in *The Village Voice*."

"No fooling!" Nicholson said. He seemed honored.

I was mute.

"His senior thesis had a very funny takeoff of the diner scene in *The Last Detail*," Bud said.

"Really!"

"Half was live-action, half was computer animation. He even managed to weave in some Bunuel. Real cutting-edge. Right, Mark?"

"Yup."

That was it: *Yup!*

"So, what do you do now, Mark?" Nicholson said.

"Musso & Frank."

Bud shot me a look. On the way over, he'd urged me to make something up—second unit director, production assistant, key grip, anything but the truth.

"No, what do you *do*?" Nicholson said.

"I play games," I squeaked.

"Video games," Bud said. "He's quite talented."

Nicholson's face was blank. This was 1981.

"*Pong*," I said.

Nicholson's upper lip was curling.

"*Donkey Kong*," I further explained.

"Hey, well, see ya around," Nicholson said, and walked away.

Chris McCauley couldn't help me at Buena Vista, but before he moved out, he'd convinced me that something other than *Donkey Kong* or *Tank*—a flight simulator like what he'd trained on in the Army, say—was where video games were headed. He was onto something.

I remembered my childhood, when the absolute coolest thing a kid could want to be, short of a major-league baseball player, was an astronaut, and I decided a combat helicopter pilot was even cooler. I had no marketing background, but my instincts told me that if I could tap into that sense of dangerous adventure, I'd be cooking. After picking Chris's brain enough to imagine I could climb into the cockpit of a Huey and fly it myself, I bought a used IBM PC with 64 kilobytes—*kilobytes!*—of RAM, a green monitor, and a how-to book on writing programs. This was financed, I should note, with my first (and only) Hollywood check, $200 for the voice of Ken on *Barbie's Polynesian Adventure*.

And now I'm going to boast—after all that's gone down, surely you'll allow me a moment of braggadocio.

So: I was a natural designer.

And I was obsessed.

I was becoming like Chris—when I wasn't at Musso & Frank, I was shut in my room, smoking the good stuff and banging away at the keyboard.

My first game was *Helo*, played like *Tank*, with one critical difference: I put you inside the chopper. Not a very realistic chopper, but enough of an advance over anything at Sonny's that once word got out, strangers were knocking on my door. I turned no one away. I even provided the weed and beer, when budget allowed—market research, you could call it.

My next venture was *Mark's Chopper*, progenitor of *Attack Ship*, CreativeWare's first title. It was a gas. I mean, you took the joystick and leaned into that screen and you were there—over Tehran, dodging lead as you raced to rescue American hostages from Islamic militants.

"You ought to start charging," Bud said one night.

"You're right," I said.

The next week I rented a room across from Sonny's and quite literally hung out a shingle.

In his piece, Charlie Goldman captured the hoopla that followed—the writeup in the *Los Angeles Times*, the lines at the door, the inquiries from Nolan Bushnell and Warner Bros., my hiring someone to run the place while I worked on an improved version, the day in late 1982 when I was visited by someone Chris knew: a guy named Phil Grace, who'd flown down from Palo Alto to see what all the fuss was about.

Only a year older than me, Phil had a middle-aged schmoozy way about him that should have been phony as hell, but somehow wasn't, at least not on first blush. I mean, you instinctively wanted to please the guy. You wanted to be his best friend, and after about a minute with him, you understood how a kid barely out of college had been able to obtain six million dollars in venture capital for his company, which made electronic chess sets.

Phil played *Mark's Chopper* and smoked hashish and when he left, at two in the morning, it was with a standing offer to go into business with him.

"We'd be perfect together, Markie-boy," he said. "You feed your artistic soul and I'll handle the rest."

Sounded good to me. Sounded like one of those producer-director dream teams you were always hearing about in southern California. There was only one hitch: Phil was heading back home, to Boston, to be near New York, which was where the real investment action was.

If I wanted in, I'd have to follow.

A few months later, I did.

And not for opportunity alone. By late 1982, word was starting to spread about some strange new killer disease. Transmitted by sex, it supposedly was a gay thing, but straight sorts didn't need long to figure you probably could catch it from some chick who swung both ways but conveniently kept that fact from you at the moment of truth. There were lots of babes like that out there then—young women willing to spread their legs in exchange for a turn at the bong, and a cigarette and strong coffee the morning after. Not that I philosophically disagreed, mind you.

Nor they, for that matter. How young we all were.

Ruth stood out from that scene.

She was in L.A. for the wedding of her college roommate to Bud, who was moving to Santa Monica, and I couldn't believe my luck when I found myself at her table at the reception.

The way she dressed, how she carried herself, the degree she'd taken last June from Radcliffe—in music, no less—piano, my mother's instrument, make of it what you will—it all bespoke Eastern refinement, a welcome change after three and a half years in Lalaland. Moreover, she wasn't some snooty high-brow. I'd met her kind in New York, and they all moved through life as if they were God's personal gift to mankind.

Not Ruth. She was funny, smart, and down-to-earth. And beautiful.

At my invitation, she dropped by my place after the reception and she thought *Mark's Chopper* was cool. She laughed at my jokes and proclaimed my Jack Nicholson imitation fantastic. I played one of my little practical jokes—told her that my apartment had been chosen for a set for a movie, a Hollywood film crew was due at midnight for a shoot—and she bought it, for a few hilarious minutes anyway. She took only a courtesy toke on a joint and didn't finish her beer, although she was into wine—knew vineyards and vintages, which was cool, even if my sophistication ended at Mateus, whose bottles made groovy candle holders. I figured with everything else I had going, I'd waltz her right into bed. What with AIDS, I hadn't been with a woman in months. I put the odds that she was infected at zero.

Sitting next to her on my couch, I was embarrassed for the first time ever by my furniture, which was vintage Salvation Army.

I tried to kiss Ruth.

She politely pushed me away.

I felt like a fool.

"Can I call you?" I said when she was leaving for her hotel.

"I'm going back to Boston," she said.

"So am I."

I was now, anyway. Have I forgotten to mention that along with being obsessive, I was also highly compulsive? There's probably a description of me in the DSM-IV.

"So, can I call?"

"I'd like that," Ruth said.

"You don't think I'm a beast?"

"I think you're cute," she said, and kissed me, lightly, on the cheek.

I've mentioned a certain afternoon in the Cape Cod dunes.

Ruth and I had her family's summer place to ourselves that Fourth of July weekend, and we spent the days drinking wine, swimming, and suntanning. I reenacted scenes from *Chinatown* and *Rocky*—I had this brief Stallone thing that summer—and I played one of my all-time best practical jokes, to Ruth's delight.

Claiming to be the Hyannis harbormaster, I called her father in Boston to say that his boat—his beloved vintage 1920s mahogany speedboat—had been rammed by the Nantucket ferry and was sinking even as we spoke. Old Syd nearly shit, right through the phone.

"Oh, Dad, can't you take a joke?" Ruth said when I'd played it for all I could. "You're such a prune!"

On our final afternoon on the Cape, there in the dunes, Ruth and I made love for the first time. When we were done, I asked her to marry me.

"Are you putting me on?" she said.

"No," I said.

"You mean *marry*—as in settle down and have kids?"

"I don't know about the kids," I said, "but yeah, I mean settle down."

"Are you sure this isn't one of your jokes?"

"I swear to God."

"We've only been going out a month," Ruth said.

"Like I need a month to know I'm madly in love?"

"Where would we live?"

"I ask you to marry me and that's all you can think of— where we'd live? This isn't the time to be practical, Ruth. I'm asking you to marry me."

"I will," Ruth said.

I wanted to believe her but didn't.

"So, it's your turn to play a joke," I said.

"No joke," she said. "Let's make love again."

Was Syd's money part of the draw? Did a childhood dressed from Filene's Basement drive me, if only subconsciously, toward acquisitiveness? Syd took great satisfaction believing that's how it was when Ruth broke the news to him. Wrong-side-of-the-tracks me, he thought, and said, was his daughter's way of finally sticking it to him.

I believe the truth was simpler: Ruth and I were crazy in love, and not yet twenty-six.

The next spring, there on Cape Cod, my father performing the service, we were married.

I examine the early days of our marriage and I find no watersheds, no points of no return, only subtle changes that were imperceptible at the time. Maybe they should have been. But as you've no doubt gathered by now, introspection was never my strong point.

We newlyweds moved into an apartment on Beacon Hill. I took tennis lessons and Ruth started a wine cellar and I began buying my clothes through the mail, Land's End and L.L. Bean attire mostly. My wife wasn't big on going to the movies, but that was cool; the video revolution was underway and you could remain a junkie without leaving home. With the wild success of *Attack Ship*, we hired an architect and built our home in Marblehead. We traded old Buicks for new Volvos and Ruth indulged in a Steinway baby grand and we bought season tickets to the Boston Symphony Orchestra. All with my money, not her father's. Which galled him.

And I have to tell you: even I, who'd already been through many iterations during my twenty-seven years, was astonished at how easily I slipped into my new adult life. Ruth wasn't keen on Phil and his crowd, mostly stock brokers and gold-seeking chicks, so we moved toward her circle: Cliffie friends and colleagues from the Harvard Development Office, where, with Syd's connections, she'd landed a position after an unsatisfying year teaching music at a private school. They were a fine enough lot, I suppose, if discussing capital campaigns was your thing. Ruth brought me to black-tie dinners, and I was a good sport about it, making small talk with drunken old fools with deep pockets and fond memories of The Yard and drunken orgies inside the locked doors of *The Harvard Lampoon*.

Were there incompatibilities?

Of course—did you think this was *Love Story*?

Ruth had escaped the worst of her father's influence, but, like him, she was shaded toward anal-retentive, being incapable of going to bed with dirty dishes in the sink. She kept the magazines in chronological order, packed her briefcase every night, all of which bugged me for reasons I would not have easily articulated. She wouldn't go near cocaine and she wasn't into weed, although, out of some sense of marital obligation I suppose, in the earliest days she could occasionally be coaxed into a few hits on a joint. She had a healthy interest in sex, even if, with the exception of that time on Cape Cod, she favored dark rooms and conventional positions.

What it boils down to is Ruth wasn't hang-loose. I do not suggest this was a character flaw, nor that my wife was one-dimensional—only that her dimensions were not those of Venice Beach. That was cool; the further I was from California, the more I came to believe how badly I'd needed structure. I'd never have admitted it to my father or for that matter Ruth, but I'd been in free fall long enough.

Still, that past never entirely faded—every so often, I'd get calls from the Venice Beach crowd. Doris Wong found me, compelled to share the news that she was president of the Los Angeles Gay-Lesbian Alliance. Things with Bud were rekindled briefly before *Hometoons* went south. I even got a couple of late-night rings from Chris McCauley, after Eisner hired him and Katzenberg promoted him. But eventually, it more or less all stopped. I wasn't bothered, not then. The more it receded, the more the beach really did seem hallucinogenic and the less I wondered: Was that really me—a guy who really believed he'd someday direct Hollywood movies? Or only a boy from Maine who refused to grow up?

Or was there a larger issue: Whether comfort and familiarity were so numbingly powerful that not only could they rewrite history but erase certain pivotal chapters altogether.

It seemed to me now, sitting at Ten Revere Way, that they could.

But only temporarily.

One chance event, one random thought, and the past could be present.

I opened the manilla envelope and read the first letter.

"Dearest Mark," it began.

"Well, I can't believe you're really away at college. I wish you were here so we could snuggle—and more! I will never forget your last night (until Thanksgiving!) in Blue Hill, how I didn't want it to end. You were asleep when the sun came up. I watched the orangey-pink that the sky gets that early come over the water and up the sand and across the sleeping bag and onto your face and I wanted to be able to stop everything there, like put us both in a picture and frame it and hang it on a wall in some magical palace in some faraway kingdom forever and ever.

"Now I'm yakking, like I do! I miss you so much and love you so much (special kiss!!!) and I know I'll be talking to you on the phone tonight but it's not the same. 37 days until Columbus Day weekend, I CAN'T WAIT THAT LONG!!!! Do you know that since kindergarten, we've never been apart that long? It's true! (Except that summer in third grade I visited my aunt in Canada. I forget how long that was.) (Stupid memory, huh?!!!)

"I'm sad but not wicked sad cause I know that no matter what happens, we're gonna be in love forever. Nothing can ever come between us, certainly not some silly thing like you being in New York and me back here (for now)..."

I had more than a hundred letters like that. Why had I saved them—lugged them from NYU to Venice Beach and back to Boston, through three apartments and a house and finally to a secure repository at Ten Revere Way? My Tony C. scrapbook—I understand that. Everyone has mementos of their youth, if only a few yellowed clippings or a dog-eared report card or some faded photographs.

But Sally's letters? Were they, as I'd told myself, just material for the screenplay I still intended to write? Or was there more to it—something I wouldn't acknowledge, maybe didn't recognize?

I read on, each letter an unfolding chronicle of the past. There was Sally during her first visit to New York. There she was after our first blowup, after finding out about Doris Wong, when she believed it would be best if we broke up. And the next letter, in which she was so happy we hadn't.

I even had a note she'd passed me in high school English the morning after I told my father I'd slept with her and didn't give a shit that we weren't married or engaged.

"I don't care if the whole world finds out," Sally wrote, "'cause what do they know anyways?"

They really would make a good screenplay, I thought, oddly reassured. *Call it* Summer Love, *something sappy like that. Maybe make her a mermaid and give it a horror twist.*

I'd read Sally's letters through to senior year at NYU when I came across the ring, taped to Sally's final missive. I held it in my hand, remembering how difficult it had been to sell Mom's silver dollars, the only way I could afford the ring—but knowing Mom would have approved, for she had adored Sally.

I remembered the last time I saw Sally, the night after her abortion.

I closed my eyes and was back there in that terrible moment.

"Who is it?" Sally had said when I rang the bell at her apartment.

"Me."

She opened the door without a word.

"I brought you this," I said, handing her a single white rose.

Sally was in her nightgown. She didn't seem sore or anything, but I didn't ask. If there is such a thing as a post-abortion etiquette, I've never seen it.

I just started talking about *Eating People*, which I'd spent the day editing, babbling on about how combining live action and computer animation was so avant-garde, and how hilarious *The Last Detail* spoof was (especially juxtaposed to Bunuel), and the hopes I had for first place in the NYU festival, and how another mention in *The Village Voice* could help ignite a career.

I guess I went on like that for five or ten minutes before I couldn't stand myself anymore.

Sally hadn't spoken a word.

"How was it?" I said.

"How the fuck do you think it was?" she said.

That freaked me out. Sally had never used the F word, ever.

"They stuck a tube into my cunt and vacuumed my baby away," she went on. "Except for that, everything was ducky."

"I'm sorry," I said.

You don't ever want to experience silence like what followed, believe me.

"If you want me to leave," I finally said, "I will."

"I don't," Sally said. "I want to dance."

She put an Eagles album on and cued up the theme song from our high school senior prom, "Take it To the Limit." The song started and she put her arms around me, and I closed my eyes and smelled her perfume: Shalimar, my final Christmas gift to her.

How many times do you slow-dance with your girl when you're twenty-one? A hundred? A thousand? Of all our times, that one is most vivid. I fought Sally's pull, but the feel of her body was strong. I wanted to make love to her. I wanted to be where the doctor had gone. It was so wrong, especially knowing Sally would have let me.

"I have to go," I said when the album ended, and the only sound was needle on dead space.

"Please stay the night."

"It's wrong."

"Everything's wrong, Mark," she said. "It can't get more wrong."

I went to the door. Our eyes met and I had to turn away.

She wasn't crying when I started down the stairs. She wasn't pleading. She wasn't doing anything but standing, silently, the ring I'd given her in her open hand.

I knew she expected me to take it and I did.

And that was the last time I'd seen Sally Martin.

I found Sally's number on the invitation to our high school reunion and dialed it, lighting another cigarette from the one I'd just finished. My hands trembled.

"Hello?" the voice on the other end of the line said.

"Sally?"

"Mark?"

"I didn't wake you, did I?"

"No," she said. "I was watching the news."

"Bet you've never gotten a call from a cannibal before."

It was a weak attempt at humor, but Sally obliged me with a laugh.

"You'd have to be crazy to believe everything you see on TV," she said.

"Or everything the cops say."

"Tell me about it. I made the mistake of marrying one. But that's over now."

"You've been on my mind a lot lately," I said.

"You've been on mine, too," she said. "Maybe it's telepathy."

"Maybe. So how are you, Sally?"

"I'm busy. Christmas is always busy, what with the kids and all."

"Don't I know it."

"Plus working so much overtime like I am. The money comes in handy this time of year."

I was afraid where that might lead.

"How was the reunion?" I said. "I wanted to go but things came up."

"I figured you'd be too busy," Sally said. "It was great. Everyone was asking for you."

"Was Bud there?"

"No. You and Bud were about the only ones who weren't."

There was a bit of a pause.

"Actually, I didn't call to talk about the reunion," I said.

My mouth felt dry, the way it was on our first date, to the Blue Hill Nickelodeon for a showing of *The Godfather*, playing on a twin bill with *Butterflies are Free*. I remember seeing Goldie Hawn in her underwear and imagining what Sally looked like in panties and bra.

"Then why did you call?" Sally said.

"I wondered if it was too late...you know, for our own little reunion. Just you and me."

"Do you mean it?"

"I do."

"When do you want to get together?"

"How's tomorrow sound?"

"Tomorrow?"

"Like in the afternoon. We could have coffee or something."

Sally hesitated and said: "I guess that would be okay."

"If it isn't, we could always do it another time."

"No," she said. "Tomorrow would be fine."

No hostility in her tone, no recriminations—could the years have been so softening?

"Did you save my letters?" I asked before saying goodbye.

"Yes."

"I still have yours. And the ring. Remember the ring?"

"I remember."

"Funny the stuff you hang onto, isn't it?"

"Funny," Sally said. *"I guess that's what it is."*

I hung up and dialed Beth Israel Hospital.

"Fair," the condition person said.

Yes! She'd been upgraded again.

"Is she able to talk yet?" I asked.

"Any details will have to come from the patient's doctor," the condition person said, and that was that.

I had one more call before leaving CreativeWare.

"Detective Malloy," I said.

A moment later, he came on the line.

"Hello, Mark," he said, "or should I say Mack? Until tonight, I never would have guessed you had such a marvelous sense of humor."

"Humor?"

"Your Channel Five interview. Cute name, Snuffy—you're a very funny guy, after all, Mark. Giving that bum your loafers and Superman tie was a real howl, too. And that airport scene— it had me in stitches! I love being played for a fool. Just *love* it."

He was getting that Terminator tone again.

"Have you talked to Allison?" I asked.

"As a matter of fact, yes," he said.

"What did she say?"

"That you're a lousy lover."

"Funny."

"Honest Injun, that's what she said."

"She's not giving you the full story."

"And what might that be?"

"Allison Manchester's a call girl."

"You mean a prostitute?" Malloy said. "A *whore*, as in someone who fucks for money?"

"And not only a call girl, but a madam whose burning desire apparently was to open the world's first digital bordello. You're an ace detective. Know anything about that?"

Psycho-cop was back again.

"She is not a whore!" Malloy shouted. "Do you hear me, you fucking dirtball? She is NOT a whore!"

"Really?" I said, calmly. "What if I could prove it?"

"How are you going to do that—with your naked-ass video?"

"No, with her computer files."

"Her computer has been seized," Malloy said, but you could sense it—a trace of uncertainty in his voice.

"But I have her backup tape," I said. "In fact, I'm going through it now."

And I was. I'd just opened a file.

The line went silent.

"As busy as I've been," I went on, "I haven't had the chance to take a look until now. Guess whose names are in here?"

Malloy didn't answer.

"How about Richard Bates, the Philadelphia Main Line heir."

Silence.

"Here's another: U.S. Rep. Donald J. Dolan. Up for re-election this year. Good luck with that now, Donny."

Silence.

"And from a very long list, let me give you one more."

"I don't know what you're talking about," the detective said.

"Let me give you a hint," I said. "It begins with the letter M."

I scrolled through.

"My, my, would you look at this," I said. "October First, the Plaza. October Third, Sixth, and Eleventh, the Pierre. The Fourteenth and Fifteenth, the Plaza again. October was a busy month on the zipper front, wasn't it, Detective? Expensive, too, at five hundred a pop. Now *here's* a funny entry: 'Wife, Deidre Malloy, is lieutenant on force.' Reading this, it would be hard to say which gives you greater interest in my case: jealousy or fear. It almost makes me sorry I rained on your parade."

"It's all lies," Malloy said, weakly.

"Computers don't lie, detective. Not with such explicit pictures, anyway."

"We still have the two in Boston," Malloy said.

For such a temperamental guy, he was suddenly quite subdued.

"That's bullshit," I said. "I didn't kill anyone, and you know it. You've been watching too many movies. Now listen carefully: I'm only going to tell you this once."

I gave Malloy a detailed account of my last seventy-two hours, with names or descriptions of witnesses who could confirm my story.

"When you've checked it all out," I said, "I want you to call your buddies in Boston. Then I want you to clear my name, on TV. Your deadline is 24 hours. You're not going to pull a Richard Jewell on me."

There was another silence.

"You will oblige me, won't you, detective?" I said.

I was beginning to regain my appreciation for the First Amendment.

Malloy didn't answer

"Or maybe I should upload these files onto the Internet," I said.

Actually, I already had, to an obscure e-mail account I doubted the cops could even find. Plus, I was about to make backups on floppy discs.

"After uploading," I said, "I will call a few reporters with instructions on how to download."

"You wouldn't do that," Malloy said.

"Only those that come with JPEGs," I said. "Do you know what a JPEG is, detective? Stands for Joint Photographic Experts Group. Non-nerds know them as photographs."

"I'll see what I can do," Malloy said.

"Before we part, I suppose you're not interested in a *real* crime," I said.

"What kind of crime?"

"Embezzlement. Maybe tax fraud, too. It involves my partner, Phil. I believe you've spoken with him."

"I have."

"Tell you what," I said. "You call your buddies in Boston, and I'll leave the door unlocked so you can seize his records. I'm sure you've already got someone on the way over, anyway. Sweet dreams, detective."

CHAPTER THIRTEEN

I intended to drive straight to Maine, not Fenway Park, but I found myself parking in Kenmore Square and walking across the turnpike to Lansdowne Street, where I heard a rock band inside a nightclub. Couples kissed in the shadow of the left field wall and cabs were queueing up for closing. It was ten to one.

This was the route we always took, my father and me, those summers we made the long drive down from Blue Hill. Lansdowne would be mobbed and I would beg Dad for hotdogs and cotton candy and peanuts and here, only here, he bought whatever I wanted. The lines through the admission gates seemed impossibly long and I was always afraid we'd miss batting practice, but Dad timed it so we never did. Once inside, I would get a Coke and Dad would get a beer—a single, smallest-size beer—only alcohol I ever saw him drink—took him to third or fourth inning to finish—and we would emerge into the sunlight and green splendor of the park.

You would think breaking into a major-league stadium would be a criminal challenge, but it wasn't: I had to climb a chain-link fence, that's all, to get into Fenway tonight.

No alarms went off and no guards came running. I made my way to the bleachers. I hadn't been there in some thirty years, not since the last time with Dad: in 1968, the summer after Mom died. Descending to the visitors' bullpen, I looked at the field, shadowless and white under a nearly full moon. Except for a single set of footprints in the snow that disappeared beyond first base—left by an off-season groundskeeper, I supposed—the field was undisturbed.

I could not be here without remembering Tony Conigliaro, of course.

He survived Jack Hamilton's beaning, as I mentioned earlier, returning in 1969 to hit 20 home runs and be named Comeback Player of the Year. In 1970, he hit 36 homers and everyone believed he was back, but he wasn't; on late afternoons, as the Fenway shadows lengthened, Tony C. had trouble seeing the ball. In 1971, he slumped badly and was traded to the California Angels, and by the end of that season, his vision still impaired, he was out of baseball for good.

"How often did I tell you," my father said, "that no good would ever come of him playing again?"

But I didn't care about the greater meaning my father found in everything. I was fourteen.

I heard car engines starting and drunken laughter, drifting over the wall into Fenway. The nightclub was letting out.

I hopped onto the field.

Easily two hundred times at Fenway, and I'd never set foot here, the sacred place, where once upon a time I really and truly believed I'd spend my adult life.

I walked to center field and stopped. A wind was blowing in from home plate—one of those winds that, on a fine summer's day, can carry a ball practically to Kenmore Square—and my thoughts returned to Tony C. Not the heroic Tony C., but the not-yet-middle-aged man who'd gotten into sportscasting when his playing days were over.

He was in Boston to audition for the analyst's spot on Red Sox broadcasts when, in a tunnel beneath Boston Harbor, a clot that had been harmlessly lodged in a vessel somewhere decided to relocate closer to his heart. His brother Billy was with him and it didn't take great powers of imagination to smell the fear in that car, Tony C. gasping for air and turning blue as the cognitive parts of his brain checked out, neuron by neuron. He didn't die that day, but during what was left, eight torturous post-stroke years I believe it was, this man who'd hit 100 home runs sooner than any player in history could not wipe the drool from his own chin.

If you wanted to slice it close to the bone, I thought, morosely, stupidly, *that would be the type of game you'd do. End Game, you could call it.* Hadn't Hitchcock and King and Spielberg and all the rest proved what an appetite the public has for death and demise?

Whatever.

I continued past second base and across the pitcher's mound to home plate, remembering the ritual from the days when I was a Little League all-star: rubbing dirt onto my palms, blessing myself, holding the bat straight toward the sky.

I remembered when, not yet a teen, I'd rehearsed it all, scene by super-heroic scene: How by senior year I would be six-three and weigh 190 pounds and be drafted from Blue Hill High straight to Triple A; how in my first year with the Pawtucket Red Sox, Boston's farm team, I'd bat .400, hit 40 homers and knock in 120 RBIs; how midway through my second year, I'd be called up to Boston.

Tony C. would still be playing, and so would Yaz and Lonborg and everyone else from that 1967 Impossible Dream team. Mom and Dad and Sally and all my friends would be there—and they wouldn't be in any bleachers, no sir, but sitting with Tom and Jean Yawkey in their fabled private box. My first game would be against the Yankees, against Mel Stottlemyre, their ace. He'd have heard of this rookie and he'd brush me back with his first pitch to let me know just who was boss. His second pitch would be low and outside, exactly where I liked it, and I would connect and I'd get that incredible rush I always got when I'd sent one out of the park and...

I heard sirens.

Distant, but coming closer.

They'll go past, I thought.

And when they didn't, I thought: *Must be trouble at the club.*

Except they were on the other side of the park, on Yawkey Way. More sirens joined in and now I clearly heard: the squawk of police radios, a major operation underway.

An alarm rang and Fenway's lights started on.

Not emergency lights but the towers—all of them—dim at first, slowly brightening. Fenway was coming alive.

How is this possible? I thought. Had a careless computer

programmer cross-wired alarm and light circuits when shutting down for winter? Did police have a way to activate the towers?

I started running.

This ball is deep! This ball is out of here! Gray rounds first! He's heading into second! He's—wait! Something's wrong folks! He's turned away from second! He's into center field! Headed toward the bleachers! I've never seen anything like it in my life! This ball is out of here and Gray is too! He's over the wall! Into the bleachers! The crowd is stunned! God help us it's Jimmy Piersall all over again in Fear Strikes Out!

I looked back. Cops were fanning out over the field. For one crazy second, I was sure I saw Malloy, leading the charge.

I cleared the gate and was lost in the nightclub crowd, suddenly hushed. Everyone was watching Fenway's lights, burning the December night.

"Are they gonna play?" I heard one guy say.

"Get real," the woman with him answered. "It's almost Christmas."

I arrived in Blue Hill at nine that morning.

How long since I'd been home? Not since 1992, when dad held a service on the twenty-fifth anniversary of my mother's death. There are places that change and places that don't, and I guess my hometown is one that doesn't. I noticed a couple of new houses on the way into town, and that the Duckpond Restaurant had burned, but really, that was the extent of it.

People in Jaguars still parked next to beat-up Ford pickups and lobstermen in their waders still exchanged good-mornings with ladies attired from Talbots. Dad often used such homespun juxtapositions to open one of his sermons.

I parked at Merrill & Hinckley market and walked past Town Hall to Blue Hill Elementary, my old school; past the library and Morton Field, where I played Little League; past Saint Luke's Episcopal Church and rectory, where I'd grown up; and through snow-covered gardens into the cemetery, where Mom is buried.

I found her grave, marked by a simple granite stone. Someone, undoubtedly my father, had left a wreath and Mom's favorite flower: a yellow chrysanthemum.

"I love you, Mom," I said. "I miss you."

God, did I ever.

Profoundly, thirty years later.

Pictures of her in health show a slender woman of delicate beauty whose smile conveys patience and compassion. Mom was a simple person with a heart as big as the state of Maine, uneducated past high school but endowed with a native wisdom no university education could ever impart. She spoiled Dad and me—not with consumer goods, the way I spoiled the adult me, but with cooking and sewing and piano and song. Mom played the organ at service and directed Dad's choir, and she tended the church gardens with an award-winning hand, and told me stories and tucked me into bed every night and came to every one of my practices and games.

I say she was simple, but I mean only that her needs were not substantial.

Mom was frightfully intelligent, well-read, conversant, like Dad, in the topics of the day—the kind of woman who in my generation would have made a name for herself in the outside world. I look back now and I see all the clues: her sense of organization, how effortlessly she juggled household and parish duties, her determination to see a job through, the cozy order she (like Ruth, I realized) brought to our lives. Nothing was ever contentious with Mom—no unpleasant surprises, no emotional jags, nothing ugly or mean. Only common sense and beauty, as in her gardens—only, every now and again, a practical joke, usually at my father's expense. On Mom's calendar, April Fool's was the naughty highlight of the year. At least I got something from that good soul who was my mother.

I've recounted how Mom got sick the summer Dad pulled me from baseball, how she wasn't up to that trip to Fenway the weekend Tony C. got beaned.

She was still in bed when we got home, shivering under afghans and quilts even though it was August. Against Mom's wishes, Dad called Doctor Henderson and he came right out and took one look and said: "I want her in for tests."

The next day, they diagnosed cancer.

I didn't learn for years that it was ovarian cancer—a malignant tumor too big to operate—for Mom and Dad wouldn't get into detail in front of me.

"Everything's going to be fine," they said, but anyone could see it wasn't. Mom wasn't hungry anymore and she couldn't sleep at night and her skin began to take on the color of newspaper left in the sun.

I remember the night she came home from her tests. It couldn't have been September yet—I hadn't started school, and blueberries were still in season.

"I want to climb the hill," she said.

"You can't do that, Mama," my father replied, "you know what the doctor said."

"Well, the doctor's not God," she said, "and neither are you, close to him as you may be. First thing tomorrow morning, we're climbing Blue Hill, aren't we, Mark? And afterwards, I'm going to bake, same as always."

"Can Sally come?" I asked.

"Not this time," Mom said. "You know how dear she is to me, but this time it's going to be just the three of us. And now I'm tired of hearing myself talk. We leave tomorrow at eight."

We'd climbed Blue Hill annually since I was old enough for the trip. I would run ahead and Mom and Dad would bring up the rear and halfway to the top, we'd stop to pick blueberries in a field Mom's grandfather bought for a dollar from a Native American, or so the story went.

The final climb started like any before. Mom sang and Dad looked for birds through his binoculars and I raced ahead, calling out the deadfalls and looking for wildcats, which we'd never seen but which were rumored to be as big and fierce as tigers. Fifteen minutes into it, a third of the way up, Mom couldn't breathe. We stopped, and she couldn't catch her breath, and I knew from his tone how scared Dad was.

"Stay here—I'll get someone," he said.

"You'll do no such thing," Mom managed, "we're going to pick blueberries."

"Mama—" he started, but she'd have none of it. I don't know what strength she summoned, or how much harm she might have done herself, but Dad helped her and even though we had to stop every few minutes, she made it. She filled her bucket and Dad and I filled ours and that afternoon, same as always, she baked pies.

Much of the rest of that fall is hazy in my mind, but not everything.

I remember we all started saying tons of prayers—as a congregation, a family, and each of us alone. A box went up in Saint Luke's for donations. The diocese sent Dad a fill-in pastor so he could care for Mom full-time, for pretty soon she was confined to bed, too weak even for her beloved piano. I would come home from school and go into her room, drapes drawn and smelling of Vick's Vapor Rub. I hated that room. Sometimes a humidifier would be hissing in there, and there was a bedpan and a night table with all kinds of pills next to my baby picture, and, before long, a pole for bottles that connected to Mom with plastic tubes.

But I don't remember ever hearing Mom complain and I know for sure she always greeted me with her customary smile and kiss. She demanded a full accounting of my day and listened with genuine interest—kids can tell the difference— and she always asked how Sally and the rest of my friends were, and would they like to come for dinner, "such as it is with Dad doing the cooking now!"—her idea of a joke, since Sunday dinner, which he always prepared, was a feast fit for a king.

Begrudgingly, I started playing soccer that fall—"It's the least dangerous sport," Dad said—but I was looking ahead to next year and a return to baseball.

Mom considered Dad too harsh on me, a belief she shared only in strictest confidence.

"Let me work on him," she would whisper when he was out of earshot. "By spring, he'll come around, you wait and see. He's never been able to say no to me yet."

Mom died the day after Christmas, 1967.

I'd been playing with my Lionel trains—my only present except for a sweater and boots, which didn't count—and I'd gotten bored and Dad was at the drugstore so I went to see if Mom wanted tea. That's all she'd been taking lately: tea with lots of honey.

"Would you like some tea?" I said.

"I'd love some," she said, her words labored, "but first there's something I want you to have."

Hands shaking, she opened a small embroidered box I'd never seen before; where she'd kept it, and how being so sick she'd managed to get it from that safe place, are mysteries to me still. Ten silver dollars, as shiny as if they'd been minted that morning, were inside.

"Wow!" I said. "They're beautiful."

"They were my grandfather's," Mom said. "He gave them to me only after I vowed to save them for someone very special. You, Mark, are very special."

"Oh, Mom," I said, "you shouldn't."

"Well, yes I should," she said. "Now be a sweetie and go get my tea. But first, a nice hug and a kiss."

When I returned, Mom was perfectly still.

"Here's your tea," I said, setting it on her night table.

She didn't answer.

"Mom?" I screamed. "Mom? Are you all right?"

I grabbed her hand. It was cold, and her fingers seemed stiff, but it was her eyes that scared me most. They were open, but she wasn't seeing with them. They were shiny but dry and she didn't blink, not even a faint flutter of eyelash, and all I could think of was the deer carcass Sally and I had found that fall near Blue Hill—how we'd looked at it, marveled over it, and finally poked it everywhere with sticks, even the eyeballs... How bad we'd been, how wicked we both felt after, how ashamed but strangely courageous.

"No, Mom!" I screamed. "NO!"

I heard Dad's VW coming up the drive then. The front door opened and Dad must have known immediately, must have recognized the presence of death, for he'd ministered to the dying since before I was born.

"You didn't say she was going to die!" I screamed. "Why didn't you save her? You're a priest!"

"I'm only human," he said, and maybe time has colored the memory, but as I hear his voice now, no one ever sounded so defeated.

I left the cemetery through what might have been one of Mom's gardens.

I wonder if anything she planted still grows here, I thought, and decided it was good I didn't know. I wanted to see my old room, in the St. Luke's rectory. I wanted to stand in it, recreate it in my mind as it was before Mom got sick: the posters of Carl Yastrzemski and Tony C., the nature books, my seashell collection, the quilt Mom made for my birthday, my Little League trophies, the comics I hid under my bed, which Mom knew about but had promised not to tell Dad. I knocked on the rectory door, but no one answered. Dad had retired ten years ago. I'd never met his replacement. I'd have to settle for a glimpse of my old school.

The door to Blue Hill Elementary was unlocked. I found the janitor and he gave me permission to visit. I wandered, surprised to remember the names of all my teachers, and where I sat in every grade, and the scene the day that poor Billy Collins threw up at lunch—the sort of stuff that lodges in your brain for no good reason.

But mostly, I thought of Sally.

Until high school, she lived across the street from the rectory. My mom and hers were best friends, and her dad was a deacon in Dad's church, and at least once a year, we all climbed Blue Hill together. Sally grew her hair long in high school, but back then she had a pageboy with bangs cut straight over her brown eyes. She favored jeans and she liked what boys liked: climbing trees, catching frogs, playing cowboys and Indians. She probably had Barbie dolls, but I don't remember them—I remember her garter snake, and her aquarium, and her CCM hockey skates, same as mine. About the only thing she couldn't do was play Little League, for girls at that time were not allowed. I bet she would have been good.

There was more than common interest to our friendship.

I understand that now, in a way you can't when you're a kid. I had lots of buddies growing up, and we did all the usual boy stuff together, but it was Sally I was drawn to on a deeper level. I don't profess to know if this is ordinary or not: a boy being best friends with a girl at such an age. We sometimes got teased for being in love, but there was nothing romantic between us at that early stage; I mean, we were only eight or nine. Sally was just different than all the rest, boy or girl—forgiving, kind, not competitive. Like Mom, uncomplicated—unacceptably provincial, as I would come to believe during my revisionist period, which started freshman year in college.

I ran to Sally's when the undertaker came for Mom. I cried and she hugged me and that helped. She sat with me at the funeral and later, she listened whenever I went on about my father, who, on the day Mom died, I'd started to hate. I really did believe he could have saved her.

"God wanted your mom," Sally would say, "and God is more powerful than even a priest."

"He could've done more," I'd say.

And Sally would reply: "He did the best he could."

But I didn't believe that, not then.

"This room is locked," I said to the janitor.

"I'll let you in," he said, "but only for a minute. I'm off at noon."

It was my fourth-grade classroom—modernized of course, the chalkboards green not black, a touchtone phone on the wall, a color TV and Apple computers in a corner. For all I knew, kids here regularly logged onto CreativeLine.

But like Blue Hill itself, nothing essential had changed: the flag, the clock, the alphabet over the board, the names of kids written in neat teacher's hand over coat hooks. In my time, the TV was black-and-white and was used mostly to watch rocket launches. Rockets were big with me then, bigger than anything but baseball. Even my father, who hated his government for its napalm and killing, took pride in the space program.

"This," he said, "was where President Kennedy wanted to take us. To where the human spirit is free to soar and everyone is equal."

I didn't know about grandiose notions like that. I only knew the excitement of thundering flame propelling steel, slowly at first, as if the whole thing were some mad scientist's experiment doomed to exploding failure—then speeding up, faster than a car, faster than a jet, faster than anything, growing smaller until it was thumbnail-sized and then a speck and finally invisible, only the voice of mission control to prove it really existed: a calm and deep voice, like I imagined God himself, The Big Guy, must sound.

Once on Memory Lane, I couldn't stop.

I remembered the summer of 1968, when Dad and I went to Bangor for the Fourth of July parade. Dad's parish group, Pax Universum, took the bus with us. My Lai was in the news—that's all Dad talked about that summer, My Lai, My Lai—and they had handmade signs—I will never forget them—that said "BABY KILLERS" and "CALLEY'S COWARDS" and "VIET CONG ARE GOD'S CHILDREN TOO."

I hated Pax Universum, which was mostly grey-haired ladies and men with ponytails and beards—men who chopped their own wood and wrote poetry and lived with women who never shaved their legs, women very different from my mom. Parade-watchers spit on Pax Universum and called them pinkos and fags and when, led by Dad, they lay down in the street in front of the Twenty-second Infantry, I ran—to the Elks float, which was carrying Johnny Bailey, Maine's only native-son astronaut.

I knew Johnny's story from the library: how he'd graduated from Bangor High, gone to the Naval Academy, flown combat in Korea, joined the Blue Angels before being chosen for the Apollo program. I wanted to be like him—a tall, muscular, crew-cut man wearing sunglasses and an orange flight suit with his name in gold. You could tell, just looking at him, that Johnny Bailey didn't drive any VW bug or hang around any guys with ponytails, and certainly didn't date women with hairy legs. I got Johnny Bailey's autograph that Fourth of July. I still had it, in the drawer with Sally's letters and the scrapbook of Tony C.

Dad bought me Estes model rockets after that.

All the rockets I wanted—rockets with two stages and three stages and multi-colored parachutes and cameras that took pictures of you below on the ground.

Don't look for the logic here—I have, never sure of what I've found. Afraid of a baseball, Dad provided me solid explosives; opposed to Vietnam, he encouraged a passion for a weapon of war. I mean, I could have been pretending they were ICBMs, for all he knew.

Sally liked rockets, too. We'd take them to the blueberry barrens and she'd be the voice of mission control and I'd have my finger on the button and we'd both feel it at ignition: breathtaking excitement, as if we were blasting off for the moon. That fall, Sally's father drove us to the Brunswick Naval Air Station for the Blue Angels show. We watched Star Trek together every week and she was with me the night the next summer, 1969, that Neil Armstrong planted a flag on the moon. Sally was going to be an astronaut, too—the very first American spacewoman.

One day after my thirteenth birthday, when my father had gone with Pax Universum to a demonstration in Portland, Sally and I hitchhiked to Bangor Airport. I'd read in the paper about flight lessons: with parental permission, kids my age could enroll. All they needed was a birth certificate and a $50 deposit. Sally helped with the money.

"So, you want to be an astronaut," the guy at the counter said.

"I'm going to be a Navy pilot first," I said. "I want to fly F-4 Phantoms."

"It's a fine aircraft, young man," the guy said. "Flew 'em myself with Johnny Bailey."

"You know Johnny Bailey?"

I was in awe.

"Sure do. Grew up with him. He's a heck of a flyer. Now let's see what you have here."

I handed him my birth certificate and a letter from dad I'd forged on parish stationery.

"Dad's a minister, huh?"

"Actually, an Episcopal priest."

"You sure he wrote this?"

"Scout's honor," I said. "You could call him."

I figured if I said that, he wouldn't.

The counter guy made some comment about how clergy must be like doctors, at least as far as their penmanship is concerned, and let it go. You could tell he really wanted me to fly.

"Okay," he said. "Step around here."

Through the window, I could see the tarmac. The National Guard flew F-101s out of here, and there they were: delta wings tucked back like bald eagles at rest. I saw a DC-9 and a slew of private planes, including Piper Cubs the Bangor Flight School flew. The Cub was a single-engine runt of a plane, but nothing ever looked more thrilling.

The instructor directed my attention to an eye chart.

"Read the top line," he said.

I started to read.

"Without your glasses," the guy said.

"Without my glasses?"

"That's the rule. Have to have at least twenty-forty uncorrected. That's down to the sixth line."

"What if I only get to four?"

"We need six, young man. Now go ahead."

I got the top two lines and could make out enough of the third to guess correctly. From the fourth line down, I got everything wrong.

"I'm sorry," the man said.

"Can't I try again?"

"Sorry," the guy said.

I was fighting tears, and something else: anger, as dark as when my mother died.

I left the school and walked to The Eggemoggin Reach Diner, where I ordered the special of the day, then called Sally from the pay phone.

She said her nursing-home shift ended at three; she would meet me at East Blue Hill Beach half an hour later. As I was returning to my booth, a driver was filling the honor box with the late edition of the Bangor Daily News, my hometown rag. I bought one. My picture was on the front page—first time since my all-star Little League days.

CHAPTER FOURTEEN

This was the story:

SOCIETY STALKER'LINKED
TO NATIONAL PROSTITUTION RING
Blue Hill Native Remains on Run
by
ROBERT D. JONES
Associated Press

NEW YORK—*Software mogul Mark Gray, 42, subject of a nationwide manhunt in connection with the gruesome holiday deaths of two Boston women, is a central figure in a high-price prostitution ring allegedly involving Manhattan socialite Allison Manchester, the Associated Press has learned.*

"Gray was the force behind it," Detective Brian Malloy said this morning, after a source who declined to be identified contacted the AP.

Disclosure of the ring came as Manchester's condition was upgraded from critical to serious at Beth Israel Hospital, where she has been hospitalized since being found unconscious and nude in her upscale Manhattan apartment early this week. Manchester, 27, was able to speak to police for the first time, but Malloy refused to elaborate on her comments. Gray is wanted on a charge of attempted murder in the attack on Manchester.

"All I can say at this preliminary juncture is that we're investigating the distinct possibility that Miss Manchester was coerced or even blackmailed by Gray," Malloy said, refusing further comment.

Nothing about Allison's co-conspirators or the many juicy details on her hard drive, including her extensive list of clients.

So, Malloy was playing hardball. No worries about the backup tape and JPEGs, perhaps he had concluded; given my brilliance with virtual reality, the public would surely believe they all were fake. Which was not out of the realm of possibility.

I read on:

Manchester's father, banker and New York Knicks co-owner George W. Manchester Jr., denied his daughter was involved in any way with prostitution.

"It's simply preposterous," he said in a statement. "I know my daughter better than anyone and I can assure you she hasn't had a date lately—never mind this garbage."

In a related development, Boston police confirmed that they have traced Gray, who remains at large, to a room in a Sheraton Hotel in that city. Gray checked out hours after a near-riot in the Copley Place Mall, caused when the suspect was identified by a security guard and several shoppers.

Gray has not been formally charged with the deaths of the two women, but sources say he is the only suspect at this point. A prominent video-games developer, Gray was this year's winner of a Wilbur, his industry's highest award.

Police have refused comment on a broadcast report that cannibalism may have been the motive of the killer. Bite marks allegedly were found on the body of two women found strangled in Boston, according to the television report.

The Bangor Daily News had reprinted a sidebar from *The New York Times* about Allison Manchester's mother, the late Libby O'Reilly, a minor actress and model from the '60s. So, this was Mom—Libby Love, as she called herself, a woman who'd gotten her fifteen minutes hanging with Hendrix and Morrison.

The paper ran an old photo. The hair, the eyes, those lips— it was Allison, all right. Reading the profile of Allison's father, George W. Manchester Jr., I felt a certain empathy.

George Jr. met O'Reilly in 1968, when he was 32. After a string of business failures largely underwritten by his father, the late banker and philanthropist George W. Manchester, Sr., the son had invested in Morning Records, an upstart company in Los Angeles. It became a hot label, signing rocks acts such as Canned Heat, Iron Butterfly and Peyote Express, among others.

"Libby had already slept her way through half those guys when she met Junior," The Times quoted Tommy Miller, lead guitarist for the '60s band Peyote Express, now the owner of a Beverly Hills sushi bar.

"I remember how turned on she was after a weekend on his yacht," Miller recalled. "She came back with a gold necklace and diamond earrings. They were married a month later."

According to the paper, Libby walked out on Manchester in 1970, less than two years after marrying.

"That's when she met Janis Joplin," Miller said. "They fell head over heels for each other. Libby dumped George one weekend. I remember her saying capitalist pigs didn't belong in the Woodstock generation. Then, of course, Janis died. Libby was heartbroken."

Heartbreak apparently propelled her briefly back to Manchester, and she became pregnant by him in late 1971.

"Everyone figured she'd have an abortion," Miller recalled, "but she didn't. I don't think it was religion or anything—she just thought a baby would be groovy."

Allison O'Reilly Manchester was born in 1972 in New York. The next year, court records showed, Libby divorced Manchester, who successfully petitioned the court for sole custody of the baby. "A kid was like everything else in Libby's life," Miller said. "After a few months, it was time to move on to the next happening thing. Unlike most of the rest of us, her looks let her get away with it—until she hit thirty and that lifestyle began to take its toll."

According to The Times, the remainder of Libby's life was a descent into addiction and debauchery.

She took up with an exiled Thai prince, gravitated toward Andy Warhol, had an affair with Edie Sedgwick, published a book of nude photographs of herself, and died, in 1985, at the age of 37, of a heroin overdose behind a building in SoHo. From what The Times could glean, Libby only ever had occasional contact with her daughter—just enough, apparently, to really do a number on her head.

Rounding out the Society Stalker package in today's *Bangor Daily News* was the local angle—belatedly, their intrepid staff had discovered a native son at the center of New England's juiciest story. Dad had declined to talk and no one had gotten to Sally or Ruth, leaving their reporter to cobble together quotes from old teachers, as in this breathtaking insight from Miss Lamoureax, who taught me in second grade: "He was so quiet."

I shouldn't bitch—after the beating I was taking in New York and Boston, pablum was welcome.

The piece ended with the appearance of an old friend:

"He was one of the brightest people I ever met," said Bud Robbins, a producer at Viacom's Paramount Pictures whose films include last summer's box-office smash The Doors and many others. Robbins was Gray's college roommate. They met in eighth grade, when Robbins moved to Blue Hill from New York City.

"He wanted to do everything and he had the talent for it all," Robbins said on the telephone from Los Angeles, where he is producing Batman V, starring Jack Nicholson, who is recreating his 1989 role as The Joker.

"I think the problem for Mark was being unfocused—at least until he got into software, where, as I understand it, he made a killing," Robbins said.

Asked if he knew of anything in Gray's past that indicated he was capable of murder, Robbins said no.

"He had so much ahead of him," the filmmaker said. "It's sad it had to end like this. He really was a star in his own movie."

I read those four paragraphs, over and over, becoming increasingly disturbed.

Not from reading Bud would be producing Jack Nicholson—there was ample irony there, but Bud had worked tirelessly, he had talent and instinct, and deserved everything he got.

And not the dig about me being unfocused—that was a polite description of my early adult life, and it kindly ignored all sorts of skeletons Bud knew were buried in my past.

No, it was how Bud spoke of me: in the past tense, as if I were dead.

So much ahead of him…sad it had to end like this….

Well, a big-time Hollywood guy like him ought to be careful: it could be over for him just as swiftly.

I contemplated calling Bud to deliver that cheery caution, but my attention was diverted. A cop had come into the diner. After buying a paper, he took the booth next to me.

Shit, I thought. *It's Officer Bill.*

Officer Bill, who'd come to Blue Hill Elementary every year to teach safe bicycling and fire prevention. Officer Bill, who administered the Lions Club eye tests and, it was rumored, played Santa Claus at Saint Luke's annual Christmas party. I would never forget him.

"Ribs?" the waitress, a young woman of about 20, said.

"Thank you," I said.

She set the plate down in front of me. I hid behind my paper.

"Scary, ain't it?" the waitress said. "Finding out a cannibal grew up in town."

"Very scary," I agreed from behind my *Daily News*.

"I guess I was born after he left. But it still gives you the creeps. What do you think—was he eating people even then? Like missing people they ain't never found?"

"Boy, I don't know."

"And his father was a clergyman! Still lives here, as a matter of fact. I've served him breakfast. Nice old guy—always leaves a good tip. Makes you wonder who you can trust anymore."

"Maybe he didn't do it," I said.

"Oh, no," she insisted. "He did it. One look at them eyes"— she tapped the front-page mugshot of me—"and you know. The thing I wanna know is what he does with the bones. It's wicked hard to get rid of bones, you know. Heck, you run a plate of them ribs there down the disposal and nine times outta ten you blow the fuse. Well, enjoy your lunch."

I was hiding in the sports pages when a voice interrupted.

"Ribs," Officer Bill said, "no matter how careful you are

eating them, they still make a bloody mess, don't they?"

I nearly choked.

"Here," he said, handing me a napkin. "You've got sauce on your face."

I wiped my mouth.

"Thank you," I said.

"We know each other, don't we," Officer Bill said.

"I'm afraid not."

"Sure we do. I remember how you used to hit a baseball. Fifth grade, and you had the swing of a high school senior, no exaggeration. Much as I respect your father, I'm not sure I agree with his decision to take you out of the game."

Officer Bill opened his own paper to the sports section.

"We'd have been reading about you here, not the front page," he said.

"I don't know what you're talking about," I said.

"Then again, I happen to know first-hand your eyesight *was* going bad," Officer Bill continued, so pleasantly you'd think we were best buddies. "Not that there haven't been fine players with glasses."

"You must be mistaken," I said, weakly.

Was I losing my mind, or had he finally gone senile? I was the Society Stalker, for Christ's sake! The Cannibal who stole Christmas! The asinine Naked Ass! I was the biggest criminal Officer Bill would ever have a shot at bringing in, and he wanted to talk ball?

"You know what I thought when I first heard about all this?" Officer Bill said.

He turned back to the front page.

"What?"

"That they'd made a big mistake."

"You really thought that?"

"I did. You know what I think now, after a goddamn week of it?"

I shook my head.

"That they've made the kind of big mistake somebody ought to hang for. Cannibalism—I laughed out loud when I read that about Pastor Gray's boy. Of course, that's the world today. These things get a life of their own and before you know it, it's like a giant snowball rolling down a hill. It gets bigger and bigger and faster and faster until nobody can stop it. That's the media for you. Look what they did to poor Princess Diana."

Now would have been my chance to bolt. But I was paralyzed.

"I've known killers, Mark. Not many, but enough to speak to the subject. I've looked into their backgrounds, talked to their parents and teachers and the folks next door—even, sadly enough, known a couple personally, from when they were knee-high to a grasshopper. In every case, you knew by adolescence where they were headed in life. You weren't anything like that. Oh, you had your moments—what kid doesn't, especially one who loses his mom at such a tender age? My guess is you met this New York lady and fell for her—the kind of falling that makes a red-blooded young man's head spin. Who wouldn't—a looker like that?"

He called to the waitress for a refill.

"The bottom line is you didn't have an ounce of luck, if that's what a pastor's boy ought properly to call it. A hundred guys cheat on their wives for every one that gets caught—and you're that one. Don't get me wrong: I'm not condoning it, just saying it could happen to anyone. Heck, that's the whole plot of half the movies and books these days. Anyway, here you are forty-whatever, if memory serves me, and you figure one last fling before it's too late—and wham! Fate crushes you like a bug on a windshield."

I liked that: *Like a bug on a windshield*. It was better than any of my metaphors.

"Of course, the flip side is: sooner or later you've got to face the music."

"I intend to," I said.

"'Cause that's part of being a man, too."

"I know," I said, "I just have a couple of things to do first."

"Related to your dad?"

"That's one of them."

"Is Sally another?"

Lord. Was my entire life an open book?

"Why would you say that?" I said.

"Just a hunch, is all. I won't put you on the spot. What I *will* do is hold off on bringing you in. How much time do you need?"

"A day. Two at most."

"No more, Mark. I'll be on real thin ice as it is, waiting forty-eight hours."

"I promise."

"Forty-eight hours or I'll have the Maine State Police here with their SWAT team. I'll bring in your dad for harboring a fugitive, if I have to."

"You have my word."

"No one goes back on his word to Officer Bill."

"Thanks, Officer Bill," I said.

I reached for my wallet, but he restrained my hand.

"The ribs," he said with a smile, "are on me."

"Thanks," I said.

"Now you get your pantless behind out of here," he said, roaring with laughter.

I drove to the mall at Ellsworth, a few miles outside Blue Hill, and bought jeans, flannel shirt, boots, a leather jacket and Old Spice, the cologne Sally gave me Christmas of senior year. Then I checked into a Holiday Inn, where I showered and shaved. Thank God, I was able to rinse most of the dye from my hair and the tanning creme was wearing off: I was dark, but no darker than from an hour or two in the sun, and the streaks were gone.

East Blue Hill Beach was deserted when I arrived.

The tide was coming in and dark clouds hugged the water. A northeast wind was kicking up and the temperature was dropping. I'd be surprised if we didn't have snow by tomorrow.

This had been our place—one of them, anyway.

Before the summer that everything changed, this was where we came to beachcomb, to picnic and swim on those precious few days the Maine water didn't turn your skin blue. Mom and Sally's mom loved the beach and if I had to guess, it was here that Sally and I first sensed that someday we'd be more than friends.

I remembered the summer after eighth grade, how girls

in our class started wearing bikinis—how relieved I was that Sally didn't. Those older girls confused me. And I remembered the next summer, when Sally grew her hair and her figure developed—how, by autumn, there was no denying: like last year's bikinied classmates, she was no longer a little girl. I was becoming less confused by then.

I'd changed myself by then, in lots of ways.

I was openly defiant of my father, ignoring curfews, refusing to help out around the house, slamming my bedroom door when I was sick of him, which was most days. I'd told him—often, and in no uncertain terms—exactly what I thought of Pax Universum, Volkswagens, Episcopalianism, God, math teachers, and his Sunday dinners.

I'd snuck my first cigarette, with Bud, and had my first booze: a bottle of port wine we smuggled out of the Saint Luke's sacristy. I'd bought my first Playboy. I'd dropped my paper route and demanded an allowance, unsuccessfully. I'd put on weight—okay, nothing like now—and was within an inch or two of my adult height. I got into Led Zeppelin, the Stones and Lennon; my hair was down to my shoulders; and I refused to shave.

Maybe it was because we'd known each other so long that Sally and I progressed to dating with so little awkwardness. I don't believe we fumbled the first time we held hands, here on East Blue Hill Beach that fall; or were nervous the first time we kissed, by a fire after pond-skating on a January afternoon, or hesitated the first time I reached under her blouse, in the back of Bud's mother's car that spring. I only remember how amazing everything felt, how right, how we stayed awake nights in our beds hurting to be with each other.

By the end of sophomore year, we were a confirmed couple.

Dad cautioned me about too far too fast, but a lot of attention I paid. Bud was steady with Jane Rogers and his stepbrother was old enough to buy booze and we all started getting tanked pretty regularly on Pabst Blue Ribbon and Boone's Farm. In August, Bud's cousin sailed up from Connecticut on his family's yacht, bringing with him half a pound of Columbian, my introduction to weed. I got my license but declined Dad's offer to take his

VW. Sally got her license and her father let her borrow his '68 Cadillac, and as soon as we were out of sight of her house, she took the passenger seat so I could drive.

And as Sally drove up to East Blue Hill that eve of Christmas Eve in the year of the madness, I was thinking that the first time we made love, Allison Manchester had not been born.

I recognized the car immediately—it was Sally's father's Cadillac. He must have left it to her when he died. It was still in decent shape, shiny finish and barely any rust. Somebody had babied it. Only the grumble of the muffler suggested its age.

"Hello, Sally," I said.

"Hello, Mark."

I smiled and Sally smiled and for a moment, we studied each other's faces.

I don't know what she saw in mine—the buffoon lately in the news, or the first boy she'd kissed, or someone else entirely, some stranger she'd agreed to meet for reasons she couldn't articulate and might regret.

And me?

I did not see the image I'd carried all these years of Sally: the brown-haired, brown-eyed young woman who brought to mind a Van Morrison tune. I saw the first traces of crow's feet and makeup applied with an unsophisticated though not clumsy hand. I couldn't tell if she'd touched up her hair, but I didn't remember henna highlights. Even her lips looked different. She was wearing lipstick. She never had before. Never makeup, either.

She's a middle-aged woman, I thought.

Like aging had exempted me.

"I brought you this," I said, handing her a white rose.

"It's beautiful," she said. "Thanks."

"Stupid me," I said. "Now it's going to freeze."

"Not under my parka, it won't," she said.

She slid the rose under her coat. I made some dumb remark about thorns and Sally laughed.

"It's wrapped," she said. "Relax."

"Want to walk the beach?" I said.

"Sure," she said. "It's been a long time."

"A very long time."

We set off, across mud flats toward the surf.

I was behind Sally, wondering, despite myself, what she looked like without clothes. I remembered the first garment I ever bought a girl: a white halter top I gave Sally on her sixteenth birthday in a box wrapped in red paper and sealed with a ribbon and white rose. I remember how she went into her bedroom and when she came out, she was wearing it and cutoff jeans, and no bra. I remembered later, her parents out for the night, how Sally took everything off, then slid my head down her body.

"So how have you been?" she said.

"Considering everything, I've been okay."

"Considering everything," Sally said, "you're lucky to be alive. You look great, by the way."

"Thanks. So do you," I said, and I meant it. Looking past the years, I saw my girl.

"I do think you look much better in real life than on TV," she said

She giggled.

"What's so funny?" I said.

"That video. You know—"

"The Naked Ass Shot, I call it. It doesn't get any more embarrassing than that, believe me."

"That's not what I thought when I saw it."

"What did you think?"

"How you always had such a cute butt."

"Nice to see some things never change, isn't it?" I said.

We both cracked up at that, and the laughter opened something, because our conversation was suddenly animated. I heard details of Sally's divorce from a small-town cop who was a decent enough dad but couldn't keep his hands off other women. I talked about Ruth and Timmy, albeit without details of his paternity, and I took a gratifying shot at old Syd. Sally told of bumping into my dad now and again; of her job in a nursing home, low-paying but rewarding helping others like that, she said; of our first-grade teacher, Miss Biddle, who'd died last winter; of Jane Rogers, who'd married at 19 and was now, could you believe it, a grandmother.

I told Sally of how I'd always hoped to move back here, or at least have a summer place. It was not the complete truth, but somehow it was the right thing to say.

"You're wearing Old Spice," Sally said when we reached a lull.

It was almost dark now.

"Is it too strong?"

"No. I'm just surprised you remembered."

"I remember a lot."

"So do I."

I looked seaward, at waves that had turned Blue Hill Bay angry. Further out, the unprotected ocean would be treacherous. On nights like this, my father always offered a prayer for mariners; when she was alive, Mom always joined in. Her grandfather, the guy who'd bought Blue Hill's blueberry fields from a Native American for a dollar, had been lost at sea on a night like this. His body had never been recovered, which meant no funeral or grave to ever visit.

"Can I ask you something?" Sally said.

"Anything you want."

"Why'd you call?"

I'd been expecting that question. I still didn't have the answer.

"I found the ring," I explained, "going through your letters."

I dug into my pocket and offered it to Sally, but she wouldn't take it.

Suddenly, the circumstances of our last encounter were with us—heavy and low, and nasty, like the clouds.

You stupid fuck, I thought. *What possessed you to do that?*

"I want you to have it," I said, struggling.

"Why?"

"Because it's yours."

"*Was* mine."

"Please?"

Sally took the ring, but she wouldn't wear it. Rather, she slipped it into her pocket.

"Things didn't turn out like we planned, did they?" I said,

and that sentence sounds monumentally stupid now, but then—then, it seemed profound.

"They never do," Sally said. "The older you get, you learn that. And when you do, you reach a place of peace."

A place of peace.

How I envied her, this girl who'd become this woman.

We left the beach and climbed quite some distance, to the top of a granite ledge bordered by pines. The wind was stronger here and I wished I had gloves and hat, as Sally did.

"Do you remember this ledge?" I said.

"Of course."

"We used to fish off here when the tide was high. What were we in—fourth grade?"

"Something like that."

"Mom was always afraid we'd fall."

"Mothers are like that. I remember the time you told me about sharks that could crawl out of the ocean. I really believed you, for a while."

"I think that was the beginning of my infantile practical jokes."

"I wouldn't call them infantile," Sally said. "Sophomoric, maybe."

We laughed.

"I have other memories of here," I said.

"One stronger than the rest," Sally said.

"Graduation night."

"It seems like a million years ago."

"Maybe it was," I said. "Maybe everything went into a time warp and here we are, back again."

I know—that sounds stupider than my last stupid comment. But if Sally took it that way, she didn't let on.

Moving closer to her, I smelled Shalimar perfume, always her favorite; in one of those inexplicably weird coincidences, it was Ruth's, too. I thought I also smelled whiskey, but I couldn't be sure.

I wanted to kiss Sally and feel the swell of her breasts. I wanted it to be summer, and sunrise, over a flat blue sea.

"We better go," Sally said, "before it's completely dark."
She squeezed my hand, fleetingly.

"You're right," I said.

"We wouldn't want to get stranded here. Not with a storm coming on."

"No," I said, "not with a storm coming on."

We walked in silence until we got to our cars.

"Well," I said, "I guess this is it."

"Where do you go now?" Sally asked.

"Maybe my father's," I said. "Maybe the Blue Hill Inn. I'm not sure I'm quite ready for Dad yet."

"But you *will* see him before he goes."

That seemed important to her.

"Of course," I said.

"Since you don't have plans," Sally said, "would you like to have dinner?"

"I'd love to," I said, too eagerly.

"I'll even cook," Sally said.

It had been an old joke, how she had trouble boiling water.

"You don't have to go to that bother," I said.

"I want to. Just don't expect any of that gourmet stuff you get at home."

"Are you kidding?" I said. "We live on macaroni and cheese. It's Timmy's favorite.

"Then maybe I have a chance."

"What about your kids?"

"They're with their father," Sally said, "until tomorrow night."

"You're sure it wouldn't be a bother?" I said.

"Do you think I would have asked if it was? Take your car. You can follow me."

CHAPTER FIFTEEN

We drove through downtown Blue Hill, past shuttered summer places and Victorian mansions with candles in the windows. Just before the intersection where Route 15 hooks east to Deer Isle, we took a gravel road that winds through woods. A mile later, we were on a cul-de-sac, and it was like being teleported into Stephen King's *Cujo*. I saw a trailer, and an old bungalow with plastic over the windows, and a tarpaper shack behind a yard littered with junk cars and rusted washing machines and refrigerators.

And I thought:

Please not one of these. I couldn't deal with that. What a bummer of an end to the script.

I was spared.

A narrow driveway cut between the trailer and the cottage, and we traveled down it some distance to a white ranch. It was a modest structure, three bedrooms at most, in need of paint, no garage, a jungle gym and swing set in the yard, apple and cherry trees to one side, a cord of stove lengths by the door. The door had a wreath with a bright red bow, and a single strand of twinkling lights was strung on the rhododendron bush by the steps.

"Home sweet home," Sally said as she let us in.

"It's nice," I said.

"You're just saying that," she said. "Compared to your place, it's a shack."

"What do you know about my place?" I said.

"Everything—it was all in that *Wired* story. You think we don't follow your career in Blue Hill?"

"Native son stars in *Silence of the Lambs*," I said.

The line fell flat.

"Let me take your coat," Sally said, stomping the snow from her feet.

We were in the largest room in the house: a combination dining and living room with carpeting worn to the matting in spots. The couch was Naugahyde, repaired with duct tape, and the Barcalounger was frayed, but so what? I knew without having to ask that Sally had made the quilts and pillows. I knew she'd cut the Christmas tree and custom-crafted the ornaments, and while they weren't exactly my taste, I appreciated the spirit behind the knick-knacks so carefully arranged on the fireplace mantel. A manger scene and advent calendar occupied the top of the TV. I noticed the baby Jesus had not been placed in the cradle yet.

"Don't mind the mess," Sally said. "Kids, you know."

"Mess? This is my idea of comfort."

"Aren't you nice."

"I'm serious," I said. "I live with the czar of clean."

"My ex-husband was like that," Sally said. "Even had the spices arranged in alphabetical order. The day he moved out, I mixed them all up. Made me feel a world better. Come on into the kitchen. I'll crank up the fire."

The kitchen was small, with a worn linoleum floor and one of those '50s Formica snack bars—but here again, she'd imparted her touch. Plants filled the windows and copper pots lined the pegboard over the Glenwood stove. Her canning filled shelves, and a fresh-baked apple pie was on the counter. She had hand-dipped candles in pewter holders and many straw baskets.

This was a safe place, an honest and real place, not some yuppie fantasy from the money-grubbing mind of Martha Stewart. Or mine, at the time the madness set in.

Sally stoked the Glenwood while I stood by the refrigerator. It was covered with crayoned skaters, water-color ocean scenes, paper snowflakes, and two $20 food stamps secured with a magnet next to a clip with five- and ten-cent coupons.

"That's what you're reduced to when your ex is six months behind on child support," Sally said.

"I wasn't looking at those," I said. "I was admiring the drawings. You have talented kids."

"Thanks. I love them terribly."

"How old are they?"

"Susan is eight. Paul is six."

"Same as my Timmy."

"I bet he's cute."

"He is."

"What else could he be, given his genes?"

She meant it as a compliment. I wondered if she noticed how pointedly I did not respond.

"Care for a drink?" she said. "I've got beer, wine, Jim Beam if you don't mind drinking the last of the ex's. I keep forgetting to tell him to take it when he drops off the kids."

"What are you having?"

"Wine."

"Make it two."

Sally brought out a bottle of 1992 Foxen Pinot Noir, from an obscure winemaker in the hills above Santa Barbara. I recognized it—Ruth had had a case air-freighted in last spring for a Harvard College Century Club event she'd organized for Harvard President Neil Rudenstine. It was an exquisite wine, thirty dollars a bottle, rarely seen outside of California—the kind of wine you'd happily become an alcoholic for, given unlimited supply.

I tried to remember if Sally had liked fine wine, or any wine. All I could recall her ever drinking was beer.

"How did you know this was my favorite wine?" I said.

"A little birdie must have told me."

It was one of her favorite lines, once upon a time.

"That's right," I said, "they mentioned it in *Wired*. Where'd you get it?"

"I have my ways."

I swirled my glass, sniffed, and tasted.

"Delicious," I said. "The best."

"Don't be shy," Sally said. "I have another bottle."

The heat from the Glenwood brought a cat out of hiding from another room and I sat at the table while Sally took a recycled Cool Whip container of her spaghetti sauce from the freezer and went to work. We ate in the dining room, on china that looked like it was probably used only at Easter and Thanksgiving. It was a tremendous meal—sauce, angel hair pasta, home-baked bread and Caesar salad, the only course for which she consulted, briefly, a cookbook.

"I suppose you grew the tomatoes for the sauce," I said.

"Actually, I did," Sally said, "the peppers, onions and oregano, too."

"Wasn't there a time when you couldn't make instant oatmeal?" I said.

"I guess motherhood does that to you," Sally said. "One of the wonderful things."

We finished the first bottle of wine and had dessert: vanilla ice cream and blueberry-apple pie. I was full, and warm, and the smell of spices and smoke reminded me of Mom's kitchen.

For the first time since Alison's email, I'd stopped running.

I found the scrapbook nosing around in the living room while Sally cleared the table and opened the second bottle of Foxen. It was in bookcase filled with paperbacks, old *National Geographic*s, and hardcover library books, mostly mysteries and how-tos.

I was looking when Sally said: "Oh, that old thing. Don't look at that."

"I already did," I said.

Sally joined me on the couch.

It was a thick scrapbook, started by her folks when their daughter was born.

There they were at her christening, her first birthday, steadying her on her first bike. There was Sally in kindergarten, on East Blue Hill Beach, on the swing set when the Martins lived near Saint Luke's. This is where I entered, around first grade. Sally had a Polaroid of me in my Little League uniform, clippings of the year we went to the regionals, a shot of me and her with a model rocket. She had my mother's obituary and a photo of a bishop visiting my dad.

I was getting creeped out.

Sally kept flipping through—past pictures from our eighth-grade dance, our sophomore semi-formal, and both proms. She had shots of us lying on the beach, hiking Blue Hill, and in her father's car. There she was the night of her sweet-sixteen birthday, in that halter top holding a white rose between her teeth. There we were in Halloween costumes senior year: she as Faye Dunaway, me Jack Nicholson. In the background, you could see Bud, dressed as Clint Eastwood. He was holding a can of Budweiser, "the beer they named me after," he used to call it.

"Bud's party," Sally said. "Remember?"

"We got plastered."

"You did your Jack Nicholson imitation."

"Pathetic."

"Not even. It was like watching *Chinatown* again. God, how I loved your Jack Nicholson imitations."

Chinatown—it was my first Nicholson film.

I saw it with Sally at the old Bangor Drive-in, long gone.

It was fall of senior year, and on any other night we'd have been in the back seat of Mr. Martin's car. This night was different. From the opening scene, I was blown away. I'd never seen anyone like Nicholson before, in real life or on the screen. The way he walked, the way he talked, how he told the joke in that great scene with Faye Dunaway, that sneer, those eyes, so cocky and full of mischief—I wanted to be him. Seventeen years old, and star-struck for the first time. Not since Tony Conigliaro had anyone had such a pull on me.

"I guess you'd rather watch the movie," Sally said partway through.

"We can go to East Blue Hill after," I said.

I don't remember if we did. I only remember the next week, how I scoured the papers for Jack Nicholson films. Capitalizing on the success of *Chinatown*, the Blue Hill Nickelodeon sponsored a Nicholson film fest and I saw every film they screened: *Easy Rider*, *Five Easy Pieces*, *The Last Detail*, and *Carnal Knowledge*. When *Cuckoo's Nest* came out, I saw it six times, once recording it with Bud's eight-millimeter camera, which I'd hidden in my jacket. Sally and I drove the distance to Portland to see *King of Marvin Gardens*. I tacked a poster of Nicholson onto my door, where once a signed eight-by-ten of Tony C. had hung.

Chinatown had the strongest pull.

After watching it, I switched from Marlboros, Bud's brand, to Camels, and visited junkyards in hopes of finding a '30s roadster. I bought a three-piece white suit and tan fedora at a second-hand shop, a look Bud copied—maybe the only thing I ever inspired him to do.

Except on war, my father was not a fire-and-brimstone kind of preacher, but my "Jack Nicholson thing," as he called it, alarmed him—especially when I announced my intention to apply only to universities with commercial film programs. If he didn't care to foot the bill for that, I said, then we could scrap college altogether. I'd head straight to Hollywood.

"You're acting like a fifteen-year-old girl," he said one day before I graduated high school.

"Fifteen-year-old girls—reminds me of McMurphy in *Cuckoo's Nest!*" I said.

I launched into my rendition of Nicholson with the superintendent on his admission to the looney bin.

"Between me and you, Doc," I said, "you get that little red beaver right up there in front of you—I don't think it's crazy at all. No man alive could resist that..."

"That's obscene," my father said.

"Like I care," I said.

"No good will come of this, Mark. Hollywood is without soul."

"I've seen where soul's gotten you," I said. "The middle of nowhere."

"Hollywood is only about image," Dad persisted. "Nothing there is real."

"Like what's real, Dad?"

"The cry of a newborn," he said. "The first light of dawn. Breaking bread with friends. Holding hands with your loved one. This obsession with money and fame they have out there—it's not you, Mark. I know you think I'm full of beans, but someday you'll see it's true. I just hope that day comes soon."

"Go to hell, Dad," I said. "I'm going to film school."

What a punk I was.

In my defense, Bud fed into this.

Bud, who was not exactly Dad's idea of a positive role model.

He'd come to Blue Hill from Manhattan in eighth grade when his parents divorced and his mother got custody of him, an older son from her first marriage, plus ownership of the summer place. Mrs. Robbins was hip—not the kind of lady who got hung up over curfews or worried herself sick when her kid started to smoke and drink. She made sure Bud got a new Mustang on his sixteenth birthday and had a telephone in his room. She overlooked his little practical jokes, like the time he, with my eager assistance, glued missals to the pews at Saint Luke's.

Bud wanted to be a moviemaker like his father, who'd made a name in industrial training films. But his vision was grander than his dad's. His idol was Robert Altman, Mr. Robbins' friend from way back. Bud wanted to write, produce and direct his own films. He wanted to live in Santa Monica and be on a first-name basis with Mia Farrow and Robert Evans. He could recite whole scenes from just about any movie you could name, and a lot you'd never heard of. He was the only kid I knew, before NYU, who'd seen a film with subtitles.

He was the only kid who, in his own way, already was a star.

"You ever hear from Bud?" Sally said.

Our second bottle of Foxen was almost gone.

"Not in a long time," I said.

"I tried to reach him for the reunion but couldn't find his address. His mother left Blue Hill years ago."

"He's in L.A.," I said. "In fact, he was in the paper today."

"Really? For what?"

"Another of those flattering stories about me."

"I don't know how I missed it."

Sally found her copy of the *Daily News*.

"Here it is," she said. "I guess I didn't read it too carefully: ...

Robbins said on the telephone from Los Angeles, where he is directing Batman V..."

Sally was pleased.

"What a coincidence! Here we are talking about him and he's in the paper! I *love* Batman! Do you think he'd let us on the set? I bet he could get Jack Nicholson's autograph!"

I said nothing.

"Don't you think it's exciting?" Sally said.

"Of course. I'm happy for Bud."

"He probably wouldn't even return my phone call," Sally said. "But you—he'd send a plane for you."

Sally refilled our glasses.

"You know what would be cool?" she said.

"What?"

"If you did your Jack Nicholson imitation."

"Forget it."

"No, really. I want you to do your Jack Nicholson."

"It's been almost twenty years."

"So? I bet it's like riding a bike. You never forget."

"Maybe some other time," I said.

"Come on, Mark, it'd be a hoot."

"No, thanks."

"Pretty please?"

"Sorry."

"With sugar on it?"

She stood and pulled me to my feet.

I pushed her away.

"I can't," I said.

Sally fast-forwarded through her scrapbook from that point on, mostly without comment. There, at the end, were clips of me in my adult life: a brief when I graduated from NYU; my wedding announcement; wire stories about the launch of CreativeWare; the *Wired* piece; a smiling photo of me and Phil in the Entrepreneurs column of *Fortune Magazine*; everything neatly centered and pasted onto the pages of her book.

It was spooky, it really was. The earlier stuff—I could maybe understand that, who doesn't keep a scrapbook when they're a kid? But this…. If you were doing the screenplay, the next scene could have been Sally excusing herself and returning with a chainsaw.

Which, I should add, I probably deserved.

"Enough of this," she said, closing the book. "Let's get back to the present. You know what Paul wants most from Santa?"

"What?"

"*Shuttle Saga*."

"He's the only kid on the planet who does," I said.

"Why do you say that?"

"It's a joke," I said. "Your son has fine taste."

"Thank you."

"If I'd known, I would have brought him a copy."

"You could have signed it."

"You bet."

"It would have made him so happy," Sally said.

"*Tomorrow*," I said, "*we'll buy one and I will*."

Sally put the scrapbook away and went to the VCR. She didn't go to many movies any more, she explained, and she hardly ever rented them, but she'd taped a sizeable library from broadcast TV.

"I have *Chinatown*," she said. "*Cuckoo's Nest*, too."

"How about we listen to some music?" I said. "My eyes are kind of tired."

"Okay," she said. "What will it be?"

"Anything you want."

Sally stood by her turntable, and for a moment I thought she was going to comment about how my music was surely all on CD, and how I probably had an exorbitantly expensive high-tech home entertainment set, which, in fact, I did.

"John Lennon?" she said. "You always liked him."

"No, thanks," I said.

"Linda Ronstadt? The Eagles?"

"The Eagles would be fine."

"How about their Greatest Hits?"

"Perfect."

Sally put the record on. We were into the second song when she said: "Do you still smoke?"

"You mean marijuana?"

"Yes."

"On special occasions, I do."

"Is this a special occasion?"

"Very special."

You can see that the wine was really starting to work.

"Good. You stay right there."

Sally went to the kitchen and came back with a big baggie—one of those Zip-Loc freezer deals that can hold about a gallon. It was full.

"I grow my own," she said.

"I might have known."

"It's kick-ass weed," she said, "so be careful. You never know what might happen."

She handed me rolling papers and said: "Here. You always did the best joints."

I managed to roll a passable number. Sally put it to her lips and I got us going with my Spiderman lighter. She inhaled, and we passed it back and forth, and my brain flew quite pleasantly apart. "Take It to the Limit" was on when Sally asked me to dance.

I haven't mentioned how Sally looked with her parka off.

She looked awfully damn fine. She was wearing a flannel shirt over a black turtleneck and in my mind's eye, I saw what was beneath.

We danced, slowly, her arms around my neck, my arms on her hips. What can I relate the feeling to—a night a quarter of a century ago in a sleeping bag on Blue Hill?

Can two decades be erased with slow-dancing? I thought, and the idea seemed both completely absurd and completely realistic.

Or maybe Sally was horny; maybe it was no more complicated than that. I wondered how long it had been since she'd been with a man, and guessed, or perhaps only wanted to believe, it had been a long time. For my part, I knew I did not want spiritual communion or a claim on her soul. I only wanted to make love to her.

It was that simple, and selfish, and sad.

Sad because the first time had been on my mind since East Blue Hill Beach.

It was the summer before junior year, before Chinatown, before college, before Bud lost his virginity to Mary Jane. Sally was turning sixteen in two weeks. Nothing was planned. We'd been close several times, and I guess we had an unspoken understanding that when the time was right, whenever that was, we'd go all the way. Sally suggested we sleep out on Blue Hill. We'd bring a tent and an eight-track tape deck and cook up some excuse to satisfy the parents, and Mary Jane and Bud would join us and it would be a helluva party up there, in the blueberry patch my great-grandfather supposedly had bought for a buck.

When Bud and Mary Jane backed out, Sally and I decided to go alone. The horizon was pink with dawn when we were finally done; an hour later, we did it again. Back in town, I bought Sally a single long-stemmed rose, all I could afford. It was white, her favorite color.

"Take it to the Limit" ended and I tried to kiss Sally. I was clumsy and rough. I was thinking, depressingly enough, of Allison.

"Wait," Sally said, pushing me away.

I sat, the taste of lipstick on my tongue, as Sally went into the kitchen. After banking the fire, she disappeared down the hall into her bedroom.

You watch, I thought, *she's into S&M. Gonna make it two-for-two.*

"Okay," she said, what seemed like an hour later. "You can come in."

I went down the hall. Sally's room was ablaze with candles placed on her dresser, night table, desk, in pewter holders on the walls. I saw neatly ironed nursing uniforms hanging in her closet but I focused on her bed, one with finely turned oak posts and an intricately carved headboard. The pillows were plumped, the covers turned down. Sally was wearing a flannel nightgown. She'd brushed her hair, spilling it over one shoulder.

"Geez," I said.

"That's it, 'geez?'"

"You're beautiful," I said. "More beautiful than ever."

"That's better," she said. "You can kiss me now."

I wanted to, desperately, but I thought of Ruth and Timmy and how much I'd put them through already, and I couldn't.

"I'm sorry, Sally," I said. "It wouldn't be right."

"It's true, isn't it," Sally finally said. "You really can't go home again."

But that was how the script should have been written, not what happened.

What happened was I said: "You're beautiful. More beautiful than ever."

"That's better," Sally said. "You can kiss me now."

I did and in maybe three minutes, we were naked on her bed. She went down on me and I on her, and she moaned, and I moaned, and then she screamed for me to fuck her.

"I don't have a condom," I said.

"I don't care," she said. "I want you to fuck me."

My head was pounding when I awoke, at half past eight, according to the baby Ben. Sally was gone. I found a note in the kitchen:

"Ran into town. Back soon. Help yourself to anything. Love, Sally."

She's gone for the cops, I thought, but that paranoia quickly shifted to another: *She's worried about getting pregnant. Went to buy a morning-after pill. Oh, man.*

I found aspirin in the medicine cabinet and took four with orange juice—where had I played that tune before—and stoked the fire. The heat felt good, made me feel almost human. Then I put coffee on and went to the living room window.

She really did live in a place of beauty. I could imagine summer, everything green, apples and cherries starting to form on the trees. I bet she kept a flower garden, like my mother's. I bet she grew mint and sat outside drinking juleps as her children played and songbirds sang and night came on, ushering her and her family toward blissful sleep.

I showered and dried myself by the stove and when Sally wasn't home by 10, I washed last night's dishes, turned the TV on and off, and walked through her kids' rooms. When Sally still hadn't returned, I started through hers.

I was gazing at the top of her bureau when I heard her car coming up the drive.

I went to the kitchen.

"I thought you were never coming back," I said.

"I never start my day without a lottery ticket," Sally said.

"Win anything?"

"Are you crazy? But you did."

She handed me the paper.

"Merry Christmas."

The headline read:

N.H. MAN NABBED IN DEATHS
OF 2 BOSTON SOCIALITES
Blue Hill Native Son
'no longer' suspect,
police in Hub affirm

"Yes!" I shouted. "Yes! Thank you, Jesus!"

I kissed Sally, hugged her—actually lifted her off her feet.

"I thought you'd like that," she said, and it didn't connect, not yet, how subdued she was.

I read the story, word by gratifying word.

The guy they'd arrested had it all: a history of acute psychiatric hospitalization, neighbors who'd heard strange noises late at night, a pornography collection rich with leather and chains. He had a state-of-the-art computer and a website, and phone company records showed daily connections to the Internet, presumably to less-than-savory corners of that vaporous world. Seems his would-be third victim had escaped in the nick of time and when the cops got him, at his apartment a few hours later, he confessed everything. What flipped me out was that he apparently was into cannibalism for real: police found bloody butcher knives, cleavers, sharpeners, a meat grinder, a chainsaw, and a copy of *Silence of the Lambs.*

Creepier still was how John Jefferson Harris had endeavored to be me—the media me, The Society Stalker.

You already know about the social status of the victims: how superficially, at least, they were clones of Allison. In both cases, Harris had led cops to the bodies with a call to 9=1=1—you know where he saw that movie. But that was only the beginning. Harris was a software engineer, employed by a small video-game firm in New Hampshire. The part of his hair, the glasses, the L.L. Bean shirt, the freaking Spiderman ties, which he'd used to strangle both girls—it was me. When the cops broke down his door, he was naked from the waist down. Police recovered a video camera, tripod and videotapes of Harris in the act. What a sick fuck.

"Classic copycat killer," a New Hampshire state trooper was quoted as saying. "Weird thing is, he was copying someone who didn't exist."

As a reflection on the metaphysics of it all, that worked fine.

I wonder what my dear friend Malloy thinks of this latest development, I thought, but I wasn't about to dwell on him now.

"Check this out," I said, referring to a shot of Harris in handcuffs. "Does he look like me or what?"

"He does," Sally said.

"He even did the naked ass thing!"

Sally didn't laugh.

"I wonder if this sort of shit went on before TV," I said.

"I wouldn't know," Sally said. "I wasn't around before TV."

"I'm sure it did. TV made it worse. Microchips have made it worse still. And to think I've been one of the so-called gurus."

I'd lost Sally. She was preoccupied, but not with the downside of the digital revolution.

"Well, it's a great Christmas gift," I said, and then I shut my mouth.

"You made coffee," Sally finally said. "Thanks."

"I did the dishes, too."

"Aren't you sweet."

"Are you okay?" I asked.

"I'm fine."

"Are you sure?"

"I'm sure. Why?"

"You seem—I don't know, quiet. Preoccupied."

"I'm fine," she said. "Maybe just a little uptight about Christmas. I still have all my shopping to do. Speaking of shopping, we have some of our own."

"Of course," I said, *"Shuttle Saga*. You didn't think I'd forgotten?"

CHAPTER SIXTEEN

Sally asked me to drive and I did.

We rode in silence. We both had things to say, that was suffocatingly clear, but neither wanted to be first. But I'd slithered away from too many sticky situations already in my adult life. I wasn't going to let this be another. We had to talk.

Where to begin?

Excuse me if I'm a little gun-shy about morning-afters?

Hard to be more superficial than that.

I don't know about you, but from the moment we walked the beach, I knew nothing could stop us?

In a strictly carnal sense it was true, but Harlequin romances start like that.

Maybe I was living one, an X-rated version.

I suppose I could have—should have—acknowledged my depravity the day of her abortion. Should have told Sally how I'd give anything for the chance to replay that scene. I could have explained that Allison had been cheap thrills, while she and I would always be connected on some higher plane—but then, how to explain Ruth? And twenty years of silence?

I don't know what to say, would have been the most honest way to begin. *I don't even know what I believe. I only know how badly I've fucked everything up.*

"Look, about last night...." I said.

"It's what I wanted," Sally said. "So, if you're experiencing some sort of moral crisis, you can relax."

Yikes.

"I want to explain why I didn't use a condom," I said.

"Don't bother," Sally said. "I'm on the pill. Believe me, you don't make that mistake twice."

This was not the person I'd been with yesterday.

"Pull over here," Sally said.

We were in front of Saint Luke's. I parked and followed Sally into the graveyard.

"I want to show you something," she said.

I thought she was taking me to my mother's grave, but after pausing there to make the sign of the cross, she continued.

She stopped two rows deeper, near a young tree.

"I planted that," she said.

A tree? She wants to show me a tree?

It was starting to snow again.

"It's an oak," I said.

"Someday, it'll be a hundred feet tall."

"It's a fine tree."

"But it's not why I brought you here," she said. "This is."

I looked down, at the tombstone by Sally's feet.

"I came here every week at first," she said. "Of course, that was before Susan and Paul. Now, I come when I can. Always today, his anniversary."

I read:

JAKE MARTIN
Sept. 23, 1979 - Dec. 24, 1979.
Playing with the Angels now.

"I wasn't going to show you," Sally said.

"I don't understand," I said. I hadn't gotten it yet.

"After so long, you figure it doesn't matter anymore. Then you find out it does. That's what happened today. I woke up and found out it does."

"Was he related to you?"

I hear myself now—*was he related to you?*—and want to cry.

"He was," Sally said.

"A cousin?"

"He was my son."

I got it then.

I did the math and I got it, but I couldn't believe it.

This is nothing but a terrible hoax, I thought. *She's gone crazy. This is not my son. My son was medical waste.*

"Not my son," I said.

"No," she said, "our son."

"You didn't have the abortion."

"I couldn't. I went to the clinic and when they called my name, I didn't go in. I knew I could never live with myself if I did."

"You had the baby."

"In Bangor Hospital. A beautiful baby boy. Three months later, on Christmas Eve of all days, he died. Crib death, the coroner ruled."

"Oh God."

The wind was getting under my jacket and my fingers felt numb.

"Why didn't you tell me?"

"I tried to," Sally said.

"When?"

"After he was born. I called you in California. You hung up on me."

"You could have called back," I said. "Or written, or sent a telegram...something...anything, for God's sake."

"It wouldn't have made any difference."

"How can you say that?"

"You're kidding yourself, Mark. You would've told me it wasn't your problem."

"No," I said, "it wouldn't have been like that at all."

"But it would have. You were in Hollywood. All wrapped up in yourself."

I had no reply to that.

"Are you interested?" Sally said.

"In what?"

"Any of it. Me. Him. What happened."

"Yes," I said. "Tell me everything."

Sally did—about spending her pregnancy in Bangor, not Blue Hill, a place she wouldn't return to for years; about labor and delivery, with her mother as coach; about Christmas Eve morning, when she found Jake cold under the comforter in his crib. She'd told only her parents who the father was—and Mr. Martin, since deceased, would have gotten on the next plane to

L.A. if Sally hadn't begged him not to.

I listened to Sally now and I heard courage, and pride, and something else—something dark and coiled I hope never to hear again.

With her finger, Sally traced the letters on Jake's tombstone.

"Do you like his name?" she said. "I almost called him Mark, but it didn't feel right."

"It's a good name."

"He was the sweetest baby. He had your eyes."

"Do you have his picture?"

"Of course," she said, opening her purse.

She handed me one of those prayer cards undertakers provide for funerals. It had a white rose border and a crucifix and photograph with this caption:

"Jake Martin, Sept. 23, 1979 - Dec. 24, 1979, Playing with the angels now."

The photograph was of a smiling baby wearing a tiny Red Sox uniform and cap. His hair was curly and brown, his eyes blue, his cheeks pink, his nose straight, just like mine. I remembered my own baby picture, which my mother kept on her night table until her dying day. This could have been it.

"He was beautiful," I said.

I started to sob then, holding the picture of my son, realizing this was all I would ever have of him.

My thoughts went haywire then, about Mom being buried so close, and Dad not long to follow, and how someday I myself could be here and Sally and maybe Ruth and Timmy, too…all of us, for all eternity.

I wondered what Jake would have looked like today and I realized he would have been older than I was when I first made love to his mom. I wondered if he would have been interested in baseball, or Estes rockets, or Spiderman action figures, or video games, or movies, or through some perverse cosmic twist might have been headed toward the ministry. I wondered if Sally and I would have married, and whether Timmy would have existed, or if I would have ever met Ruth, maybe passed her on the street someday, a complete stranger, and be hit with some echo from another life, some crazy karmic parallel universe that I'd inhabited in a dream, and...

I was a blubbering mess.

Sally kneeled and began to clear the snow away from the base of the stone.

It had to be a small coffin, I thought. *Like in Sarajevo, the rows and rows of tiny coffins, laid out for burial after a shelling.*

Sally uncovered a floral arrangement, explaining that she'd left it on his birthday, another day she always tried to visit. She took a candy cane from her pocket and set it in the basket, there among the frozen petals of a white rose.

"Merry Christmas, Sweetie," she said. "Mommy loves you."

Sally handed me a Kleenex. She had a package of those in her purse, too.

"Not bringing you would have been crueler," she said. "If you'd found out—everything gets found out eventually, no matter what it is—you'd never have forgiven me."

Suddenly, I wanted to leave.

"Things happen for a reason," Sally said. "Sometimes we just don't know what the reason is right away."

Her tone had a dreamy, far-off quality.

"When I read about all your troubles," Sally continued, "I felt like a door had opened."

"To what?"

"I didn't know—until you called. That's when it fell into place, why all of this was happening."

"Why?"

"I'm afraid to say," Sally said. "I might be all wrong."

"Please tell me."

"And if I'm wrong?"

"Could you be more wrong than me?"

Sally took my hand.

"It's another chance, Mark," she said.

"For what?"

"For us. I know how nutty it sounds, after everything. But that door's closed now—the life you had. Ruth won't take you back, you know she won't—she's not the type, and after all you've put her through, who'd blame her? I'm not so stupid to think we don't have lots to work through, but we could, I know we could. Didn't we once or twice already?"

Sally spelled it out—how her kids would love me, and I'd warm to them, and I'd be close enough to Marblehead to see Timmy as often as the judge allowed, and of course he'd be welcome anytime in Blue Hill. She'd give me the basement and I could run a computer consulting firm, a videotape company, a Jack Nicholson fan club, whatever. And if I needed some time to get my act together, well, she had a job. What was one more plate at the table?

There could even, she hinted, be another Jake. She wasn't too old. Her biological clock hadn't quite run out.

"Do me one favor?" Sally said. "Don't answer now."

I suppose I could have given her that. I could have weighed the pros and cons, maybe talked to a lawyer, sounded out Ruth. I could have tried believing there was some magic to bring us back to a time when your biggest decision was the style halter top you'd give your girlfriend on her sixteenth birthday. I suppose I could have.

I went to speak but Sally put her hand over my mouth. I gently pried it away.

"I can't," I said.

"Will you at least sleep on it? For old times' sake?"

I watched the snow spitting against Jake's grave, saw brown oak leaves rustling in the wind, and I thought, not for the first time: *What an odd turn of phrase: For old times' sake.*

"I'm sorry, Sally," I said. "I can't."

She didn't answer, didn't look at me.

Kneeling at Jake's grave, she bowed her head, then stood.

"Here," she said, handing me the ring.

"But it's yours."

"Take it," she said.

I did.

Sally wrapped her scarf around her head. She hadn't worn a hat and her ears were red.

"I'll take you home," I said.

"I don't want a ride," Sally said.

"I'm sorry, Sally."

"Why?" she said. "Did you really think I was serious?"

I watched her disappear into the snow.

I knelt myself now, intent on a prayer. It had been years since last I'd said one. What came to mind was "Now I Lay Me Down to Sleep," which Mom had taught me.

I placed the ring next to the candy cane and watched as snowflakes covered them both.

CHAPTER SEVENTEEN

Dad had retired to a house in Buck's Harbor, twenty minutes out of Blue Hill on Eggemoggin Reach. It was across the road from the water: a traditional white Cape with an incongruous picture window so the previous owner, a summertime deacon at Saint Luke's, could keep an eye on his boat. The deacon had left Sea Watch, as the place was known, to Dad in his will. Dad had lived there a decade now. I'd visited only twice.

I knocked and my father opened the door.

"Hello, son," he said.

He sounded as if he'd been expecting me.

"Hello, Dad."

"Come in," he said.

A fire burned in the fireplace and I smelled a roast in the oven. Dad hung my coat and I followed him into the kitchen.

"Hungry?" he said. "I was just about to have my dinner."

"No thanks," I said.

"I hope you won't consider me rude if I eat."

"Not at all."

"You reach my age," he said with a smile, "and the noon meal takes on new meaning. Can I get you coffee?"

"Coffee would be fine."

Dad set the table and served. He moved slower than the last time I'd seen him, when he'd visited Marblehead last spring. He'd suffered a minor stroke over the summer, an event he shared with me only after he was out of the hospital, and you could see it was still affecting his coordination.

"Let me help you," I said when he had trouble removing the roast—it was veal—from the oven.

"No need to," he said, "I manage just fine."

Dad made gravy, and finished the cream sauce for his baby onions, and zapped a pan of sweet potatoes in butter and maple syrup in the microwave.

"All that fat's bad for the heart," I said.

"Nixon and Johnson were bad for the heart," Dad said with a smile. "A little cholesterol is nothing by comparison."

I remembered all those Sunday afternoons, the Pax Universum folks making themselves at home while Dad fussed in the kitchen with his veal, or turkey, or leg of lamb, or ham.

Dad would say grace, and over dinner, he'd kick off discussion of one of their issues. The topic often was war, but not always. Dad had been first in his class at the Harvard Divinity School, and he could expound on Thomas Aquinas, Kierkegaard, More, Fox, a bunch of other philosophers and theologians I steered clear of in college. His peacenik friends couldn't get enough, and after Mom died, when there was no one to move things along, there were Sundays Dad's sessions went late into the night. I'd come back from Sally's or Bud's, and they'd still be there, drinking decaffeinated coffee and going around and around, as if they really did believe a bunch of do-gooders from small-town Maine could change the world.

I know now that good people like that, from Maine or anywhere, can.

"I suppose I needn't ask how you are," Dad said when he was seated. "You can't pick up a paper or turn on the boob tube these days without seeing something about you."

"It's been an experience," I said.

"You know what my first reaction was?"

"I won't even guess."

"I thought: I haven't seen that bottom since his diaper days!"

He laughed, and I couldn't help but laugh, too. I'd forgotten how funny my father could be, when he was in the mood.

"You're a regular riot, Dad. I should have brought you one of those T-shirts they're selling."

"The coed naked you-know-whats?"

"The coed naked you-know-whats."

"Seriously," he went on, "my first thought was: My son's not a murderer. That's what I told the officers who came by."

"When were they here?"

"Two days ago. I refused to answer any of their questions. 'You'll need a judge's order before I say another word,' I said. Turned out to be unnecessary, judging by today's headlines."

Dad rose.

"Ice cream?" he said.

He'd barely touched his dinner.

"I've got Ben and Jerry's."

"No thanks."

"You should eat something. Stress is not good on an empty stomach. The acid eats the lining away. Ulcers are the worst."

"I appreciate the advice," I said, "but my appetite's had a mind of its own lately."

Dad cleared the table and rinsed the dishes and I thought of the dishwasher I'd offered to buy him and the wide-screen TV and satellite dish and VCR. He'd refused it all.

"I was up in the attic a little while ago," he said, "poking around for the manger scene. I happened onto your train set. Do you remember it?"

"Of course."

"It's a Lionel. Still runs—I know, because I tested it. I thought Timmy might like it."

"I'm surprised you saved it," I said.

He paused, and in that pulpit voice of his said: "I should have saved more."

I knew what he was referring to—my glove and bat, the posters of Tony C., my baseball magazines and Red Sox programs. He threw everything out during a sudden fury in the spring of 1968, when I was hounding him to get back into ball—everything but my scrapbook, spared because I'd left it at Sally's. I know how cruel Dad's reaction sounds, and the truth is, it was cruel. Dad was never angrier, before or after—never close.

But something had snapped and he became someone else, a monster who terrified me, until my own anger came. I never forgave him, despite his apologies and what he did the very next day, which was go out and buy replacements for everything.

"I was terribly wrong, you know," Dad said.

I shrugged.

"We all make mistakes," I said.

"Some far more grievous than others," Dad said. "Will you accept my apology?"

I didn't know if he'd forgotten how often he already had.

"Yes," I said.

"I'm so sorry."

"We were both different then."

"I wish I could do it over."

"You know what?" I said. "You can't. Time moves in only one direction."

I didn't intend it as a cheap shot—I was thinking of Sally, and me, and my son.

"No," Dad said, "but it's never too late to seek forgiveness. Or to forgive. Or to remember that redemption follows crucifixion, a truth I believe applies to us both."

I was certain Dad was going to quote Scripture, but he didn't.

The dishes were done. We went into the living room and Dad threw a log onto the fire and went to the china cabinet for a bottle of brandy I didn't know he kept. I could see the harbor through the picture window, barely. The storm was settling in for real and no one was on the water. I looked at Dad's desk, cluttered with large-type books, receipts, and cancelled checks, many to charitable organizations and the Episcopal Church.

"Almost tax time," Dad said, and I remembered when I was 13, how he'd been arrested for withholding that portion of federal taxes he calculated went to Vietnam. Only the diocesan lawyer's intervention had gotten him out of jail, after a highly publicized weekend during which, not for the first time, I wanted to run away.

Dad set the brandy and two glasses down.

"Care for one?" he said. "I'm not sure it's the best thing on an empty stomach. Nor am I sure it's the worst."

"Why not," I said.

"Mama would have liked this view. There isn't a prettier spot on the coast of Maine. She loved the water, your mother did. She always said it put her at peace. Do you remember?"

"How could I forget?"

"It's thirty-one years next Christmas," Dad said. "Hard to imagine you could miss someone so much after so long. The choir sang at Mass this morning. When I closed my eyes, I could almost hear her voice. Do you remember our Christmases?"

"Like yesterday."

"How I cooked while she played her beloved piano?"

"I visited her grave this morning," I said.

"Did you see my wreath?"

"Yes."

"Thank God. There's been a terrible problem with vandals lately. I'd hate for Mama to be without her wreath on Christmas."

My eye traveled to Mom's piano: an ancient Kimball upright that had been handed down from her grandmother. Mom always dreamed of owning a baby grand, but she never complained that circumstances did not allow her one. What she did was put a pickle jar on the mantel and squirrel away spare change, pennies and nickels, mostly, for her "Steinway Fund," as she called it. She died before it was full. Dad used what was there to buy her tombstone.

We sat in silence then, for I don't know how long. I finished my brandy and Dad his and he poured us another. We'd never shared a drink before, never mind two.

"Go on," he urged, "it'll fortify you."

"For what?"

"For climbing Blue Hill."

I thought he was kidding, or drunk.

But to my knowledge, Dad had never been drunk, and he wasn't acting it now. He didn't sound demented. He sounded resolute, as if he'd pondered this a long time.

And there was no mistaking his eyes. They were as steely as the day IRS agents led him out of Saint Luke's in handcuffs while a photographer for the *Bangor Daily News* snapped away.

"You're kidding," I said.

"No, I'm not," he said.'

"It's a blizzard out there."

"City living's spoiling you," Dad said, smiling. "What this

is is a good old Downeaster, no more, no less. Now, I intend to climb Blue Hill. If you won't accompany me—well, I guess I'll have no choice but to go it alone."

We parked at the base of the mountain. Dad struggled leaving the car and I doubted he'd have been able to get out if I hadn't helped him.

"This is worse than when we left the house," I said as Dad got his balance.

"Maybe to a city slicker."

"This is crazy."

"You've more than made your point," Dad said. "Now let's go—the day's getting away from us. Don't lock your doors, I'm afraid the locks will freeze."

We made respectable progress the first few hundred yards, a stretch that is gently sloped. Dad walked unassisted and the pines surrounding us broke the wind and the snow hadn't drifted much, was only a smooth three or four inches deep. We nipped from a flask Dad had filled with his brandy and we were determined in our silence.

It was one-thirty on the kind of wintry afternoon when night is impatient to fall.

A bit further, we hit a deadfall.

Dad tried getting over it by himself, but it was too much—even he conceded that after a clumsy try that left him sputtering. I straddled the trunk and as Dad swung his body over, I bore his weight. He was thinner than I remembered and I thought, although it was probably only my imagination, that I could feel the brittleness of his bones.

"Damn arthritis," he said, then added: "Don't take that to mean I want to turn back. This is actually easier than I expected."

A bit further still, we were on an open stretch of mountain. The wind had blown the snow deeper than two feet in places and knocked down pines. A ranger would have had trouble getting through.

"I don't know, Dad," I said.

"It gets easier past here," he declared.

"How do you know?"

"The Big Guy told me," Dad said.

I grinned, but he didn't; he really meant it.

"Let's take a five-minute breather," he went on, "then give it all we've got. We'll make the top by three."

We took shelter behind a boulder. Dad drank from his flask. I wanted to tell him that alcohol and sub-freezing temperatures were a deadly mix, but he'd had his fill of my observations so I didn't. His face was flush, whether from effort or wind or both I could not tell, but I didn't mention that, either. I didn't tell him how worried I was that his gloves, and mine, were soaked. I listened to the wind and it sounded like the wildcats I always imagined awaited us on our family climbs more than three decades ago.

The snow was so heavy that I did not notice, until Dad was set to push off again, that just beyond this boulder was the path leading to Mom's grandfather's blueberry field.

I lost my grip bringing Dad over the last deadfall and he surely would have broken his hip if the drift hadn't cushioned his fall. I said nothing and neither did Dad, but his face showed pain. He put his arm around my waist, and we hobbled on, under a canopy of pines that was strangely still and unblanketed with snow.

Ten minutes more, we reached the summit.

"After all I've given Him," Dad said, "the Big Guy owed me."

There is a fire tower at the top of Blue Hill and a ranger's hut and, on good days, the finest coastal vista south of Bar Harbor. We found the leeward side of the hut and I eased Dad down. His lungs sounded like Timmy's, or Mom's on her final climb. Brandy brought him around. His breathing returned to normal and a satisfied look crossed his face.

I wonder if he really would have attempted this without me, I thought, but didn't ask. I waited for him to speak and hoped it would be soon, for afternoon was surrendering to dusk.

"This was Mama's favorite spot in this world," he finally said, like I didn't know. "I think she really believed on a clear day, you could see forever."

"You just about can," I said.

"Our first kiss was here," Dad said, "on a clear day like that.

I was still in divinity school."

Dad's gaze grew distant and I could see he came here regularly in his mind.

"You were the apple of her eye," he said. "I was always afraid she'd spoil you, but she'd have none of it. 'It's impossible to spoil those you love,' she used to say. It was the only issue we ever had words over. The only one."

"You did what you thought was right," I said.

"No," he said, "I was a coward."

"What coward goes to jail for his beliefs?"

"Those were easy beliefs—that senseless killing and wars are wrong. Only the Nixons and Johnsons of the world don't see that. My cowardice was with you. I wanted control."

"You were protecting me."

"No," Dad said, "I was smothering you. Long after it was time, I wouldn't let go."

"I was a brat," I said.

"You had the most powerful imagination," Dad said. "So unlike me. I embraced principles and rules but imagination scared me. Instead of encouraging you, I tried to rein you in. That was wrong. What was more wrong was thinking I could live my dreams through you."

I remembered the first anniversary of Mom's death, where those dreams were rooted.

The bishop came to Saint Luke's to concelebrate her service, and afterwards, Dad hosted a reception. He and the bishop disappeared for a spell and I happened on them, alone in the vestibule. The bishop was tearing into Dad for his anti-war activities—how the publicity was hurting collections and bringing dishonor to the Presiding Bishop and Executive Council.

"If you want a future," the bishop said, "the shit stops now."

I almost fainted, hearing a bishop talk like that.

"I can't," my father said. "The war is wrong."

And the bishop said: "You do understand the Council has very high hopes for you."

And Dad said: "I have to do what's right."

And the bishop declared: "Then so be it. I hope you like the boondocks."

Only much later would I understand what had slipped away from my father that day.

What detached from him became affixed to me, however wishfully, until after I'd left for college. In his plan, I would receive my doctoral degree in divinity and be ordained in the Episcopal faith. I would not be content with a small-town parish, but would take an assignment in a city. I would climb the church hierarchy, using my growing influence for social causes: working to end poverty, racism, hunger, misogyny and homophobia.

I would be savvier than Dad was, more diplomatic, and I would make it to bishop, but I wouldn't be satisfied there. The longer my father protested Vietnam the more he became convinced change on the big issues could come only from Washington.

And so, in his dreams, one day I would become a Senator, even if it meant leaving the priesthood, and I would chair powerful committees and my words would move mountains. Dad never spelled this scenario out so definitively, but the gist of it became abundantly clear over time. It didn't seem to matter that there was an inverse correlation between his desires and mine—that the harder he pushed, the more I ran.

The snow was piling deeper.

"I've been doing all the talking," Dad said. "It's your turn now."

"I guess I don't have much to say."

"Please," Dad said. "I didn't drag us up here in a blizzard for one of my sermons."

We laughed.

"So, it *is* a blizzard!" I said.

"Maybe a little one."

"Really, I think you've said it all."

"I know you too well to believe that," my father said.

I reflected a moment and said: "Okay. You want to know the biggest thing?"

"Hollywood."

"No," I said, "baseball."

"That would have been my second guess."

"You were mean."

"I was thinking only of you. Kids get badly hurt—even die—every year in baseball."

"And a thousand times more get hurt crossing the street. What kind of logic was that?"

"I didn't say it was logical," my father said. "I've already conceded I was over-protective."

"Baloney," I said. "You were jealous."

"Of my own son?"

He was incredulous.

"You didn't make it in baseball and so you weren't going to let me."

"You're wrong," Dad said. "Nothing ever made me prouder than watching you play."

"Well, it doesn't matter now," I said.

The last light was draining from the sky and the wind had picked up another notch. I figured we had five minutes, ten at most, before we had to start down or face grave peril.

"I visited another grave this morning," I said. "Sally took me. Sally Martin."

"She told me she might."

"She told you?"

"Yes. And for this one and only time ever, I will violate sacred responsibility and tell you where: in the confessional. She's been coming about every other week since she was a kid. I've known about Jake since before he was born."

I was stunned. I still had the capacity for that.

"How come you didn't tell me?" I asked.

"I wanted to, sorely—but I kept my vows. And Sally was explicit that if anyone shared her secret, it had to be her, when and if the time came. It's been a heavy burden for me to carry so long. Far heavier, of course, on Sally. Except for her parents and cousin and the undertaker, who has long since passed, I'm not sure anyone knew Jake existed. Except for the grave, of course, one of many whose stories will never be told. Sally is a strong woman. Stubborn, but strong."

"I'll never get over it," I said.

"No moral being could," my father said.

I found his use of that word, "moral," uplifting. It seemed to offer me a chance for redemption.

"I would've come back immediately if I'd known," I said. "Sally doesn't believe me, but it's true. I'm not saying I would've married her—I mean, maybe I would have, I don't know. But I think of him, the things we could've done...."

I trailed off, my thoughts scattering on the wind.

"I suspect you blame yourself in some way," my father said. "You shouldn't. The Lord gave us Jake and the Lord took him, for reasons known best to Him. As I've said all too many times, the Big Guy can work in strange and mysterious ways."

"Was he christened?" I asked.

"Yes. By me, in a chapel in Bangor."

"So, he's happy now."

"And will be for all eternity—he's at the Lord's side. Does that help, even a little?"

"Yes," I said.

"He was the image of you."

"Do you think he would have liked me?"

"He would've liked the person I'm talking to now."

In the movie version of my adult life, of course, this is where Dad would have hugged me. Tears in my eyes, I would have accepted his embrace, and the words would have rushed out of us, words of forgiveness and acceptance, a blessing on us both.

Not only redemption, but a resurrection.

But my father said nothing.

We did not hug.

"Do you know about Timmy, too?" I finally said.

It was the most unexpected development of our marriage, how close Ruth had grown to Dad—although, the better you knew Syd, the more you understood. Ruth was the one who made sure my father visited Marblehead every spring. She kept asking him to live with us. I can't envision how far my father and I would have drifted apart without Ruth.

Dad nodded.

"You've never mentioned that, either."

"There's been no need to," he said. "You're a wonderful father. There's not a single thing I'd change."

"You're mocking me."

"I'm as serious as I've ever been."

"Not even all the toys and the ballfield and the pool?"

"Not even all the toys and the ballfield and the pool. Ruth is a fortunate woman. And you are a fortunate man."

"How could I have forgotten?"

We both laughed at that—crazy, fool's laughter the storm carried away.

There was much more I felt compelled to tell my father now, but it was almost dark; even if we started down immediately, our descent would be treacherous.

"We should do this more often," my father said.

He had a wink in his eye I hadn't seen since I was a kid.

"Maybe next time in a Nor'easter," I said, and we laughed again.

I helped Dad to his feet, but he didn't start off immediately. He drew my attention to a heart and arrow carved into the hut. My parents' initials were faded, but legible.

"Forty-nine years they've lasted," Dad said. "I don't know what I'd do if the Park Service replaced the hut."

"I'd haul you up here to carve them again."

Dad reflected a moment.

"Mama would be proud of you," he said, and while I didn't agree, I kept my objections to myself.

Carolers were moving through downtown Blue Hill when we arrived from the mountaintop. Dad identified them as the Saint Luke's choir.

"You were in that choir," he said. "Sally, too."

"I remember."

"They're singing at Saint Luke's for the Christmas Eve concert," Dad said. "Would you care to go?"

"Not this year," I said. "I have some matters to attend to."

"Then stop here," Dad said in front of Merril & Hinckley,

"but keep that heater running, my bones are still freezing."

I helped him out of the car and he went in—alone, at his insistence.

When he returned, he handed me an envelope with Ticketron labeling.

"Sorry it's not wrapped," he said.

The envelope had three tickets to a Red Sox-Yankees game in June. They were bleacher seats.

"Our favorite homestand," I said.

"How long since we've been?"

"Twenty-five years, at least."

"Does Timmy hate the Yankees as much as us?"

"More," I said. "It must run in the family."

Suddenly, my father was crestfallen.

"Stupid me," he said.

"What?"

"I forgot you have season tickets."

"Not anymore," I said. "I'm getting rid of them."

"Really? Why?"

"Too expensive," I said. Already, I was envisioning my life post-redemption.

Dad brightened.

"Well, merry Christmas, son."

"Merry Christmas, Dad."

Ruth had left a message on Dad's answering machine.

"Sorry to keep bothering you…" she began.

"Bothering me!" Dad said. "As if it were possible."

"…but Timmy is in the hospital."

"Not again," I said to myself.

"He's okay," the message continued, "but he could use a visit from his dad. If Mark calls, will you please tell him? I still don't know where he is, but we've gone into all that. Thanks. Oh—I almost forgot. Timmy's in Boston Children's, not Mass General. My father's really gotten out of hand since Mark's troubles and I couldn't handle having him around so I transferred Timmy there. Please keep it a secret. Merry Christmas Eve, Papa. Love you. I'll call tomorrow."

"How often has she been in touch?" I asked.

"Twice a day, at least," my father said. "She's been beside herself with worry about you. She reminds me of your mother that way."

I dialed the hospital and they patched me through to Ruth at Timmy's bedside. He was napping: Thank God, all signs pointed to discharge tomorrow.

"I'll have to pay in cash," Ruth said. She explained that our insurance didn't cover Children's and our Visa had been declined. I told her of my suspicions of Phil.

There was silence and I wondered if the storm had knocked down the lines.

"So that's what got you all weird when you heard his message," Ruth said. "You know, for a smart man, you're awfully stupid sometimes."

"Sometimes?" I said, and we both laughed.

"Is everything all right?" Dad said when I was done.

"Everything's fine."

"I don't think you should leave until morning," he said. "The roads are horrible. Timmy can wait a bit longer for a safe dad."

"That's what Ruth said."

"And you're going to ignore her."

"If I take it slow," I said, "I'll be fine."

"It's dangerous."

"So was climbing Blue Hill."

"You've got me there," my father said. "Now don't forget the trains for Timmy."

"Thanks," I said.

"Be careful," he said.

"I will."

"Godspeed, son."

There was a time I would have at that, one of his favorite sayings.

"Godspeed," I said.

Then I hugged him.

CHAPTER EIGHTEEN

Highway crews in Maine and New Hampshire were on top of the storm, but Massachusetts, as usual, was a disaster. The storm had stalled off Boston and radio announcers were making comparisons to the Blizzard of '78, which had shut the city for a week. Hey, I wasn't complaining—the weather had knocked me out of the news, not a word anywhere. I left Storrow Drive and turned onto Beacon Street, reduced to deep ruts between cars buried in snow.

Phil lived at Beacon and Dartmouth. I stopped outside his building.

The curtains were open and I saw a Christmas tree and mistletoe and people: Lisa, Phil, CreativeWare's chief financial officer, our vice chairman, others I didn't recognize. They looked festive, and when I rolled my window down, I could hear a stereo and drunken laughter.

It came back to me then: the day long ago that Phil, my new partner and friend, had brought me by to look at this place—how my enthusiasm helped persuade him to buy it.

Attack Ship had been on the market less than a month, but based on the initial response we'd tripled our forecast, and would soon triple it again. Ruth had just been named assistant director of development for Harvard. The week after Phil bought this building, Ruth and I put a down payment on a lot in Marblehead. Life was good.

I had plenty of things I wanted to say to Phil now and I didn't care if I spoiled his party or anything like that, but you know what? I didn't have the heart for it, not then, and maybe I never will. What's past is past—trite, yes, but true. Plus, I had more urgent tasks and I was late.

So, I continued up Beacon to Kenmore Square, deserted and dark. I crossed the turnpike to Pro Time, the sports memorabilia shop across from Fenway, and broke the lock with a tire iron. No alarm rang. I opened the door and went in. An emergency light enabled me to see.

They had plenty of autographed balls in a felt-lined display case—balls signed by Canseco and Greenwell, even Yaz and Tony C., but not Mo Vaughn.

"Now what?" I said.

I rummaged through the rest of the store, on the chance they kept the Vaughn stuff somewhere else, but all I found was a Red Sox program with Vaughn's signature, which I used to forge his autograph on a brand-new ball. Timmy would never know, because I would never tell him—another of my harmless white lies, you see. This one, however, with virtue.

I placed the last of my cash—nineteen dollars—on the register with a note of thanks and a promise to call later to see if $19 had covered repair of the lock.

My car was stuck and after furiously attempting to free it, I gave up and walked the remaining ten or so blocks to Children's. It was nearly 2 a.m. when I got to Timmy's room. He was asleep. So was Ruth, in the chair by his side.

I kissed her forehead and said: "I'm home."

"Oh, it's you," she said drowsily, and then her eyes opened. "It's you! What are you doing here? You were supposed to stay at Papa's."

"You know I can only take so much of my father," I said with a smile.

"Was the driving awful?"

"I've seen better."

"You poor thing. Your nose is red."

"Call me Rudolph. At least my ass is warm."

Ruth laughed. Humor indeed is therapeutic.

"Are you really home?" she said.

"I really am."

Timmy stirred but didn't wake. I laid my hand on my son's

forehead and I'll tell you: Nothing ever felt so good.

"I guess this will have to wait until morning," I said, showing Ruth the baseball.

"Thank God! That's all he's been saying: 'Daddy's coming home for Christmas and Santa's bringing my ball.'"

"You know what I'd give anything for?" I said.

"A Glenfiddich."

"You bet."

"Would you settle for coffee? There's a machine downstairs."

We took the elevator to the lobby, deserted save for a guard. We passed the chapel, closed for the night, and I decided maybe I'd visit tomorrow if the mood fit. We went to the wishing pool. The TV was on, bringing the latest report on the storm.

"Speaking of news," Ruth said, "I've got some. I got fired yesterday."

"Shoot me now," I said. "Please."

"That's not self-pity I detect, is it?"

"No, I believe it's called self-loathing."

"You know I'll be able to find something in half a second," Ruth said.

"Sure," I said. "Put 'Wife of Society Stalker' at the top of your resume and the phone will ring off the hook."

"Actually," Ruth said, "I'd probably do better with 'Wife of Cannibal.'"

We laughed—laughter that built on itself until we were in tears.

Outside, dawn was breaking over snowy rooftops.

I held Ruth's hand and didn't let go.

POSTSCRIPT: DECEMBER, A YEAR LATER

By now, you've probably had your fill of the stories, I know I have—how a New York grand jury declined to indict me, how the prosecution for the real Society Stalker, John Jefferson Harris, subpoenaed me to appear at his trial, how I was on the stand for two days. Harris was one toasted cookie, and a hell of an accomplished hacker.

He'd kept a digital scrapbook of me, transcripts of my

many online appearances, and copies of every piece of e-mail I'd sent or received for more than a year—although Allison had pushed him over the edge, he'd been stalking me long before she came along. Asked by one reporter why he'd gone for me, he'd answered only: "Because he was fucking with my ego."

It was a chilling echo of Mark David Chapman. Harris, of course, was acquitted by reason of insanity. I just hope the attendants have the good sense to keep him away from a PC. And that someday, science finds a way to cure people so severely sick.

Allison recovered completely, to face twenty-six counts of solicitation. Despite threats of lawsuits, her clients' names were published everywhere and Rep. Donald J. Dolan, who lost reelection, was hardly the only one ruined. Allison's father hired Alan Dershowitz to head the defense team and just last week, as the trial date was set, old Dersh began making the rounds of the morning news shows. God, he annoys me—is there any case he *won't* take?

Malloy turned out to be the best story.

My good friend had indeed been enamored of Allison's services but that was not the full extent of his troubles. God love Charlie Goldman—his brother-in-law, that captain on the New York force, initiated an internal investigation of their hotshot detective. Seems Malloy had a fondness for cocaine that exceeded Allison's. His firing made the front page of *The Post*—TOP COP CHOPPED was the headline—they sure know how to write 'em, don't they?—and several of his own naked-ass pictures some enterprising police insider lifted off Allison's hard drive (I swear it wasn't me) found their way onto the Internet (OK, it *was* me—you know, that old saying about revenge being a dish best served cold).

All that garbage Malloy fed the press about me apparently was nothing but a crazed attempt to save his marriage, futile as it turned out; I'm told his wife walked out on him the day my other good friend Doug Fenning broadcast a shot of the detective's own personal derriere. I keep trying to reach Malloy to see if I can be of assistance, but so far, he hasn't returned my calls.

Let me repeat: What a wonderful thing the First Amendment is.

Following an FBI investigation, a federal grand jury indicted Phil and CreativeWare's chief financial officer for embezzlement and tax evasion; both men made bail and are awaiting trial. They face hard time, but odds are they'll cop pleas and get off with fines and probation. The fat cats always manage to not get screwed, even after they've screwed others.

CreativeWare was granted bankruptcy protection, which gave it a new lease on life, but I decided not to go on. And not because of *Shuttle Saga*, one of the biggest bombs of all time—I mean, you don't want to know how much space it took up at the landfill. I just didn't have it in me anymore. My lawyer is negotiating to sell CreativeWare's assets and his best guess is I'll come out with three or four hundred thousand dollars, perhaps five percent of what I would have been worth if Phil had been an honest man.

I'm not complaining.

I'm not even going to keep much of it.

I have some substantial debts to take care of, and money is part of my repayment plan, albeit the smaller part.

So, it was over in Massachusetts. At the last minute, old Syd offered to pay off our mortgage and keep us in Marblehead, but I told him to blow—politely, of course, that's the new me. We sold the Marblehead house and had enough left over for a down payment on a modest place in Maine.

We've been here now since May.

Not Blue Hill—you can appreciate why that would be too cozy—but half an hour away, on Deer Isle, where Ruth was fortunate to find a job as a fundraiser for the Eggemoggin Oceanographic Institute. Down by the basement oil burner, in the shadow of the electrical panel, I run a software consulting firm from a single desk. You'd be amazed at the amount of work there is in a backwater place like coastal Maine. Nowadays, even lobstermen need computers.

Without wanting to, I became a celebrity on the Internet.

A real one, not the naked-you-know-what one.

The way I'd eluded the cops, that Fear Strikes Out scene, Phony Phil—some weird karma sprang up that resonated within cyberspace, for reasons I don't pretend to understand.

I followed it for a while, long enough to see that despite her legal troubles (or perhaps because of them), Allison was morphing into some sort of multi-media goddess—$39.95 buys her X-rated CD-ROM, from Twisted Productions.

I guess it couldn't have ended any better for her, could it? I mean, with Dershowitz on board, she's guaranteed to beat the rap. She's gotten way more than her fifteen minutes of fame and word is she's close to marketing a credible virtual reality game. Just last week, someone claiming to be her e-mailed me expressing the desire to meet online for "old time's sake"—God, I really hate that line—and that was the day I closed my account.

You want me now, try a postcard, or Deer Isle directory assistance. I'm in the book.

Of course, the mainstream press got its rocks off, too, but I refused substantial cash offers to appear on *Hard Copy* and in the *National Enquirer,* just as I refused invitations to appear live online and said no to lawyers interested in representing me in Richard Jewell-like litigation. *Variety* ran something about a movie deal Bud Robbins was trying to put together with Jack Nicholson, but I didn't bother to find out if it was real or Hollywood hype.

The only one I've talked to is Charlie, because I'd given him my word to help him with his—and because I rather like his brother-in-law. God only knows how the book will turn out, but you know what? I don't give a rat's ass anymore. I really don't. I hope Charlie makes himself a million. He's an ass-kisser, no question about it, but he's an ass-kisser with a heart.

Timmy has a new doctor now, and he switched my boy to a medication that's kept him out of the hospital for half a year, longer than ever. Things improved enough that he could safely climb three quarters of the way up Blue Hill, to my great-grandfather's blueberry field; he wanted to go all the way, but we're playing it on the safe side.

Knock on wood: If we hold this course until spring, Timmy can try out for Little League. If he can and he wants to play, you better believe I'm coaching.

And if he can't, that'll be okay, too. I've got things in perspective now.

The morning of September 23rd was sunny and warm, and after seeing Timmy off to school, I got into my Corvette. I'd vowed to sell the damn thing, but Timmy and Ruth—even Dad, go figure—had talked me out of it.

I drove to Saint Luke's, where I visited Mom's grave. Then I went to Jake's. His oak tree was ablaze in color, but not a leaf had yet fallen.

Sally came up behind me.

"Isn't it magnificent?" she said.

"I was just thinking that," I said.

"It's amazing how it's grown."

"Even from last year."

Sally knelt, blessed herself, and said a silent prayer.

I'd already said mine, and it had come easily.

"I saw Ruth for the first time last week," Sally said when she was done. "She's very pretty. Very…together. Of course, I already knew that."

"Where were you?" I asked.

"Merrill & Hinckley. I knew it was her because she gave her name for a charge."

A special order of Foxen Pinot Noir, I believe her purchase was, to celebrate our anniversary.

"Thank you for the check," Sally went on.

"What check?"

"Come on, Mark. It's me you're talking to."

I'd sent a bank draft, anonymously, but I don't know who I thought I was fooling.

"My first impulse was to return it," Sally said. "But then I remembered nursing-home wages and decided my kids deserve a college education someday. I won't take any for myself. That wouldn't be right, would it?"

"No," I said, "I guess it wouldn't."

We didn't speak after that.

Our eyes met, but nothing passed between us.

I knelt at Jake's grave with head bowed and didn't get up until I heard Sally's car, still in need of a muffler, disappearing into the distance.

Timmy would be home soon from school, and Ruth and I would be discussing dinner.

My dad was coming over. After we'd eaten and tucked Timmy into bed, we'd be watching a movie. Dad had requested *Chinatown*.

He'd never seen a Jack Nicholson film and he figured that would be a good start.

ABOUT THE AUTHOR

This is G. Wayne Miller's 19th published book. He is also a Providence Journal staff writer, a filmmaker, a podcaster and a visiting fellow at Salve Regina University's Pell Center for International Relations and Public Policy, where he is cofounder and director of the Story in the Public Square program. He also co-hosts and co-produces the national Telly-winning PBS TV/ SiriusXM Satellite Radio show, *Story in the Public Square*.

Miller has been honored for his writing more than 50 times and was a member of the Providence Journal team that was a finalist for the 2004 Pulitzer Prize in Public Service. Three documentaries he wrote and co-produced have been broadcast on PBS, including *The Providence Journal's* "COMING HOME," about veterans of the wars in Iraq and Afghanistan, nominated in 2012 for a New England Emmy and winner of a regional Edward R. Murrow Award.

Visit Miller at www.gwaynemiller.com

ALSO BY G. WAYNE MILLER

BOOKS

NON-FICTION

The Work of Human Hands: Hardy Hendren and Surgical Wonder at Children's Hospital, 1993.

Coming of Age: The True Adventures of Two American Teens, 1995.

Toy Wars: The Epic Struggle Between G.I. Joe, Barbie and the Companies That Make Them, 1998.

King of Hearts: The True Story of the Maverick Who Pioneered Open Heart Surgery, 2000.

Men and Speed: A Wild Ride Through NASCAR's Breakout Season, 2002.

The Xeno Chronicles: Two Years on the Frontier of Medicine Inside Harvard's Transplant Research Lab, 2005.

An Uncommon Man: The Life and Times of Senator Claiborne Pell, 2011.

Top Brain, Bottom Brain: Harnessing the Power of the Four Cognitive Modes (with neuroscientist Stephen M. Kosslyn, PhD), 2013.

Car Crazy: The Battle for Supremacy Between Ford and Olds and the Dawn of the Automobile Age, 2015.

Kid Number One: A Story of Heart, Soul and Business, Featuring Alan Hassenfeld and Hasbro, 2019.

The Growing Season: Frank Beazley and the Meaning of a Life, 2020.

FICTION

Thunder Rise, 1989.
Since the Sky Blew Off: The Essential G. Wayne Miller Fiction, Vol. 1, 2012.
Summer Place, 2013.
Asylum, 2013.
Vapors: The Essential G. Wayne Miller Fiction, Vol. 2, 2013.
The Beach That Summer: The Essential G. Wayne Miller Fiction, Vol. 3, 2014.
Drowned: A Different Kind of Zombie Tale, 2015.
Blue Hill, 2020.

FILMS

On the Lake: Life and Love in a Distant Place, 2009.
Behind the Hedgerow: Eileen Slocum and the Meaning of Newport Society, 2010.
The Providence Journal's Coming Home, 2011.

SCREENPLAYS

The Glamour Girls, with Jessi Sundell Cramer, 2008, WGA registration # 1288636
Summer Love, Harvardwood Books and Unlimited Publishing LLC, 2008, WGA registration: #1216146
Snyder, with Drake Witham and Drew Smith, 2008, WGA registration: #1217682
King of Hearts, 2009, *with Drew Smith*, WGA registration #1062014

Curious about other Crossroad Press books?
Stop by our site:
http://store.crossroadpress.com
We offer quality writing
in digital, audio, and print formats.

CPSIA information can be obtained
at www.ICGtesting.com
Printed in the USA
BVHW032132171120
593603BV00019B/67

9 781952 979965